THE PACT

ROBERTA KAGAN

ISBN (eBook): 978-1-957207-22-3
ISBN (Paperback): 978-1-957207-23-0
ISBN (Hardback): 978-1-957207-24-7
ISBN (Large Print): 978-1-957207-25-4

Title Production by The Bookwhisperer.ink

DISCLAIMER

This is a work of fiction. Names, characters, businesses, places, events, and incidents are either the products of the author's imagination or used in a fictitious manner. Any resemblance to actual persons, living or dead, or actual events is purely coincidental.

PROLOGUE

The crash of shattering glass exploded through the silence in the tiny attic where seventeen-year-old Anna Levinstein slept with her family.

Her eyes flew open. Her body bolted upright on her cot. *Could that noise have been another nightmare?* She looked around the room and saw the terror on her parents' faces and the sorrow on her brother's, and she knew...

This was no dream.

"What was that sound?" her mother's lips moved, but she did not speak. Her face cracked with fear. It was the middle of the day, but they had all been asleep. "What was that?" she repeated without a sound.

No one answered.

Then, in a soft voice, Anna's father said to his wife, "Lillian, I think they're looking for us. I think the Nazis are in the house."

"Dear God," her mother said.

Anna's brother Anselm started coughing. He always coughed whenever he was nervous. Frantically, Anna stood up and ran to him. She covered his mouth with her hand. "They must not hear you," she whispered to him. "If they hear you, they'll know where we are."

Anslem nodded. His face was scarlet as he tried to stifle the coughing.

"He's choking," her mother said.

Another crash came from downstairs.

"They're searching the house. They are looking for us," her father said frantically. "You must keep Anselm quiet."

Anna and her mother held a pillow over Anselm's face to dampen the sound of his cough. "Be careful, Anna. We must let him breathe, or we will kill him," her mother said. Anna nodded.

"Jew swine, where are you?" They heard a man's voice coming from downstairs, and it reaffirmed what they feared: the Nazis were searching for them.

It was horrifying to hear the Nazis tearing the house apart and even more frightening because she could not see what was happening. Her imagination was running wild. Each time she heard glass breaking or heavy things being thrown on the ground, Anna jumped.

Sweat began to drip into her eyes. She wanted to wipe it away, but she couldn't dare to move her hand from the pillow she held over her brother's face.

Then there was a moment of silence. Outside, Anna heard the sound of a siren, a Gestapo siren. It grew loud and then softer and softer until it faded out.

Have they gone? Is it possible they decided we were not here and left? Anna prayed. *Dear God, could it be that they have gone, and we are safe?* A spark of hope filled her with joy, but it was only momentary. Not even a second later, Anna trembled when she heard the heels of Nazi boots as they ascended the stairs toward the tiny hidden attic where the family hid. Each loud step as the boots hit the wooden floor reverberated through her body. Anna's father sighed as he walked over to stand beside the rest of his family. He put his arm around Anna and held her mother's hand. "They're heading right for the attic. It looks like they know there's a hidden attic here. Someone must have turned us in," he said sadly.

"But who? Why?" Anna's mother asked, her voice filled with despair.

Anna's father shrugged his shoulders. "I don't know, Lillian. I don't know. But no matter what happens, at least we are together."

With each deafening step, Anna felt more and more desperation. She wished she could jump out the window and run away, but it was too high. Besides, she would never leave her family to face this alone. They were just waiting now. There was nothing else to do. There was nowhere to go, nowhere to hide. *The Gestapo agent is getting closer. Could it be they don't know about this attic? Is it possible that they are just checking upstairs in the house? Maybe they will go away.* Anna's young, idealistic mind sought comfort.

But the comforting thoughts were obliterated by a ferocious kick to the hidden door. It burst open as it flew off its hinges, revealing the terrified Jewish family.

Anslem coughed harder as Anna released the pillow. There was no point in silencing him now. They'd been discovered, and now they must face whatever the Nazis had in store for them.

"Jews," a giant man in a Gestapo uniform said. "We knew you were here, you sneaky rats."

There were two of them. Two Gestapo agents came to arrest her defenseless family. But only the giant entered the attic. The other one stood behind him. Anna felt herself fill with panic. They were helpless.

Anna glanced up into the giant's eyes. She was hoping she would see some sympathy. But she saw no humanity, none at all. His eyes were dark and hard, devoid of emotion. Anna's heart beat fast, and her chest ached. *What are they going to do with us? Are they going to shoot us right here, right now? I am so scared. Dear God, help me; I am so afraid. What does it feel like to die? Will it hurt? And what about my family? I can't bear to watch them die or, worse, watch them suffer. The Nazis might take us away. But where? Maybe somewhere to work? But will we be together if they take us, or will they separate us? Dear God, please help us. I beg you, please.*

"Don't hurt us. Please, please don't hurt us," Anna's mother pleaded. Anna saw her mother's knuckles turn white as she clung to Anselm's shoulder.

The giant slapped Anna's mother across the face with the back of his hand. "Don't speak to me, Jew. Don't speak unless I tell you to." Then he looked Anna up and down and said to his partner, "Too bad it's illegal to fornicate with Jews. I'd like to have my way with that young one."

Anna felt her breath catch in her throat. *No, please, not that. Please, God, not that.*

The giant was mumbling obscenities. Filthy terrible obscenities. Anna wanted to cover her ears with her hands, but she dared not move. Then the giant's voice grew muffled, and she couldn't hear him. In her mind, she heard her bubbies voice. It was strong and clear, even though her bubbie had been dead for years. "Be brave, Annaleh. Be brave."

But I am not brave like you, bubbie. I'm scared.

"I know, Annaleh. That's when you must look deep into your heart to find courage. Your parents were brave. They escaped pogroms in Russia. You come from strong stock. It's in your blood. Be brave..."

"Let's go. Move, *mach schnell!*" The giant said, nudging Anna's father with the butt of his rifle. "Right now, you lazy pigs. All of you."

Anna held on to the side of the bed and eased herself up, but then the room went dark. She reached up and touched her face. It was wet with tears. She didn't even realize she was crying. Then, silver and black floaters appeared in her eyes, and they were all she could see. Her heart pounded loudly in her ears. She could no longer see or hear the giant, but she knew he was there. Anna lost all strength in her legs and fell to the floor, fainting.

CHAPTER ONE

June 1929, Austria

It was the last day of school before summer vacation began. Elica's third-grade class buzzed with excitement as they waited in the hallway for the teacher to come and open the classroom. As Elica approached, all the girls said hello, hoping she would stand with them and be a part of their crowd. Elica was by far the prettiest and most popular girl at school. Everyone wanted to be her friend. Even though the boys had not yet become interested in girls, they, too, looked at Elica with a certain reverence that was reserved for truly beautiful girls.

Elica was always polite. She smiled at them as if she were a queen or a princess when she was little more than a poor girl who was the daughter of a factory worker and a maid. She looked around at all the faces in the hallway until she saw Bernie.

"Bernie!" Elica said as she rushed over to her.

"I am so glad it's the last day," Bernie said.

"Me too. I can't wait to get out of here for the summer."

"We'll have so much fun," Bernie smiled. "Maybe I can even get you interested in playing sports."

"Don't count on it," Elica said. "Last time we played, I chipped my nail polish; believe me, it's hard to get nail polish. I had to swap stuff with the older girl who lives upstairs before she let me use hers."

Bernie laughed, "Should I ask what you had to give her?"

"My red hair ribbon. I've regretted it ever since."

Just then, a heavy-set girl with blonde hair and a thick nose began pushing a small boy slightly built. "Don't come back to this school next year. You hear me? We don't want Jews in our school." The large girl said.

"Leave me alone," the little boy yelped, "please, just leave me alone."

"Leave me alone," the large girl imitated him. Then she punched the boy in the face, knocking off his glasses.

"Looks like Dagna Hofer is at it again. She's beating up Michael Feinstein."

Dagna kicked the boy in the stomach, and he winced in pain. The entire class was watching, but no one moved. They were afraid of Dagna. Even the boys.

"I have to do something," Bernie said. "I can't let her kill him. He's so small and skinny, and she's huge."

"I know she is. Aren't you scared of her?"

"Not at all," Bernie said, but Elica could see that Bernie was afraid of Dagna. "But she'd never hurt you, Elica. Dagna follows you around like a puppy."

"I know she's strange. She wants to be my friend in the worst way."

"Everyone wants to be your friend because you're so pretty. You look like a movie actress."

Elica laughed, but her face told Bernie she was enjoying the compliment.

"Hey, why don't you come with me and talk to Dagna? She'll

leave Michael alone if you tell her to. She would never listen to me, but she'll listen to you, Elica."

"You really want me to talk to her?"

"Yes, I do. I mean, think about it. Anna is Jewish, and she's our best friend. We should stand up for Jews. It's not right for Dagna to beat Michael up for no reason. I mean, just because he's Jewish."

"You're right," Elica said.

"I know I am. He's crying, and everyone is just watching. No one is helping! We have to do something."

"Let's go," Elica said, and she walked over to where Dagna stood over the boy. "What are you doing?" Elica asked.

"He's a Jew. He doesn't belong in our school."

"You have no right to treat him that way. I am very disappointed in you," Elica said. She used the sentence that the teacher Frau Hauptmann used when she wanted to make one of her pupils feel guilty about their bad behavior.

"I'm sorry, Elica," Dagna said.

"You should be."

Then the teacher opened the door to the classroom, and the last day of school began.

After school that same afternoon, Elica and Bernie walked almost a mile to the more affluent part of town. They waited outside the Jewish school for their best friend, Anna.

Anna saw Elica first and waved to her. Both Elica and Bernie waved back. "Let's go to our special place," Bernie said.

"All right, but I have to go home and change," Anna said. "I can't believe school is out for the summer. I am so happy."

"So are we," Bernie said.

The girls walked towards Anna's home.

"We had a terrible thing happen with Dagna today. Do you remember her?" Elica grunted.

"Of course. How could I ever forget her? She's like a monster," Anna said.

"Well, Dagna was beating up a boy in our class, and Bernie

wanted to defend him. I was really proud of Bernie. She's so brave." Elica smiled, looking at Bernie.

"Bernie is always brave! I love that about her." Anna smiled at Bernie and added, "I wish I went to school with you girls. I miss so much by going to the Jewish school."

"We wish you did, too," Bernie said.

They were in front of Anna's house. "Do you want to come in?"

"No, we'll meet you at our special place in an hour," Elica said. "I don't want to see my mother. She'll ask me too many questions. She's always telling me I have to be careful around you because she's your family's housekeeper."

"I'm sure she'll be busy working. But I understand how you feel. You're my best friend, and we know each other through and through. So don't worry, just always be yourself around me. That's why I love you. I'll be there in an hour."

CHAPTER TWO

The three eight-year-old girls sat under the welcomed shade of a leafy elm tree. It had been an unusually hot day. But now, the sun was no longer high in the sky, and the temperature had just dropped, giving them some relief from the day's heat.

Anna chewed her fingernail. Her parents expected her home before dark, and she knew her mother would be worried and angry that she'd stayed out so late. But when Elica and Bernie told her to come to the park for this meeting, Anna didn't want to be the only one to say she had to be home. Her friends meant a lot to her, and she wanted to fit in, so she stayed, even if it meant receiving punishment for disobeying her parents.

Elica shook back her long blonde braids. In her right hand, she held a lit candle. "Today, my dear friends, we will make a blood pact," she said, her voice official and serious even though she was only a child. "No matter what happens, we will be blood sisters and always stick together. Through thick and thin."

"Blood sisters?" Bernie questioned.

"Blood sisters," Elica nodded.

"What's a blood sister?" Bernie asked.

"I think I know what it means," Anna said. "I think it means we must cut ourselves and mix our blood. Isn't that right?"

"You're right. That is exactly what we must do, and as we cut ourselves and mix our blood, we must make a pact. A pact to always stand by each other, no matter what happens in our lives. Even though we were born to different parents, we are true sisters. We have a pact. We are blood sisters forever," Elica said. "Now, I brought this little tin box. This will be our secret box. If we want to leave a letter for each other, we can leave it here. We will also leave notes about our deepest feelings. We will share things in this tin that no one else will know about. It will be very special because it will be our secret."

"But what if someone finds it?" Bernie asked.

"They won't because we will bury it, and no one else will ever know where it is." Elica put the tin box down on the ground. "All right, let's cut ourselves. Are you ready to be blood sisters?"

"I hate to cut myself," Bernie said, grumbling.

"Don't be such a baby. We have to do this. Do you want me to do it for you?" Elica said.

"Yes. Please. I can't even look. I hate the sight of blood," Bernie said.

Elica took the knife she'd brought from home and quickly cut Bernie's hand. Then she turned to Anna. "Do you want me to cut you?"

"I can do it," Anna said, taking the knife and quickly slicing a surface cut into her palm.

Elica nodded, then she took the knife from Anna and cut herself.

The girls put their hands together until each had blended their blood with the others. "We must have a secret name. Our secret name will be Sister's in Blood," Elica said.

"Sisters in Blood," Bernie repeated.

"Sisters in blood," Anna said, smiling.

"Yes, that name will be our secret, and we will only speak it aloud when we are alone. Does everyone agree?"

Anna and Bernie nodded.

Elica smiled at them. "Good. Now, go home and clean up your wound. But don't tell your *mutti* or *vater* how you got the cut. They would be mad if they knew we had cut ourselves," Elica said.

"That's true," Bernie answered, "and it still hurts."

Then, out of the darkness, came a familiar voice. The girls recognized the voice right away. It was Dagna. She walked over to them, a half-smile on her face.

She was a short, heavy-set red-faced girl the same age as the others. "You can be sure they would be very angry," Dagna said. "After all, you just cut yourselves and mixed your blood with the blood of a Jew."

"Shut up," Elica said. "Anna is our friend, and she is our sister now."

"She's still and always will be a Jew," Dagna said.

"Get out of here. Go home," Bernie said.

"Don't forget, I know your secret," Dagna said. "I know you have Jew blood in you."

"Shut up," Elica growled.

Anna felt small and ashamed. The girls had always been careful not to mention Anna's religion, even though they all knew that being Jewish made Anna different. But Dagna had just burst that bubble. She had just given voice to all of Anna's insecurities, and right now, Anna wished she could crawl into a hole in the ground and disappear.

Dagna giggled. "Oh, don't be that way, Elica. You needn't worry. I won't tell a soul. You can trust me to keep your secret. All I want is to be a part of your club."

Elica glanced at Bernie. Then she shot a quick embarrassed glance at Anna. None of them liked Dagna, but they knew she was right. Jews were not popular, so their parents would not be happy to learn that they'd mixed blood like this. "What do you think?" Elica asked Bernie.

Bernie shrugged.

"Anna?"

"I don't know. Maybe I should just leave the group."

"You can't. Not anymore. You're our sister now and forever," Elica said.

"We already mixed our blood," Bernie said. "Besides, it's not fair that you should have to leave."

"I don't know what to do. I don't want you to allow someone into the club just because of me," Anna said, looking away.

Elica glared at Dagna. Then she handed her the knife. "Well, I can't see any way out of it. So, here is the knife. Go on and cut yourself. Then you can be in our club."

"I'll do it. I'll mix blood with you and Bernie, but not with that Jew."

Anna's face grew red. She stood up and clumsily brushed off her skirt. "I should get home. It's late." She turned away so that Bernie and Elica could not see that she was crying.

"Don't cry," Bernie said to Anna. Then she stood up and put her arm around Anna's shoulder. "It's all right. Don't leave. Elica and I don't care what Dagna thinks or says." She steered Anna to sit back down.

"Go ahead, tell on us if you have to. Just get out of here," Elica growled, staring into Dagna's eyes.

"I will tell if you don't let me in the club."

Dagna sat down defiantly. Bernie walked over to Dagna and kicked her in the shin.

"Ow, what did you do that for?" Dagna asked.

"Because I hate you. That's why," Bernie said, "you make everything ugly."

Elica stared at Dagna. Then Anna said, "just let her in. I don't care if she mixes blood with me or not. I just don't want you two to get into trouble, and if she tells on us, you will."

"Fine," Elica said, slamming the knife down onto the ground, then she glared at Dagna, "cut your palm."

Dagna quickly sliced her hand. She winced in pain and looked at Elica and Bernie defiantly. Then she put out her hand and mixed blood with Elica. Next, she mixed it with Bernie. "Not you," she said to Anna.

Anna shrugged. "That's fine with me. I never liked you anyway."

"Jew," Dagna said.

"Stop it. Right now, or you're out of this club no matter what you threaten to tell our parents," Bernie said, her eyes fixed on Dagna.

"Sorry," Dagna said, but she didn't look sorry. She looked smug, "So, now we are sisters. We will always be friends forever."

"Yes," Elica admitted, then adding under her breath, "even though we don't really like you that much."

"But blood is blood," Bernie said, "And I suppose we are sisters. Blood sisters. Those are the rules of mixing blood." Then she gave Anna and Elica a look that said she wasn't happy about having Dagna as part of the group. Turning to Dagna, Bernie admitted, "Even though you are my blood sister, I still hate you, and I hope you bleed to death."

"No matter what you think of me, I am one of the Blood sisters. You'll see. You'll be glad I joined, Bernie. Both you and Elica are little runts. You can't defend yourselves. But I am big and strong, and if anyone bothers either of you, I'll make them sorry they did."

"What about Anna? She's the smallest and skinniest of all of us. If you want to be our friend, you have to be nice to Anna too. After all, she is also our sister. If you don't treat her nicely, we won't accept you," Bernie said firmly.

"I don't like her. She's a Jew, and if you don't treat me nicely, I'll tell on you. I'll tell your parents that you cut yourself and mixed your blood with a Jew. I am warning you; they won't be happy," Dagna said.

Bernie and Elica glared at her, but they knew she was right.

CHAPTER THREE

Two years later.

Anna watched a boy in the sandbox as the four blood sisters sat side by side on the swings at the park. The boy was the same age as they were; Anna knew this because she knew his family. They lived across the street from Elica. The boy's name was Tim, and she'd overheard her mother say he was born with some sort of mental defect. She wasn't sure what that meant. But as she watched him drooling, picking his nose, and laughing to himself, she knew he was very different. It was a terrible *rachmones*, a pity, her mother had said. Now, as she was watching Tim, she could see why.

The other girls weren't paying much attention to him. But Anna couldn't help but feel sorry for the boy.

Dagna was kicking the sand under the swings when Elica interrupted the silence. "I have this dream," Elica admitted excitedly. "There is this doll that I saw in the window of Zimmerman's toy store. She is the most beautiful doll I have ever seen, and I want her more than anything in the world. Every night before I go to sleep, I pray to God that somehow she will be mine."

"Your parents are poor. Your mother is a maid, a maid at Anna's house." Dagna glared at Anna, who turned bright red with embarrassment. "It must be nice to have a maid," Dagna said to Anna, who didn't answer. Then she turned her attention back to Elica. "Your mother is a maid, and your father hardly works. When he gets work, it's in a factory that hardly pays much. So, come on, you know as well as I do they don't have money for fancy dolls," Dagna said.

"Maybe they will get it somehow on my birthday. If not by then, maybe by Christmas," Elica said, wrapping her arms around her chest. "You don't know. Maybe they're saving money to buy it for me."

"Be serious. You have four brothers. I am sure your parents have to find enough money to buy them new shoes all the time. Boy's feet grow so fast," Dagna said.

"I don't care what you say. I can dream, and I still want that doll. She is the prettiest doll in the world. If she was mine, I would name her Mary. Have any of you seen her? She's in the window of the toy store."

"I don't like dolls. So, I didn't look. Sorry." Bernie shrugged.

"What about you, Anna? Did you see her?"

Anna nodded. "Yes, she's quite beautiful. She has light blonde hair like yours, Elica, and the same color eyes as yours."

"I know. That's why I should be her mom. We look so much alike."

"Yes, you do," Anna said.

The four girls swung silently for a few moments. Then Elica started singing, and Bernie joined in. Dagna stumbled with the words, but Anna didn't sing. She was lost in thought. What Anna didn't tell Elica, couldn't bear to tell her, was when her parents asked her what she wanted for her upcoming birthday, and before she'd known that Elica wanted the doll, Anna had told her parents that she wanted that very same doll. But now that she had discovered that Elica wanted it, she hoped her parents would not get it for her. In fact, when she goes home for lunch today, she will tell her mother that she has changed her mind and that she really doesn't want the doll at all. Anna knew it would hurt Elica's feelings if Anna received that doll. It would slap Elica in the face with the fact that Anna's parents could afford to buy the doll, and Elica's could not. These thoughts brought back memories. Memories of how Anna and Elica had first met.

Elica's mother was the maid at Anna's home. Until Elica was old enough to go to school, her mother begged Anna's mother to allow her to bring her daughter to work with her. Elica's father had been employed at one of the factories. He worked long hours, and no one was available to watch their child. Anna's mother was reluctant at first. Anna overheard her mother telling her father that she was afraid that having the maid's daughter around would not be good for Anna. But her father had shrugged it off as nonsense.

"Frau Frey has always been a good maid to our family. She has a little girl who needs to be with her mother. How can we not understand this? We must allow her to come with her mother. It's a *mitzvah*, Lillian," her father said.

They were Jewish, but not at all religious. Sometimes they went to the synagogue on high holidays, but did not celebrate the Sabbath each week. Even though they were not religious, her father was a warm-hearted man who loved to participate in *mitzvahs*, good deeds.

"If you say so. I just don't know if we should allow our daughter to become so friendly with the *goyim*, the non-Jews," her mother said.

"Anna is so young. What is it you're so worried about? Are you afraid she will find some *shagitz*, a wild non-Jewish boy, and get married?" her father, Michael, asked.

"It's not that I think she is going to marry one of them. I realize she is too young to worry about that. It's just that I would prefer for her to associate with other Jewish children, not spend her time with a little *shiksa*, a non-Jewish girl. If that little girl is here every day, I am sure they will become good friends."

"A friendship is always a good thing. No matter if people come from different backgrounds or not."

"Of course, a friendship from afar is good. But don't you think there is going to be resentment? This child of Frau Frey comes from a poor family. She will see all the nice things our daughter has, and she will grow to be resentful."

"Stop, Lilian. You should hear yourself talk. It's ugly to be so unkind. We are blessed and fortunate. Try to find it in your heart to be kind and generous to those who have less than we do. We'll give Frau Frey a raise. We can afford it. So, please."

Lilian said, "if you insist, Michael."

"I insist we try," he said.

At the time, Anna had not fully understood what they were saying. But as she grew older, the words her parents had spoken stayed in her mind, and she came to see how clear the divide was between the wealthy and the poor.

Elica, Bernie, and Dagna were talking about something, but Anna wasn't listening. She was still lost in her own thoughts.

Anna closed her eyes and remembered the first time she saw Elica. It was the afternoon following the day she'd overheard her parents talking. Anna's father suggested that Elica's mother, Allis Frey, bring Elica to meet the family. "If all goes well," Anna had heard her father say, "your daughter can come to work with you and play with Anna while you work."

The next day, Anna's father called her to come down to the living room. When Anna walked into the living room, she saw Elica and thought Elica to be the prettiest girl she'd ever seen. Her parents sat across from Elica's mother, who held Elica on her lap. She was beautiful, like a porcelain doll. Her long golden curls were in a half ponytail with a little pink ribbon, and her eyes were soft pale blue. She blinked, and Anna glimpsed her long eyelashes as Elica looked away. Elica seemed to be very shy. Anna smiled at Elica.

"Hello. It's so nice to meet you," Anna said.

"It's nice to meet you, too," Elica replied.

Anna found herself beaming when her father turned to her mother after a few seconds and said, "I don't see any problem with this."

Her mother didn't answer. She just shook her head and shrugged.

Then, to Anna's pure delight, she heard her father say, "Of course, you can bring your daughter with you, Allis. She'll play with Anna."

At first, Elica was very shy and withdrawn. But Anna had been persistent in helping her to open up. Whenever Elica arrived with her mother, Anna would rush over and invite her to the playroom. It was there that Elica lost all sense of shyness. She seemed to enjoy Anna's endless selection of toys. So, as the weeks went by, a friendship grew between them.

Anna loved the days when Elica came to play with her. Both girls admitted that they hated Frau Frey's day off. Time passed, and Elica and Anna became inseparable. Then both girls started school, and that was where Elica met Bernie. When she first told Anna about Bernie, Anna was jealous. But then Elica insisted on introducing Bernie to Anna. She arranged a meeting between the three of them after school one day. They were to meet at the park. At first, Anna was not happy about meeting Bernie. But once she met her, Anna found that she liked Bernie despite herself. Bernie was kind and funny, and she always won when they played any athletic games. But she was generous, outspoken, and fair. Soon, the three were best friends.

But from the beginning, from the first time Anna had seen Dagna, she knew Dagna had a mean spirit. She was not a pretty girl, but it was obvious that she wanted so much to be part of the group. Yet Dagna was openly cruel to Anna. And although she'd found a way to join the blood sisters, she always remained an outsider.

Just then, a group of five boys, the tough fellows from the school Bernie and Elica attended, walked into the park. They were speaking loudly, and it brought Anna's thoughts back to the present moment.

One tall, slender boy with stick-straight hair the color of cinnamon carried a bat and a ball.

"Hello," he said, glancing at Anna, "I'm Oliver. I don't think we've ever met. But you sure are pretty."

Anna blushed as she shook her head. "No, I don't think we have met."

"You don't go to school with Elica and Bernie. Do you?"

Anna shook her head.

"No, she goes to the Jew school," Dagna blurted out.

"Who asked you?" Oliver said to Dagna.

"You don't have to be so rude," Dagna said indignantly.

"Neither do you," Oliver answered.

"Hello. It's good to see you," Rolf, a handsome, tall, dark-haired boy, interrupted. He was smiling at Elica.

Elica blushed and looked away.

The other boys elbowed each other until one of them fell down. Then they all started laughing.

"You fellows are such clowns," Bernie said.

"Are we?" Rolf asked in a condescending tone. "Why don't you let your hair grow? You look like a boy. Didn't your folks ever tell you that girls are supposed to be well groomed and pretty, not scrappy with short, straggly hair?"

"Shut up, Rolf. Bernie's mother is all alone. Her father is dead," Dagna said.

"Really, I'm sorry. I didn't know," Rolf said, but his voice lacked sincerity. "As always, thanks for sticking your nose where it doesn't belong, Dagna. No one was talking to you. Besides, you couldn't look pretty even if you spent a month trying to groom yourself. You're just downright ugly," Rolf said. The other boys began to laugh again, but Oliver wasn't laughing. He was looking at the ground, glancing up shyly at Anna.

Anna looked away.

Then Rolf cleared his throat and tried to sound as if he cared as he said to Bernie, "No, really, I mean, you can't blame me. How was I supposed to know this stuff?" But he wasn't looking at Bernie. He was watching Elica, who was red-faced and could not meet his gaze.

The tension was high. Anna could see that Elica liked Rolf, and he liked her. But she was sure that Elica's loyalty would be towards her friend and not some boy who didn't matter. Bernie didn't want people to know about her business. Anna knew her well enough to know that. She usually had a comeback for any hurtful comment people made, but talking about her parents left Bernie speechless.

Bernie seemed to be searching for something clever to say to put Rolf in his place, but Rolf had lost interest in the girls. He looked away from them, his fascination turning to something else.

Meanwhile, Oliver moved closer to Anna. He spoke quietly so the others couldn't hear him. "I like you, Anna. Someday, I am going to marry you."

Anna's face grew hot. She turned away, embarrassed and not knowing what to say. Then Rolf's loud laughter interrupted the awkward moment.

Rolf had spotted Tim in the sandbox. "Look who's here. The neighborhood idiot," Rolf said.

The boys began laughing. Dagna was laughing, too. But Anna could see by observing Dagna closely that it was a nervous laugh. *Dagna's glad that they aren't criticizing her anymore. She's glad that they are fixing their cruelty on poor Tim. I hope this doesn't end badly. But I don't know what to do to stop it.* Anna thought.

"Should we have a little fun with the idiot?" Peter, one of the boys, suggested.

"Hey idiot, are you having fun playing in the sandbox like a little baby?" Rolf said, and the boys broke into laughter again. Even Oliver laughed, but Anna thought she could see that he didn't like where this was going either. He was only laughing to hide his own feelings of discomfort.

Tim had filled a bucket with sand and was trying to build a sand-castle, but the sand was too dry. It fell in a heap when he turned the bucket over. Peter stepped into the sandbox and kicked the sand into Tim's eyes.

"Don't," Tim moaned.

"Don't," Rolf mimicked him. "Why not?"

"Just leave me alone." Tim sounded like he was ready to cry.

"Nope, we're not going to leave you alone, idiot," another boy said.

"Leave me alone, or I swear I'll tell."

"Awww, I'm scared. Real scared," Rolf said sarcastically.

"Just leave him alone," Oliver suggested, trying to turn Rolf's attention away from Tim. "Come on, let's go play ball."

"This is more fun." Rolf nudged Peter, and they both laughed. Then Rolf kicked sand at Tim, and suddenly Tim was angry. He stood up and began beating his fists on the trunk of a tree. His knuckles were bleeding, but Tim didn't stop. Then he ran over to Rolf and started hitting him with bloody hands.

"Take it easy, you idiot," Rolf said, pushing Tim away. Tim fell and grabbed onto Rolf's legs. He was pounding his head against Rolf's knee.

"Leave me alone. I told you to leave me alone," Tim said. Drool was dripping from the side of his mouth down his chin.

"He's disgusting," Peter said. "He's drooling all over you, Rolf."

Rolf tried to break free, but Tim was strong and held on to Rolf's legs. He bit into Rolf's calf. Rolf let out a scream. "He bit me. The little bastard bit me," he said.

Peter picked up a rock and threw it at Tim. It hit Tim in the face. Tim let out a scream and released Rolf. Then he put his hand up to his cheek where he'd been hit. Blood flowed freely. Tim looked at his fingers covered in blood and began to wail.

Bernie glared at Rolf and his friends. "You hurt him. Can't you see he's not right in the head? How dare you do something like this? What are you thinking?"

Bernie went over to Tim. She unbuttoned the bottom of her white blouse and began to wipe the blood from Tim's face. He cooed under her gentle touch. She shook her head at Rolf. "You are a sadist," she said.

Rolf looked at Bernie with the slightest bit of guilt in his eyes. Then he turned to his friends and said, "I've had enough of this. Let's get out of here and play ball."

Bernie has a way of bringing civility to every situation. Look at her. Even Rolf feels guilty under her scrutiny. Anna thought.

After the boys went to play ball on the other side of the park, Anna and Bernie helped Tim to get up on his feet, and then, with Elica by their side, they walked him home while Dagna trailed behind.

CHAPTER FOUR

I t was Anna Levinstein's twelfth birthday, and her parents decorated the house for her birthday party. For weeks before the party, her mother had tried to encourage Anna to invite all children in her class at the Jewish school Anna attended. Anna invited several Jewish classmates, but to her mother's disappointment, she insisted on inviting Elica, Bernie, and even Dagna.

"They won't be comfortable with your Jewish friends, and your Jewish friends won't be comfortable with them," Frau Levinstein said. "There is a difference in the way we live and the way the *goyim* live. Your girlfriends will feel out of place here. You wouldn't want that now, would you?"

Anna took a long breath. "Mom, I know you mean well. But Elica and Bernie are my best friends. I just wouldn't, I just couldn't, have a birthday party without them."

Her mother shook her head. "And what about that Dagna? She's a coarse little thing. What kind of family does she come from?"

"You know what kind of family she comes from," Anna said. "Her parents are poor and uneducated. You tell me this all the time about my friends. So, I don't know why you are asking me this now."

"I am asking you because I want you to realize that although you like them, these girls are lower class, Annaleh. They are going to bring you down."

"I don't care about their class. I don't particularly care for Dagna, but Elica and Bernie are my best friends."

Anna's mother just shook her head and walked out of the room.

The children arrived at eleven thirty that morning. The party was a luncheon, and Frau Levinstein had gone out of her way to have it catered by a kosher restaurant. Although she did not keep kosher in her home, she thought that perhaps the families of Anna's classmates might keep kosher. She wanted to be sure that they were able to enjoy the food. The party room looked lovely, with white tablecloths and pretty party favors at each place setting. On a table in the corner sat a sheet cake, beautifully decorated with icing flowers in blush pink, which was Anna's favorite color. Another table covered with a white tablecloth and a pink bow sat beside the cake table. This table was for everyone to place the gifts they'd brought.

The girls wore pretty cotton dresses, which looked like they came from one of the fine department stores in town. The boys wore jackets and ties, which they continually fiddled with, trying to make them less uncomfortable.

Frau Levinstein was right. Anna's non-Jewish friends stood out in their inexpensive, well-worn dresses. But Anna didn't care. In fact, she didn't even notice. As soon as she saw Elica and Bernie, she ran over to them and gave them both a big hug. Then she noticed Dagna standing alone and hugged her, too. "I'm so glad all of you could come," Anna said, beaming.

"I brought you a gift," Bernie said.

"Thank you," Anna said, taking the small box wrapped in brown paper.

"It's not much."

"I don't care. I'll cherish it forever," Anna said, "because it's from you."

"I wanted to bring you something, but my mom said there wasn't enough money for me to spend on gifts," Elica said as she looked down at the floor.

"It's all right. I don't care about the presents. I'm just glad you could come and celebrate my birthday with me," Anna smiled brightly at Elica.

Dagna didn't bring a gift. Her dress was even shabbier than Elica's and Bernie's, and her hair was matted and uncombed. She looked around at the well-groomed children uncomfortably.

Anna walked over and put her arm around Dagna's shoulder. "I'm so glad you could come," she said. Anna whispered softly to Bernie and Elica, "I've decided that you two are going to sit on either side of me at the head of the table."

CHAPTER FIVE

A bell tinged, and everyone found their place cards, and within a few minutes, they were all seated at the table. Each place setting had a small package of candy-covered nuts tied with a pink ribbon.

Anna glanced around the room. Her mother had insisted she invite everyone in her class. And now, forty children were seated in a large airy room. "You don't want anyone to feel left out, do you?" her mother had said when she was hand-addressing the invitations.

What could Anna say? Of course, she didn't want anyone to feel left out. But she hardly knew any of these children. Except for her good friends, Elica and Bernie, she was a loner. She was a shy girl who loved spending time in her room with her two cats and a pile of books. In fact, nothing gave her more joy than a trip to the library, where she knew she was bound to meet a whole group of new bookish friends.

Frau Levinstein had hired two additional maids besides Elica's mother to serve at the birthday party.

There were platters and platters of thick white bread and fresh fruit. There were thick spicy beef sausages, bowls of mustard, and appetizing bowls of vinegar potato salad.

Anna saw Dagna and Bernie's eyes light up when they saw all the food, and for the first time, she realized they did not have access to food like this at home. The thought made her sad, and she wanted to get up and hug them both. But she dared not. Her mother would have been furious if she had abandoned table manners. Her mother had been so adamant that she learned and practiced.

Then Anna noticed Elica. Elica was trying to avert her eyes from her mother, who was serving the food at the table. Elica looked uneasy and embarrassed. Anna had never considered that Elica would be ashamed of her mother being the maid. She had never really even thought about it. But now, it struck her like a bolt of lightning. Suddenly, she was aware of the class division between herself and her closest friends for the first time. She knew this divide would grow larger rather than smaller as they grew older. All the children were eating, talking, and laughing. It was her party, but Anna couldn't eat. In fact, she felt like crying.

CHAPTER SIX

After lunch, a magician came to entertain the group. He did magic tricks. Then he suddenly pulled a bunch of flowers out of a hat, which he handed to Anna. She smiled and thanked him. He bowed and told jokes, which made everyone laugh. Anna tried to laugh. She tried hard to lose herself in the joy of her birthday. Even as a child, she was a deep, thoughtful girl, and she was afraid that her friendships with Elica and Bernie might not withstand the teenage years to come. This made her sad.

"Shall we open the presents?" Frau Levinstein asked Anna, "Or shall we have cake first?"

"Let's have cake." Anna smiled. Then she got up and walked over to her mother. "I would rather open my gifts later, alone. I don't want to open them at the party."

"And why is that? You always enjoyed opening your birthday presents, Anna. Don't you feel well?"

"I'm fine. It's just that I am afraid that my birthday presents might make my friends feel uncomfortable. I know that Elica and Dagna weren't able to bring gifts."

"Oh, I see," Frau Levinstein said, "you are starting to see that you and these friends of yours come from different worlds, aren't you?"

"I don't know. I just don't want to open the presents until I am alone."

"All right. It's your birthday. However, your father and I are going to give you your gift right after everyone finishes their cake."

Anna cringed. She knew what her gift was. She knew because the other day, Elica had mentioned that she walked by the toy store and saw that the doll she'd wanted so badly was gone. "Someone bought her," Elica said. "I wanted her so much. I even named her. I was making doll clothes out of an old sheet for her too. But now, she's gone."

"Maybe your mom bought her for you," Dagna said. "Isn't your birthday coming up?"

Elica's birthday was two weeks after Anna's. In fact, that was one of the first things they'd discussed that had brought them closer together. "Yes, but I doubt my mother would spend much money on a doll for me. We can't afford it."

Just hearing these words made Anna cringe inside. She knew for sure who had bought it.

Everyone finished their cake. Then Anna's mother brought a large box wrapped with pretty pink paper and a matching bow. "Happy birthday, darling," her mother said. "This is your gift from your papa and me. He can't be here today, because he had to go to work to take care of some things. But you know your papa loves you and wishes you the happiest birthday."

Anna smiled, but inside, her stomach was grinding. She didn't want to open this box while Elica sat across the table. She knew that Elica was going to be devastated when she saw the doll. Frau Frey stood on the fringes of the group. There was a worried look on her face. Anna realized that Elica's mother knew what was in the box. In fact, she'd probably wrapped it. Anna thought that Elica's mother felt very sad and inadequate.

"Open your present," Anna's mother said, oblivious to the situation.

Anna's hands trembled as she carefully removed the paper from the box. She felt dizzy and hoped she wouldn't vomit when she took the lid off the box.

"Hold her up so everyone can see her," Anna's mother said, taking the doll away from Anna and holding her up so everyone in the room could see.

The girls gasped. But Anna didn't care. She couldn't take her eyes off Elica, whose face had turned white. Elica got up and ran out of the room. No one noticed except Anna and Frau Frey, Elica's mother.

Bernie got up and followed Elica, and then Dagna followed Bernie.

Anna assumed her friends had left because she did not see them anymore that afternoon.

The party ended, and all the children went home. Anna was tired and upset as she walked upstairs to her room, where Frau Frey had carefully placed all of Anna's unopened birthday gifts. The floor was lined with lovely presents wrapped in pretty paper. Anna glanced at the gifts. She knew by their shape that some of them were books. And she loved books. In fact, if she could spend a day any way she wanted to, her first choice would be to spend it with Elica and Bernie. But her second choice would be to stay home alone and read. Anna loved to read. She already owned plenty of books. At least once a week, one of her parents took her to the library. But she still wondered which books lay amongst the pile of gifts. The idea of a new book, a new story, always made her excited and ready to go on a literary journey. But then her eyes fell upon the doll. It was the most beautiful porcelain doll she had ever seen.

Frau Frey had placed the doll so she was sitting up on the pink bedspread that covered Anna's canopy bed. The doll had long golden hair that waved and curled around her heart-shaped face in small pin curls. Her gorgeous blue eyes and her perfect bow-shaped red lips were painted on. She wore a white lace dress and a matching bow in her hair. Anna let out a gasp. *I love her.* She thought as she gently touched the lace of the doll's dress. *She is perfect. The most perfect doll I have ever seen. What shall I name her?* But then she remembered Elica's sad face as she received the doll as a gift. Suddenly, all the joy of owning the doll was gone. Even though Anna was only a child, she somehow knew this doll would come between her and her best friend.

The difference in schools and their families' financial situations had already begun to unravel their friendship. It was apparent how uncomfortable Elica had felt that afternoon. Bernie, not so much, because pretty dresses weren't as important to her. Anna had seen Elica looking around at what the other girls were wearing, and she wished she could give Elica half of her own wardrobe. But how could she? To offer to give Elica her clothes would be to offend Elica, and the last thing Anna wanted to do was to hurt her best friend's feelings.

Suddenly the excitement of the day was dwarfed by her fears. The thought of losing her best friend because they had been born into different worlds made her sad and afraid. Anna touched the doll's hair gently. She loved the doll; Elica wasn't the only one who had wanted it. Anna had longed for it too when she saw it in the window of the toy store. But now, as she was facing the reality of the divide growing deeper between herself and Elica and Bernie, she realized that all the toys in the world couldn't replace her friends. And suddenly, the doll was no longer of any importance.

CHAPTER SEVEN

1940, The Attic

Anna lay on the concrete floor of the attic. She was drifting in and out of consciousness. The room was spinning, still spinning. Her head ached, and she felt like she might vomit. But then, for a single moment, she closed her eyes, and her mind was clear. *Who could have done this, and why? Who knew we were here? And who would have been so cruel as to turn us in?*

CHAPTER EIGHT

1932

The following week was Elica's birthday dinner. Anna went over to Elica's home to celebrate Elica's birthday. She brought a gift, and even though her mother didn't approve of their friendship, she allowed Anna to have dinner at Elica's home to celebrate Elica's birthday. So, on the day of Elica's birthday, Anna's mother sent food home with Frau Frey. "This is for your daughter's birthday dinner this evening," Lilian Levinstein said.

"Thank you so much, ma'am," Elica's mother said.

"I wanted it to be special for Elica," Lilian said. "And since Anna will attend, I didn't want you to have to use your food to feed her."

"Yes, ma'am," Frau Frey said.

Anna arrived at Elica's apartment at five o'clock. Frau Frey opened the door when Anna knocked. She looked even more weathered in her old house dress than she did in the crisp black and white maid's uniform she wore each day at Anna's house. Although Anna had only been to Elica's home a handful of times, it always felt strange for Anna to have a meal at Elica's home. Seeing Frau Frey with her own family was so different than seeing her in her maid's uniform. Although Frau Frey was always kind to Anna, she always seemed a little uncomfortable around Anna. Anna felt that Frau Frey didn't like her. Anna was sure that Frau Frey didn't approve of the friendship that had grown so deep between the girls any more than Anna's mother, although she never said a word about it.

Anna thought that perhaps Frau Frey blamed herself because she had been the one who had gone to Anna's parents asking them if she could bring her daughter to work with her. Now, it seemed like Elica was not satisfied living the life her parents were able to give her. Even Anna could see how much Elica yearned for a better life. *She loves my clothes and my toys. She has told me many times that she wishes we went to school together. I think that Frau Frey is upset because being around me has made Elica want things that her parents can't afford to give her.*

"Hello, Anna." Frau Frey frowned as she opened the door. "I see you brought your new doll with you."

"Yes," Anna said, not wanting to share her intentions because she knew that Frau Frey would tell her not to give the doll to Elica. In fact, she would probably forbid Elica from accepting Anna's gift.

"Elica's in the bedroom," Frau Frey said.

The house was small and cramped, and Elica's room was no bigger than Anna's closet. When Anna entered Elica's room, Elica looked up and saw the doll in Anna's arms. Elica's eyes grew large, then she turned pale.

"I got her, especially for you," Anna said as cheerfully as she could, but her voice was shaking. She was nervous.

"No, you didn't. Your parents gave her to you for your birthday. Remember, I was at your party. I saw your *mutti* give her to you."

"Yes, that's true. But what you don't know is that I asked my parents for the doll as a gift so I could give her to you," Anna lied. "I knew how much you wanted her. So, I told them I wanted her as my birthday gift."

Elica stood silent for a moment. Then her shoulders slumped.

"Oh, Anna," she said, then tears fell down her cheeks. She ran over and put her arms around Anna. "You didn't have to do that for me."

"I wanted to."

"But it was your birthday gift."

"I know, but just look at her," Anna said, pointing to the beautiful doll. "She looks just like you, Elica. It's only right that you should have her. Besides, you know me, I like books much better than dolls, anyway. I got a few new ones for my birthday."

"I know you do. I don't like to read much, but I love it when you read to Bernie and me."

"I love to read to you, too. And I am so excited about the new books. I haven't read any of them yet."

"So, about the doll," Elica said gingerly, touching the doll's hair, "are you sure you want to give her to me?"

"Of course, I am sure. I want you to have her. Since she looks like you, you should be her mama, not me." Even as Anna handed the doll to Elica, she secretly wished she could keep her. But the light in Elica's eyes was worth the sacrifice. Anna decided that her friendship was worth far more than any doll.

That evening, after dinner, when Anna was getting ready to leave, Frau Frey handed her a thin slice of cake wrapped inside a small towel. "For your brother, Anselm," she said.

"Oh, thank you so much. He'll love this," Anna said.

Anselm was two years younger than Anna. He was born with a blood disorder, and although the doctors did not expect him to live past ten, Anna's mother refused to believe them. She took him to doctors and specialists, hoping to save him.

"You forgot your doll," Frau Frey said.

"No, I loaned it to Elica."

"Oh?"

"Yes, just for a short while," Anna lied. Behind Frau Frey's back, Anna winked at Elica and smiled.

Then, without speaking aloud, Elica mouthed the words, "thank you. I love you."

CHAPTER NINE

A few weeks later, Anna came home from her piano lesson to find the doll she'd given Elica sitting on her bed. Shocked, she walked over and picked up the doll. Then she looked around the room, thinking that perhaps Elica was here playing a hiding game. She looked under the bed, then in the closet, but no one was there. "Elica?" Anna said, "I give up. You can come out now."

No answer. Puzzled, Anna glanced over at the doll again. Then there was a knock on her bedroom door. "Anna, can I come in?" her mother asked in a gentle but firm voice.

"Yes, mother."

Frau Levinstein had just returned from a charity luncheon and was still wearing her dress and high heels. "I want to talk to you. Please, sit down."

Anna sat down on the bed. She knew her mother was angry with her; she knew it had to do with the doll. It was an expensive gift that her parents had given her, and she assumed her mother couldn't understand why she would give it to Elica. Anna's mother sat beside her. "Frau Frey brought your doll back this morning. Apparently, your friend Dagna told Frau Frey that you had given the doll to Elica for her birthday. Is this true?"

"Yes, it is, mother."

"Why? I don't understand. I thought you wanted that doll so badly. You told your father and me that you wanted it for your birthday. It was a very expensive doll. She is handmade and hand-painted. Why would you give her away?"

"Because I have other dolls, and Elica has none. I wanted her to have this one. I didn't know she wanted it when I asked for it. But I saw how hurt she was when I got it, and I just couldn't keep it. Do you understand at all? Elica's friendship means more to me than a doll." Anna's eyes were becoming glassy with tears.

"I understand what you are saying, and believe me, I think it is very kind of you. But, Anna, you must realize it is not good to buy your friends. Real friends don't expect that from you."

"I wasn't trying to buy her. I just wanted to give her something nice. Something she never had."

"Yes, I understand. But this sort of thing is exactly what I was afraid of when your father was adamant about allowing Frau Frey to bring her daughter with her to work. I knew that the class separation would be a problem, eventually. It would be impossible for her not to see that you have so much and she has so little. I was afraid that this divide between the two of you would make you feel like you had to make this better for her. Almost like you are guilty of having so much more? This is what you feel, isn't it?"

"Maybe, sometimes it is. But I don't see why it was any of Dagna's business what I did with my doll. She had no right to speak to Frau Frey about it. It was my birthday present. The doll belongs to me. Doesn't that mean I am free to do with it as I please?"

Her mother sighed. "Yes, I suppose it does. But you must realize Dagna told on Elica and you because she was jealous, too. This is hard to explain because you have such a kind and good heart. You are my little *gutte neshuma*, a good-hearted child. You always wanted things to be fair and for everyone to be happy. But real life isn't that way, my child. It just isn't, and sadly, these girls are poor. I know you like them, but they will always notice that you have more than they do, and that will always be a problem."

Anna's mother hesitated for a moment and took a long breath. "When I was young, my bubbie used to say that jealousy was the most dangerous emotion. She told me that when someone is jealous of you, they are often inclined to do cruel things. This worries me. I know your father thinks it's perfectly fine for you to pal around with the maid's daughter and her friends. He thinks I am being snooty when I say I don't think it's a good idea. But the reason I don't like it is not because I believe we are better. It's because I am afraid for you. I am afraid of how this might all play out in the future. As I said, jealousy can be blinding. It can make people act in ways they would not normally act, and quite often, the envied people get hurt. Sometimes they get hurt badly."

"Mother, Elica, and Bernie would never hurt me. As far as Dagna is concerned, she is different. Dagna is not a real friend to any of us. She just follows us around. She has always been a troublemaker, but she's not the only troublemaker I have met. I've seen plenty of troublemakers at the Jewish school, too."

"I am aware that there are troublemakers everywhere. But this Dagna has a mean spirit. I see it in her eyes, and it scares me because I can also see that she is jealous of you. I don't like it. I just don't like it," her mother said. Then she took Anna's hand and held it between both of hers. Sighing, she continued, "Annaleh, I know you don't understand me. You might be too young to understand this fully. You can't see any of this ever happening with Elica or Bernie because, right now, they are your best friends. But as you grow older, the class division between you girls will become more and more apparent. The jealousy will grow. Believe me when I tell you, it will."

"I hate class divisions. I hate money, and I hate jealousy," Anna said, pulling her hand away from her mother, tears flowing freely from her eyes and streaming down her face.

"Yes, I am sure you do. However, when you are older and see

things more clearly, you'll be glad you are on this side of the divide and not one of the poorer children."

Anna stared at her mother. She wanted to tell her how obnoxious she was sounding. But she knew that no matter what she said, it wouldn't matter. Her mother was stubborn, and she'd made up her mind. So, instead of arguing, Anna nodded and decided to talk to her father about the situation when he returned home from work later that evening.

CHAPTER TEN

That night when her father entered the house, Anna ran into his arms as she always did. "Papa, how was your day?"

"Good, good, my *shaina maidel*, my beautiful girl. Nu, and how was yours?" he asked as he took off his hat.

"Good."

"You went for your piano lesson today, Anna? How did it go?" her father said. Then he turned and hugged Anselm.

"All right. I'm getting better all the time. My teacher says I am exceptional for my age."

"Of course you are. You're my brilliant daughter, and you always make me so proud," her father said, smiling. Then he turned to Anselm. "And you? How was your day, young man?"

"I had a good day," Anselm said. He rarely complained, even when he had suffered and his condition caused him to need emergency medical attention. But today had been a good day. He had not had episodes of coughing up blood. It had been a little easier than usual for him to breathe. Frau Frey had taken him for a short walk, allowing him to be outside in the garden for almost an hour.

"Papa, can I talk to you?" Anna asked.

"Of course, you can always talk to me, *mayn kind*, my child. What's the matter?"

She told him everything that had happened, how she gave the doll to Elica. She told him what had happened with Dagna and, finally, what her mother had told her about jealousy and the future as far as her friends were concerned.

He listened without saying a word as she told him all about the doll. When she'd finished, he ran his fingers over the stubble growing on his chin. Then he said, "Well, the truth of the matter is, the doll was given to you as a gift. It is your doll, but I understand how your mother feels about all of this. However, if you want to give the doll to your friend, it is your right to do so."

"So, I can give it to Elica?"

"If that's what you truly want."

"Yes. It is. But you will need to tell Frau Frey I have your permission, or she won't let Elica accept it."

"I see," he said. "All right. I will speak to Frau Frey if that's your decision."

Anna's mother had been listening by the door. She walked inside. "Michael," she addressed her husband, "I don't understand you. I told her she may not give the doll to Elica. Now you say she can? You are going against my wishes?" Lilian Levinstein said to her husband. Her face was flushed, and her fists were clenched. "I told her she may not do this. Now you say she can?"

"Yes Lilian, I must say that she can because we gave the doll to Anna as a gift. That means that the doll belongs to Anna, so ultimately, it is her decision to do what she wants with it."

"She's only a child. How can she make any kind of decision?"

"Because that is what growing up is all about. We are here to guide our children, Lilly, but not to force them to do what we say."

"You infuriate me," Anna's mother said. "You are too lenient with this child. I am afraid your leniency is going to result in big problems for Anna later in life." Then she turned and walked out of the room.

That night, Frau Levinstein did not come to the table for dinner.

CHAPTER ELEVEN

Anna did not say another word about the doll. But her father came to her room the following morning before he left for work. He knocked on the door. "I spoke with Frau Frey. She understands I am allowing you to give the doll to Elica. So, you may do so this afternoon."

"Thank you, Papa," Anna said, hugging him. "I am so glad you understand."

School was out for the summer. So, Anna got dressed and walked over to Elica's home. She knocked on the door. Elica answered it. "I had to give her back to you," Elica said. "My *mutti* said so."

"I know. Dagna told her." Anna rolled her eyes.

"How do you know?"

"My parents told me," Anna said.

"Come on in," Elica said.

Anna walked in, "But I have good news. I spoke with my father, and he said that the doll was a gift to me and so it's mine, and I can give it to you if I want to. He spoke to your mother and told her it's all right for you to keep the doll."

"Really?"

"Yes, really," Anna said, handing the doll to Elica.

There were tears in Elica's eyes. "Oh, Anna. I love her so much."

"I know you do. That's why I wanted you to have her."

After Anna left, Elica went to the tiny room in the back of the house where she slept. It was more like a closet than a bedroom. But it was hers. On the small cot where she slept, she placed the doll of her dreams, the doll she had wanted since she'd first seen her. Elica knew her family could never afford to waste money on such a thing. So, until Anna had made this possible, Elica was certain that she would never own the doll. But she couldn't help praying and wishing. She thought of Anna and smiled. *Anna is my best friend in the entire world, and she made my dream come true.* Gently, Elica touched the doll's hair. It was the same color as her own. In fact, she thought Anna was right; the doll looked just like her. The only difference was that the doll had a nicer dress than Elica had ever owned. She closed her eyes and thought for a moment. *This is the first time in my life that my dreams have come true. This is my doll, and she is right here beside me. I can hardly believe it. I walked by the toy store window for months just to look at her. Now, she is mine. I was going to call her Mary, but I've changed my mind?* Elica looked at the doll. *I'll call her Anna because Anna gave her to me.*

CHAPTER TWELVE

1935

At fourteen, the girls had begun to grow up. They shared secrets about which boys they thought were handsome and what they dreamed of for their futures. They kept secret notes about the boys they liked in the tin buried in the secret place where they met at least once weekly. Even though Elica had always wanted pretty things, suddenly, lovely clothes and nice shoes were no longer just things she liked to look at. Now they were of the utmost importance. The fact that her family could hardly afford to give her much of anything made life very difficult and often painful for her.

Bernie didn't care much for clothing or fancy things. However, she was forced to work after school because her mother needed financial help. She hardly remembered her father, but she told her blood sisters that she wished he were still alive. "I wouldn't have to work nearly as hard if I had a father like the rest of you."

Even with all the changes in their lives, Anna, Elica, and Bernie remained strong, with Dagna hanging tight at their heels. But the more discontented with her life that Elica became, the more Dagna tried to win Elica's favor by stealing gifts to give her. Clothing, cosmetics, and costume jewelry made Elica squeal with delight.

When they were little girls, Anna's family money had little impression on the friendship between her and Elica. Now that the girls were older, Elica had begun to make snide remarks that sometimes hurt Anna's feelings. Comments like, "It must be wonderful to have anything you want, whenever you want it. I can't imagine what it's like to never have to wear hand-me-downs. But then again, I've never had a life like yours. After all, my mother is your maid."

Anna didn't know how to answer, so she said nothing. Then the moment passed, and Elica was her friend again.

Life was changing for Anna too. She began making friends at the Jewish school she attended and her piano lessons. A nervous, talkative girl named Judith, who constantly twisted her hair and was always worried about disappointing her parents, befriended Anna when their music teacher insisted that they play a duet. Judith on violin and Anna on piano. Anna found Judith difficult to work with because she rambled on a lot, but when she actually played her instrument, she was brilliant. Anna found she liked her because of this. Anna also became friendly with Debra, a girl in her science class. They had been paired together during lab time. Debra reminded Anna of Bernie. She was fearless, like Bernie, and had the same strong stomach. When they were forced to dissect a frog, Anna felt like she might vomit. But Debra only laughed and told Anna to sit down and look away while she did the dissection. Anna was relieved and grateful.

But none of these new friends felt as close to Anna as Elica and Bernie did. These girls were more like acquaintances. But Elica and Bernie were her sisters, her blood sisters.

On a frigid winter morning, Anna awoke before dawn. She was nauseated, and her stomach cramped. Her underwear felt wet. She got out of bed. The floor was cold, and the chill on her feet shot through her entire body as she walked to the bathroom. She sat down to urinate, and when she did, Anna's heart jumped with shock when she saw a large stain of bright red blood on her panties. Gasping, she ran to her mother's room and shook her until she awoke.

"Mother, I am sick. I am afraid I might be dying."

Her mother sat up, still drowsy, and stared at Anna. "What is it? What's wrong?" she asked.

"I am bleeding from where I pee."

"Oh, dear. Yes," her mother said calmly. "I've been meaning to talk to you about this. First, let me show you how to take care of it. I have some rags I will give you. Then we'll go to the kitchen and have a cup of tea. Just you and me. We have a lot to talk about."

"But am I alright? Should we wake papa and tell him about this?"

"No, sweetheart, there's no need to wake your papa. You're going to be just fine," her mother said, smiling. "Come on, let's go."

Anna followed her mother. She couldn't help but feel surprised at how calm her mother was, considering what she'd just told her.

They went into the bathroom, and her mother said, "This is perfectly normal. You have become a woman."

Anna just nodded. She wasn't sure what all of this meant.

But her mother was kind, and she showed Anna what to do.

After her mother showed her how to take care of her bleeding. She said, "All right, come, let's go to the kitchen."

Anna followed her mother to the kitchen. Then she stood watching while her mother put a pot of water on the stove to boil. "Sit down, Annaleh," her mother said. "It's all right. Now I am going to explain everything. I am going to tell you all you need to know about this blood on your underwear."

"Am I sick? Am I going to die? There is so much blood, and it's so red. It scares me."

"I know. I remember my first period. It can be scary. But it's also a blessing. I will explain. But first, I am going to do something that is going to seem very odd right now," her mother said. Then she slapped Anna hard across the face.

"Mother? Why did you do that?" Anna felt the sting. She put her hand up to her cheek, and tears started to form in her eyes as she looked into her mother's eyes. "I don't understand any of this."

"I know that. It's an old tradition. A mother must slap her daughter the first time she gets her period." Her mother smiled. Then she took Anna's face in her hands and kissed her gently, where the skin was red from the slap. The tea kettle began to whistle. Her mother stood up and poured them both a cup of hot tea. Then she sat down and took Anna's hands in her own. "You are a woman now, Anna. You are not a little girl anymore. That blood is a gift from God. Because once you bleed, it means that your body is mature enough to have a child."

"So, this bleeding is normal?" Anna asked.

"Yes, very normal." Her mother smiled.

"But, I don't feel well. I feel queasy, and I have stomach cramps."

"I know. But it is a gift nonetheless. Someday, when you are married, you will have a beautiful son or daughter, and you will find that you are very grateful to be a woman and to have a period."

Then her mother explained all about love and marriage and how babies were conceived. Anna listened, embarrassed but intrigued. When her mother had finished explaining, Anna found she felt closer to her mother than she ever had before.

CHAPTER THIRTEEN

Once Anna began to menstruate, she found she was often moody. Sometimes she would be on top of the world, and everything seemed to go her way. Other times she was miserable for no reason other than that a small pimple had erupted on her chin. She studied her appearance in the mirror for hours. What had once been acceptable was now questionable. Was she too short? Was she too thin? Would she look better if her eyes were blue? Were her lips too full? Anna told Anselm that she was secretly afraid she was ugly and would never meet a boy and get married. He told her she was the prettiest girl he knew, except for Elica.

Anna knew Anselm had always had a crush on Elica. He'd shared that secret with her, and she had never told anyone, especially not Elica. But Anna knew Anselm was taken with Elica because she was the only young girl who had ever been kind to him. As much as the Levinstein's tried to hide it, everyone in their close-knit community knew about Anselm's illness. Most girls turned away when they saw him. Anna assumed Elica was not bothered by Anselm because she'd known Anselm since they were children.

As time passed, Anna noticed strange changes in her body. Hair had sprung up almost overnight, between her legs and under her arms. Even the hair on her legs grew thicker and darker. She realized she spent more time daydreaming than she had ever done before. She often wondered what it might feel like to be kissed. Elica, Bernie, and Dagna were all close in age and went through the same things. They discussed the changes in their bodies and minds when alone in the park. They had all experienced their first menstrual cycle and talked about how painful and annoying it was. Dagna and Elica told the others what they thought about the boys they went to school with. "I wonder what it would feel like to have a boy kiss you. I mean, really kiss you, like they kiss in the movies. You know what I mean?" Elica said.

"I wonder, too," Dagna said.

"Elica! Would you let a boy kiss you?" Anna said, her face flushed with embarrassment.

"Yes, don't you wonder what it would feel like?" Elica said.

"No! Never!" Anna said, turning away, embarrassed. But she wondered.

Bernie did not join in the conversation; she only sat quietly and listened. She never showed interest in boys. But Anna noticed Bernie watching Elica with a strange look on her face. *It is as if Bernie is in love with Elica.* Anna thought. *But that's not possible because they're both girls.*

The divide between Anna and her friends was growing more apparent. As the months passed, Anna began to feel even more like an outsider because she went to a different school. She had never met or seen any of the boys Elica and Dagna were talking about. An odd sort of loneliness came over Anna. It wasn't that her friends were purposely leaving her out. They were being separated by that class distinction her mother had told her about.

Dagna, Elica, and Bernie went to school together in a lower-class neighborhood. The boys they met, who were their schoolmates, were the sons of the men who worked at the factories and lived in the same neighborhoods they did. Her friends belonged to the same church and went to church dances together. They often invited Anna to the dances, but her parents would not allow her to attend. And She didn't go to any of the dances from the Jewish school that she attended because she couldn't convince Judith or Debra to go with her, and she was too shy to go alone.

CHAPTER FOURTEEN

The blood sisters were still a strong club. They continued to have meetings. However, the meetings were much shorter and less often these days. Still, they went to their secret spot, and often they still left notes telling their most private feelings in the little tin that they kept buried. Everyone seemed to be busy with homework and part-time jobs. The different schools and different lifestyles had created a gap between them, leaving Anna longing for the way things used to be. She had her new friends, Debra and Judith, who she spent time with, but it was not the same. She felt lost and alone, as if a part of her were dying, and she could not find a way to revive it. The loneliness was almost unbearable. There was no one she could talk to about this.

Her father was very busy with work, and her mother would never understand. Anselm had not been doing well lately. He had more episodes, and the doctor said his condition was growing worse. So, Anna decided it was best not to burden him with her problems. However, the most painful part was that Elica was both the problem and her best friend and confidant. If she could have chosen anyone she wanted to talk to, it would have been Elica. But Elica was changing, and Anna saw that she couldn't talk to her either.

Having always been an avid reader, Anna searched and finally found comfort in her books. She began to read a lot more. To fill her need for more books, she went to the library. There, amongst her fictional friends, she found solace. At least once each week, after school, she walked into town and up the concrete steps of the large brick library building. The musty smell of old books made her feel warm and welcome. Running her hands over the leather-bound book jackets as she wandered the shelves gave her a feeling of stability that she didn't feel anywhere else in the world. Then she lifted the books that caught her eye and read the descriptions until she made a few choices. With her books in hand, she sat at a table and read just enough of each book until she could decide which one she would take home for the week. It just so happened that on one such day, a handsome dark-haired boy with soulful eyes sat down across the table from her. She looked up to see who was sitting across from her. The boy looked directly into Anna's eyes, and he smiled.

"Hello," he said.

"Hello," she managed, hoping against all odds that she wasn't blushing. Her face felt hot.

"I'm Daniel Goldenberg," he whispered, trying not to disturb the other readers.

Anna found herself intrigued. "I'm Anna Levinstein."

"It's nice to meet you," he said.

Daniel was a good conversationalist. He asked Anna questions about the books she'd chosen and the books she'd read. And he told her about books he'd read recently. Soon they were talking freely, and she found that she forgot to be uncomfortable. He was easy to talk to.

An old man who was sitting at the same table as Daniel and Anna was giving them both dirty looks because they were talking so much. "This is a library. You are supposed to be quiet here," the old man hissed.

"I'm sorry," Anna answered.

"Let's move to a table in the back," Daniel suggested.

"Good idea," the old man said sarcastically.

Daniel got up and carried his books and Anna's to an open table in the back of the room.

"This should be better. We are alone here, and we won't be disturbing anyone." Then he added, "That old man is just so cranky."

Anna giggled a little. "Well, he was reading before we started talking, and in all fairness, when I am reading, I hate to be disturbed."

"I know, it's true. I feel the same way," Daniel said.

In that very first conversation, Anna learned that she and Daniel came from similar backgrounds. His father was a successful factory owner, and both of them were non-religious, even though they were Jews. Like Anna, Daniel enjoyed reading. The more they talked about the books they enjoyed, the more they found that their love of books brought them closer together.

From that day forward, whenever Anna went to the library, she always looked around to see if Daniel was at the library when she arrived. Often, he was there. As soon as their eyes met, he would motion to her to join him. Then the two of them would go to an open table in the back of the room, where they would once again lose themselves in conversation. One afternoon, when Anna went to the library, she looked around but didn't see Daniel anywhere. So, instead of sitting at a table, she scanned the shelves and found several books. Then she got in line to check them out. The line was long that day. She was waiting patiently when Daniel walked through the door. He saw her, and his face lit up with a big grin.

"How are you?" he said as he walked over to her.

"I'm doing pretty well," she answered.

"I was hoping I would find you here today. I brought something for you. I just finished this book, and I think it is excellent. There's another week left. Do you want to read it?" Daniel showed her a copy of the short story *Death in Venice*. When Anna saw the book, she was so excited to read it.

"I've been dying to read that. But I haven't been able to get my hands on it. Can I have a look inside?"

"Of course. It was wonderful. The writing was superb. I told you I had brought it for you. I took it out from the library, but I still have another week before it has to be returned. If I return it, they will give it to the next person on the list, and you will have to wait. But if you want it, I will give it to you, and you can return it in a week."

She took the book from him and began reading the inside jacket.

"It was so well written that I had no trouble envisioning everything the writer described." Daniel cleared his throat and went on.

"I've heard so much about this book. I've been on a waiting list for it for over a month now."

"I know it was very hard to get," he said, then ran his fingers through his hair. "So, just take it and read it. So long as you promise to return it by next Monday, I don't want to lose my library card or get fined."

"Of course I will," Anna said. "It was so nice of you to think of me."

"I'll wait in line with you," he said.

"You don't have to do that."

"I want to."

"I saw you at school the other day. I called out to you, but you didn't hear me."

"I am sorry I didn't hear you. I didn't realize we attended the same school," she said.

"I knew we did. I knew that you and I went to the same school the first day that I met you. I have often seen you in the hall outside Frau Weisman's history class. I always wanted to talk to you."

She felt her face grow hot. "I didn't realize. I mean, I didn't see you. I am sorry."

"It's all right." He smiled. "Would you like to go get a soda or something?"

"I'd love to, but I can't today; I have to get home." She had promised her mother she would be home by five, and it was already four-thirty.

"Can I walk you home, at least?"

She glanced up at him. "I suppose that would be all right."

"Next," the librarian said.

Anna walked to the desk and handed the librarian her stack of books. "I'll only be a minute," she said to Daniel.

"I don't mind waiting," he answered, and when she saw the twinkle in his eyes, she smiled too.

His smile is infectious. Anna thought.

CHAPTER FIFTEEN

As they walked out of the building and into the bright afternoon sunlight, he asked, "Have you read *Heart of Darkness*?"

"Yes, I have."

"What did you think of it? Personally, I found it to be quite disturbing."

She nodded. "Yes, it was very disturbing. So much cruelty. I felt sorry for the Africans. The book was certainly a hard one to read. It seemed as if the author felt that the people in Africa were not human. I didn't like that at all. Just because people are different doesn't mean they are less human than others."

"Yes, I felt that too. It made me sick to see the way they were treated."

"In fact, I noticed a lot of similarities between the way the Africans were treated and the way the Jewish people have been treated throughout history. I realize that the people in Africa in this book were from an uncivilized tribe. Even so, they should have been treated with human kindness. The similarity I found to the Jews was that the Africans and the Jews were both hated and feared for no reason. Throughout history, there have been pogroms and destruction of Jewish settlements for no other reason than that they were homes to Jewish people. In *Heart of Darkness*, the hunters think it's perfectly all right for them to mistreat the Africans because their skin is a different color and their culture seems primitive. I felt that was so wrong."

"Yes," he said, sighing. "I felt that way too." Then he smiled at her and added, "But there was something positive that came out of reading that book, for me at least. I found that I would love to see Africa one day. Not to explore the tribes so much as I would love to see the animals and nature. I think that Africans are treated terribly, and I feel that's very wrong. And I would never condone taking advantage of anyone, regardless of skin color or religion."

"I completely agree," she said.

"But the idea that Lions and gorillas roam free in nature is exciting to me. Can you imagine such a place? I would love to see it."

"I must admit, I did find that part of it intriguing," she agreed. "But it's a little scary, too."

He laughed. "Yes, it is a little bit, I suppose. But that's what I love about reading. You can go to places that are scary and dangerous without ever leaving the safety of your room."

She let out a laugh. "You're so right. It's true."

"So, what other books did you take out today?" he asked her.

"*The gift of the Magi*, by O. Henry and *The Wonderful Wizard of Oz*. Have you read either of them?"

"Yes, I read the *Wizard of Oz*. I enjoyed it a great deal."

"I've heard that it is very good."

"At first, it appears to be a children's book. But if you look deeply, there is a lot of important symbolism. Very well written."

"I will read it right after I finish with the *Death in Venice*."

"I read that one, too," he said, smiling.

And before they knew it, Anna and Daniel had arrived at Anna's house.

"Well, we're here," she said, smiling. "This is my house." They stood on the sidewalk in front of the house. Then she turned to go. As she walked away, she said, "Thank you for loaning the book to me."

"Wait," he said, his voice cracking, "perhaps I can meet you at the library next Monday, and we can share a soda after you return the book. My treat, of course."

She smiled, and she could feel that she was blushing. "All right," she agreed. "I'll go to the library right after school on Monday."

"I'll do the same," he said with a smile.

"Goodbye." She smiled. Then she turned and walked inside. Once in her living room, she peeked out the window and watched him walk away.

CHAPTER SIXTEEN

"I met a boy!" Anna announced the following evening when she and her blood sisters met at the park. "His name is Daniel, and he's very handsome."

"Jew, no doubt," Dagna said.

"No doubt," Anna said sarcastically as she gave Dagna a look of disgust. "He goes to my school."

"Well, that's exactly what I would expect. Two Jews who deserve each other," Dagna said.

"Stop it, both of you," Bernie said. "I'm so tired of this hatred between you."

"I don't hate her. She just thinks she's better than us. She would never date a boy who wasn't a Jew."

"That's not true." Anna defended herself.

"Oh, isn't it? What would your parents say? The last time we were at your house, I heard your mother say something about stupid *goyim*. I know what that word means. It's a not-friendly word for gentiles."

"My mother is not me. I make up my own mind," Anna said fiercely.

"You sure do make up your own mind. I mean, nothing your parents say influences you," Dagna sneered. "But, when it came time to go out with a boy, you found another Jew, just like I always knew you would."

"This stops right now, Dagna. We are all old friends. Let's treat each other better, or one of us could be out of the group. You know who that would be, don't you?" Bernie threatened.

"Oh? And what would your drunken mother say when she found out you had mixed blood with a Jew? I hear her boyfriend sometimes beats the hell out of you, as it is. But let's see," Dagna said, holding up her hand, "how many boyfriends has she had living with you two in the last year? Five, six? I think it was at least that. Let's face it, Bernie, your mother is a drunk and a whore."

Bernie stood up and glared at Dagna. "Stand up and fight, why don't you, you big fat slob? I'll beat you until you can't open that lying mouth of yours," Bernie said. She was almost in tears.

"That's enough. Sit down, Bernie," Elica said. Then she turned to Dagna. "Now, as for you, just shut your mouth. Leave Bernie and Anna alone."

Bernie stood with her legs apart and her fists clenched. She was ready for a fight. Dagna looked terrified.

"Sit down, Bernie," Elica yelled, "sit down." She stood up and put her arm around Bernie's shoulder. Bernie melted and sat down.

"Now, don't ever do that again. Do you understand me, Dagna? Bernie has enough trouble at home right now. She doesn't need more problems from you. Say you're sorry."

"I'm sorry, Bernie," Dagna said under her breath.

"Now, tell Anna you're sorry too."

"No. I won't."

"You will, or you can just go home," Elica said firmly.

"I'm sorry, Anna," Dagna reluctantly spoke.

"Fine." Elica turned to Anna and smiled. "Now, I'd like to hear all about your new boyfriend."

"His name is Daniel. He's nice. He likes to read. We met at the library."

"I thought you said he went to school with you? Now you are saying you met him at the library. So, which is it?" Dagna asked sarcastically. "Sounds like you're confused. Just wondering, is he real or just a figment of your imagination?"

"He's real," Anna said, "and we did meet at the library. We like the same books. And it just so happens we go to the same school."

"I think it's nice," Bernie said.

"Yes, it feels nice," Anna agreed. "He and I are meeting back at the library next week. Then we are going out for a soda."

"That sounds like a real date," Elica said. "I wish I had a date."

"You? You're the prettiest one of all of us. You could probably have all the dates you wanted," Dagna said to Elica.

"No, I'm not," Elica said, blushing.

"Oh yes, you are," Bernie said, her voice sincere. "I think you're beautiful."

Elica blushed.

"And I think you're a lesbian, Bernie." Dagna turned to Bernie with hate in her eyes. "My ma says you're funny, queer. Not right. She told me to be careful of you. The fact is, I think you like girls, and you just better stay away from me."

Bernie's face turned bright red. She looked away. "It's not true. Don't say that about me," she said, her voice cracking. "It's just not true. You are such a nasty person, Dagna."

"Dagna, don't say that about Bernie," Anna said. "You have no right to say such a thing."

"All right." Dagna smiled. "I won't say it. But all of you know it's true."

"Shut your mouth, Dagna," Elica said.

"Maybe you like Bernie too. Maybe you're a lesbian, and you just hide it better."

"Why don't you just go home? We don't like you. No one here wants you here," Bernie yelled at Dagna. Her face was red, and she seemed so ashamed that Anna wondered if there might be some truth to Dagna's accusations.

"You are just jealous because Elica and I have a wonderful friendship when none of you are around. Isn't that true, Elica?" Dagna said, looking at Elica.

"Please, just stop, Dagna. I don't want to do this," Elica said.

"But, it's true." Dagna stood up and walked over to Elica. She touched the necklace that Elica wore around her neck. "I stole this for her," Dagna said. "You like pretty things, and because I am your friend, I will do whatever I have to in order to get them for you. Even put myself at risk of getting arrested."

"You don't need those things, Elica. You are beautiful without some necklace. Stealing is only going to get both of you into big trouble with the police," Bernie said.

"She doesn't need them, but she likes them. Look at that star around Anna's neck. I think it's gold. Real gold. It must be quite nice to have money to buy things like that. But Elica and I don't have that kind of money."

"Why do you have to bring Anna into it?" Bernie said. "She's wearing a Star of David. Do you know what that is?"

Dagna shrugged. "I don't care. All I know is she doesn't fit in here, and lately, with the way you are looking at Elica with moony eyes, you don't fit in either, Bernie."

"I've had enough," Elica said. "Go home, Dagna."

"You're telling me to leave? I can't believe you would do that. I do so damn much for you."

"I don't like these fights. I've told you that before. If we can't all get along, then you have to go," Elica said.

Dagna stared at Elica. Then she said, "If that's the way you want it, I'll go home. But remember, I know things about you that no one else knows. I know you stole that new blue sweater. I also know you stole money from your mom once to buy a soda, and I know you and Bernie mixed blood with a Jew."

Elica took a deep breath. "I hate when you do this," she said.

"But you love it when I steal for you, don't you? And that's because you want nice things. You want things Anna has, but you can't afford to buy them because you come from poor parents. But you know I can get them for you. Because I am not scared to do things that are illegal for a good friend."

Bernie shook her head. "I've had enough. Let me make this easier for everyone. I'll go home. I don't want to hear any more about this. But before I leave, I want you to know that I don't like this stealing. It's going to get you both into trouble. I hope I am wrong, but I think you are going to be sorry for doing this, Elica."

"Lesbian," Dagna hissed. "A misfit and a Jew. You don't need friends like these, Elica. Besides, they don't do anything for you. All they do is give their lousy opinions."

"It's getting late, and this conversation is getting too hot for me. I think I am going to go home, too," Anna said.

Elica didn't protest. She nodded as if Dagna's knowledge of her illegal activities had defeated her.

CHAPTER SEVENTEEN

1936

Things were changing; the blood sisters were growing into young women. Anna could feel the divide between herself and her friends growing wider. It made her sad to think that the time might come when they would have grown so far apart that they would be like strangers. In her mind's eye, she saw herself as an older married woman, running into Elica when she was town shopping. She could see them both pushing their babies in carriages. *Would we just say a polite hello, and act as if our years as close friends had never happened? Would we walk away from each other and return to our lives without a thought about the past? And what about Bernie? Would she have a child too? If I asked her if she would want to stop and have a cup of tea with me, maybe she would just nod and say something meaningless, like "Good to see you, but I am in a bit of a hurry." The thought of losing our friendship makes me terribly sad. But I don't know what I can do to prevent it.*

On Monday after school, Anna walked to the library to return the book and meet Daniel as she had promised. As she strolled through the familiar streets, she looked around. *Maybe I am getting too old to play blood sisters in the park with my friends. Perhaps I should start thinking about my future, getting married, and having a family. After all, my father would say that every girl's purpose in life is to marry and have children. Could this innocent meeting with Daniel mean anything more? Could we someday be married?* The idea made her nervous.

Is it possible that he is thinking these same thoughts? Daniel is handsome, well-read, and seems intelligent. But I am just a teenager, and the idea of being a wife and mother is overwhelming. Still, I know I will probably be engaged within a few years. Most of my cousins were engaged by seventeen and married by eighteen. Some were even younger. I think my parents would like Daniel. He is everything they want for me, and I like him too. But I just can't imagine being married to him. The very thought of it is scary. I can't imagine myself running a household the way my mother does.

When she entered the library, Daniel was sitting at a long table that was close to the door. He saw her immediately and waved. She waved back and walked over to him.

"Were you worried that I wouldn't bring the book back?" She winked at him as she asked in a whispered voice so as not to disturb the other people inside the library.

"Nope, I trusted you. You have a good face. A trustworthy face."

She laughed a little. "Well, you made a good bet. Because here I am, and here is your book." She handed him the book.

"So, what did you think of it?"

She sat down. "You were right. The writing was beautiful. The descriptions transported me."

"I know. I felt that way too."

"Shhh, quiet," the librarian said.

Daniel looked at Anna and smiled. She returned his smile. Then he said, "Shall we get out of here and go to a place where we can have a soda and talk freely?"

She nodded.

There was no line at the book return desk, so he handed the book to the librarian. "Thank you," he said.

Then he and Anna walked to the door. He opened the door for Anna, and they both walked outside.

"I'll race you down the stairs," he blurted.

"All right."

"Go!"

He won. But they were both giggling like children by the time they reached the bottom of the high staircase.

Then they strolled to the ice cream parlor, where they sat across from each other. Daniel ordered two sodas.

"I can run, and I'm an excellent dancer, too," he said. "Do you like to dance?"

"Me?"

"Yes, you, silly. There's no one else here. Of course, I am asking you?"

"I'm not very good at it, I'm afraid. But I'd love to learn."

"I'll teach you. My mother insisted that I take dancing lessons. She said a man who can dance looks cultured."

They both laughed. "My mother said the same thing about piano lessons," Anna said.

"So, can I assume you can play?" he asked.

"I suppose you would say I can."

"I see you are a girl who doesn't brag. You are so modest about your talents."

"Not like you." She teased him.

"I only brag because I feel inferior to your beauty," he said.

"Did you also take flirting lessons?" she asked.

"No, this charm of mine comes naturally."

Then they both burst out laughing.

When they'd finished their sodas, he said, "All right, I'll tell you the truth. I could say my charm came from my father. However, if you ever met him, you'd find he wasn't charming at all. Perhaps it comes from my cousin. He's my best friend, and he's only a few years older than I am."

"How's that?"

"Well, all the girls like him. So, I try to say the things he says and hope they will have the same effect."

They were both giggling until it grew dark outside. "I should be getting home. My parents will be worried," Anna said.

"I'll walk you to your house."

They walked together and talked about the characters in *The Wizard of Oz*. "Which one did you feel most represented you?" he asked.

"Me? Dorothy," she said. "How about you?"

"The cowardly lion."

"I don't believe you. You have plenty of courage."

"It's all false. I'm always feeling insecure. I often wonder if I am good enough."

"Good enough for what?"

"For my father. He expects me to take over his business someday. I am barely passing my studies. I'm always a disappointment. Just ask my father; he'll tell you." He hesitated, then added, "I hope you still like me."

"Did I say I like you?" She smiled and winked.

"I hope you do," he said.

"I do," she said, and she felt herself blush. "Of course I do."

They had arrived in front of her house.

His face turned red. "I'm sorry. I didn't mean to put you on the spot. I just thought..." he trailed off.

"I'm just joking with you. Of course, I like you. Would I have gone for a soda with you if I didn't?"

"So you do?" he asked clumsily.

"Sure. Yes. Of course," Anna said, feeling awkward. But in fact, she did like him. She liked his honesty and found his insecurities to be sweet and endearing.

"Then maybe you will meet me again on Monday next week at the library, and we can have a soda again?"

"I'd like that," she said.

"So it will be about the same time next week?"

"Yes,"

"I'll meet you at the library."

"I'll be there," she said.

Once she was inside, she ran to the window and watched him. He jumped in the air twice. She giggled as she observed him running towards home.

After that afternoon, Anna and Daniel met each week at the library, where they shared their latest read. Then they walked to the soda shop and enjoyed a soda together.

CHAPTER EIGHTEEN

One afternoon in late spring, Anna returned home from school. She walked into the house and hung her light coat on the rack. "Frau Frey is my mother home?" she asked.

Frau Frey came out of the kitchen and greeted her. "She's at a charity event," she said, then she added, "can I get you something to eat or drink?"

"Oh, no, thank you. I am going to do my homework."

"Is Anselm feeling any better?" Anna knew her brother had missed school again because he was ill.

"The doctor came this morning and gave him something. He's resting."

Anna nodded. *Poor Anselm. He's always so sick.* She wished he would get better.

After Frau Frey went back into the kitchen, Anna went into her bedroom. She sat down at her desk and opened her math book. If she finished her homework quickly, she would have time before her father got home from work for dinner to start reading the new book she'd taken from the library earlier that week. Anna cherished those lazy hours when she had finished her homework and could devote her time to a novel.

As she began to work on her assignment, she thought she heard a knock at the front door downstairs.

Probably a salesperson, or maybe a telegram for papa. Her father sometimes received telegrams from companies who supplied his business. She heard Frau Frey open the door and say, "Bernie? What in the world are you doing here?" Of course, Frau Frey knew Bernie very well because Bernie had visited Elica often at her home.

"Hello, Frau Frey. I'm here to see Anna," Bernie said respectfully to Elica's mother.

"I didn't know that you and Anna were friends," Frau Frey said.

"Yes. We have been friends for years."

"I assume Elica introduced you. Is that right?"

"Yes, ma'am," Bernie said.

"Does Frau Levinstein know about this? Does she know that you and Anna have become friends?"

"I'm not sure. But I would think that Frau Levinstein does. After all, I've been to Anna's birthday parties."

"I didn't realize that you and Anna were friends. When I saw you at the parties, I thought Elica brought you with her as a guest. You and Dagna."

"No, Anna and I are good friends."

Anna could hear the conversation. She was rather certain that if she didn't come out of her room, Frau Frey would try to send Bernie away without allowing her to see Anna. Although Frau Frey never mentioned the class divide, it was always just bubbling under the surface. She was kind to Anna and made it clear her home was always open to Anna. But somehow, Anna always felt that Frau Frey would have preferred that Elica and Anna started to part ways as they were growing older. She was sure it was because Frau Frey knew Anna's mother didn't approve, and Frau Frey was concerned about something happening that might cause her to lose her job.

But in the back of her mind, Anna felt a tiny pang of worry that Frau Frey didn't want Anna and Elica to be friends because Anna was Jewish, and it might put a stigma on Elica. However, right now, none of that mattered. Bernie had come to speak to Anna about something, and Anna wanted to know what Bernie had come to tell her. So, Anna knew she must go to the living room right now, so Frau Frey could not prevent Bernie from seeing her.

Anna closed her book and laid down her pencil. Then she stood up, stretched, and hurried into the living room. Bernie was standing by the front door. It looked as if she was just about to leave.

"Anna!" Bernie said, delighted to see her.

"Hello." Anna smiled. "Did you come to see me?"

"Actually, yes."

"Well, come into my room and have a seat. I'll get us a snack."

"What would you like, Anna? I'll bring it to you," Frau Frey said. But Anna caught a look of anger as Frau Frey's eyes met Bernie's.

"Do we have any more of those little cakes? The one's mother bought at the bakery a few days ago?"

"Yes. There are plenty."

"How do little cakes and tea sound to you?" Anna asked Bernie.

"Perfect."

"Good." Anna smiled, then turned to Elica's mother, "We'll have those, please, and some tea. Thank you, Frau Frey."

Frau Frey nodded. She did not look at Bernie again.

Anna led Bernie into her room.

"May I sit on the bed?" Bernie asked. "It's so pretty." Bernie ran her fingers along the pink bedspread. "You're the only girl I know who has a canopy bed."

"Of course. Please sit down. My mother decorated this room."

"It's pretty. It suits you."

"Thank you. I like it too," Anna said.

Frau Frey knocked on the door a few minutes later.

"Come in," Anna said.

Frau Frey carried a large tray covered with small, pretty pastries and a pot of tea. "Can I get you anything else?" she asked.

"No, thank you," Anna said. It was always uncomfortable to give orders to Elica's mother. But it was especially awkward with Bernie there.

Once Frau Frey left the room, Anna stood up and closed the door. She had a feeling Bernie wanted to speak to her privately, without Frau Frey's prying ears.

"Have some tea and cake," Anna said.

Bernie poured herself a cup of tea and took a small yellow cake with white and blue frosting. After she took a bite, she said, almost in a whisper, "I wanted to talk to you about Elica."

"Perhaps we should finish our cakes and tea and then go for a walk where we can talk privately," Anna said. "I can't be sure that Frau Frey isn't listening."

"Yes, you're probably right. I think that would be a good idea." Bernie agreed.

After they finished eating, Anna informed Frau Frey that she and Bernie were going for a walk. Then they slipped on their coats and left the house.

"You've never come to see me alone, I mean without Elica, before," Anna said. "I'm glad you came, but why?"

"I'm worried about Elica."

"I don't understand. Explain, please."

"Well, how do I start?" Bernie hesitated. Then she took a deep breath and said, "You know how pretty Elica is."

"Of course. She's always been the beauty of our group. The first time I saw her, I thought she looked like a beautiful doll." Anna smiled.

"Well, lately, she's grown very popular with the boys at school. That would be all right, except she's... well... I don't know how to say this."

"It's all right. Just say it. It's me, Anna. We're blood sisters. You can tell me anything, right?"

"She's getting a bad reputation. She's very promiscuous."

"You mean she's kissing a lot of different boys?"

"It's worse than that."

"Tell me everything."

"She was going out with this older boy. He was almost twenty."

"Oh, my goodness. Twenty is much too old," Anna said.

"Yes, I agree. Anyway, Elica told Dagna, and me she had intercourse with him. Then he disappeared. He was involved with some sort of political group. I don't really understand much about all of that. She tried to explain to us, but I was more worried about her. Anyway, she said that he had to leave the country. I know she was very hurt. For a week, she didn't go to school. I tried to talk to her, but she wouldn't see me. After that, she started dating other boys, older boys. She said that intercourse was nothing, that people made it to be far more important than it was. Then she told me that she had started having sex with a lot of different boys. Some of them give her money and gifts. I am afraid she is going to get pregnant or hurt in some way."

"Intercourse? Really?" Anna was shocked. She stopped walking and looked directly at Bernie. "Why didn't she tell me? She told you and Dagna, but not me?"

"She didn't want you to know. She said you wouldn't understand. She said you were too refined. Life was too easy for you. You wouldn't know what it was like to need money and gifts from boyfriends."

"I may not need money or gifts from anyone. But I understand all right. I understand that Elica's getting herself into trouble."

"At school, she acts like she is sophisticated. Like she is above the rest of us. She wears fancy clothes that she and Dagna steal from the local stores. She wears red lipstick and flirts shamelessly with all the boys. Even some of the male teachers. All the girls want to be like her. They think she is like a film star, and all the boys want to date her.

73

They spread rumors about having had sex with her. I am so worried. Elica is running with a fast crowd. Some of them are older people who are out of school and work at the local factories. I know she goes out drinking with them sometimes. In fact, I must admit, I feel bad because she hardly has time for me anymore."

"I didn't know anything about this."

"Of course not. You're not around all the time anymore. We go to different schools. And because of that, school has separated the three of us."

"Yes, I know, and I wish it hadn't. I miss our group, our time together, when we just sit, talk, and laugh."

"Me too. Things were so much better a few years ago," Bernie said, sighing. "And to make matters even worse, Dagna would do anything for Elica. She doesn't care about the long term and is desperate to be accepted by Elica. You know how she is."

"Yes, I know. She's always wanted to be like Elica."

"She can't be like her. She isn't pretty or popular. So, if she can't be like her, she at least wants to be Elica's best friend. And she has found a way to make herself an important part of Elica's life. She's done this by stealing things for Elica. Pretty clothes, jewelry, lipstick, and mascara. You know how Elica always wanted more out of life than her parents could give her. Well, Dagna has finally won Elica's loyalty by giving her these things."

"I see. And you still care about Elica and want to help her."

"I care about her very much." She hesitated. Then she added, "Perhaps too much. Sometimes my feelings for Elica are so strong that they actually hurt me."

"What do you mean?"

Bernie started crying. "I'm sorry. I didn't mean to start crying and make you feel sorry for me."

"I don't understand."

"I know you can keep a secret. I've known you for a long time." Bernie hesitated. "I have something to tell you."

"Of course, I can keep your secret. I promise not to tell anyone."

"I don't like boys. I mean, I don't hate them or anything. I just don't feel the way the rest of the girls do about them."

Anna didn't say anything.

"I am so ashamed to tell you this, but I have to tell someone, or I will burst with anxiety. I am not normal. I am not like other girls. I wish I was, but I am not. Anna, I hope you won't hate me when I tell you this. But Dagna was right when she called me a lesbian. Hearing her say it made me feel sick inside. But the truth is, I can't help it. I am in love with Elica. I have been in love with her since we were little children."

"I see," Anna said as she let out a small sigh. They walked in silence for a long moment. Then Anna asked, "Does Elica know?"

"I don't think so. She might wonder. But if she ever found out for sure, she probably would never speak to me again."

Anna nodded.

"I don't expect her to return my feelings. I know I am a mess. But, even if she and I could never be, I still want to help her before she gets into trouble. Elica is going down the wrong road. I can see it. But I can't help her alone. I need you because she trusts you and thinks you're smart. I think so too. If she listened to anyone, it would be you."

"Smart? Me? I don't know about that."

"You are. Don't you remember we always said Elica was the prettiest, I was the strongest, and you were the smartest?"

"And Dagna was the most manipulative," Anna said.

"Exactly, and she has turned out to be just that."

"So, tell me, Bernie, how can I help?"

"I'm not sure. I just couldn't bear to watch this happening to Elica. I had to talk to you. We both know how close we have been over the years, and I was hoping you might have some ideas of what to do."

Anna thought for a moment. Then she asked, "Do you think we should talk to her mother about it? Frau Frey has always been so nice to me."

Bernie shook her head. "No, definitely not that. Her mother is only nice to you because she works for your parents. She's much tougher on Elica and me. There's a side to her you never see. She can be very mean."

"I can't imagine."

"I know. That's because she's always acting sweet and kind when you're around. But she's not like that when talking to Elica and me."

Anna was stunned by this. She wasn't sure what Bernie meant. When Anna was very young, Frau Frey came to work for the Levinsteins. She'd known her for as long as she could remember, and she'd never seen Frau Frey get angry or raise her voice. "I'm not sure how I can approach this with Elica. She is aware that I know she is stealing. But until today, I didn't know about the boys," Anna said.

"I had to tell you. I know Elica would not have liked it. But you had to know. I am getting worried. If she gets pregnant, her parents will kill her."

"Do you think we should have a club meeting for old times' sake? Maybe I can talk to her there."

"Sure. I'll try to arrange something. She isn't as willing to see me as she used to be. But I'll be persistent and let you know when," Bernie said.

"Have you seen Dagna and Elica steal things?"

"Yes, I've been with them twice when they went on one of their shopping sprees. It was terrifying. I was so afraid that Elica would get caught. The only good thing about it is, Elica doesn't do the actual stealing most of the time. Most of the time, it's Dagna who steals things to give to Elica. But if they are together, I am afraid that they will both be arrested."

"I see," Anna said. "Well, I'll do whatever I can to help."

"I'll arrange the meeting."

CHAPTER NINETEEN

Two days later, as Anna was hurrying to school early in the morning, Bernie approached her. "I talked to Elica, and she has agreed to a meeting after school today at our secret spot," she said, smiling.

"That's wonderful. So, were you able to arrange it?"

"Yep."

"I am so glad Elica agreed to come."

"So am I. But Dagna will be there too, unfortunately."

"Don't worry. We'll figure out something. I'll see you there."

"All right," Bernie said, and then she left and turned the corner. She headed towards the school she attended.

Anna couldn't concentrate on her lessons that day. All she could think about was what she might say to convince Elica that she was going down the wrong path. *How can I help her? I doubt she is going to listen to me. She has become so distant from me. I don't know what to say to her anymore. But I have to do something. She is still my best friend.*

The four girls arrived at the spot within minutes of each other. They greeted each other warmly, but the deep affection and honesty that had been a part of their childhood were no longer there. They were young women now. Until today, Anna had not noticed how much Elica had changed. *Perhaps I haven't seen it because I didn't want to. But now that Bernie has told me about what is going on in Elica's life, I can see clearly how different Elica has become.* Anna thought sadly. Elica was still beautiful; there was no doubt about that. But what was once innocent beauty was now cheapened by a sweater that was too tight and a skirt that was too short. Her soft, full lips, which were naturally pink, were smeared with blood-red lipstick, and there was mascara around her soft blue eyes. Anna couldn't imagine that Frau Frey had not noticed these changes.

"Hello, everyone," Anna said as she put a bag down on the blanket Bernie had brought them to sit on. "I brought some pastries."

Dagna grabbed the bag and looked inside. Then she pulled out the largest pastry and began eating.

"Thank you for bringing these. It was very thoughtful," Bernie said, taking one and setting it down in front of her.

Anna offered the bag to Elica.

Elica smiled and shook her head. "Thank you, but not for me," Elica said. "I don't want to ruin my figure."

This was new. Elica had never worried about getting fat before.

Anna took a pastry and sat down on the ground beside Bernie. Anna began nibbling at it unenthusiastically as she watched Dagna finish hers and take another one greedily. The girls sat quietly. Anna searched for something to say.

"It's been a long time since we met like this," Anna breathed. Then she turned to Elica and said, "I've missed you."

Elica smiled. "Life keeps me busy."

"I'll bet it does." Anna tried to smile, but her heart was heavy. Elica had changed, and she felt like she hardly knew her.

"What does that mean?" Elica said defensively.

"Nothing, just that school and life can be overwhelming," Anna said, trying hard to say the right thing.

"I want to quit school and get a job. School bores me. Besides, my parents could use the money," Dagna said.

"Mine too, and that's what keeps me from quitting. If I had a job, my parents would take all my money if they could. Still, I've thought about quitting. I'm tired of the boys at school. They're like children. I would prefer to date men who are out in the working world. Men who have a little money can take a girl out for dinner or buy her a present or two," Elica said.

"It's probably best if you finish school. We only have one more year after this one. During that time, perhaps it would be helpful if you could learn some secretarial skills. Then you would be able to get a better-paying job after graduation," Anna said.

"Yes, I suppose," Elica said.

"Factory work is hard," Bernie said. "You have to stand on your feet and always be alert, or you could get hurt or even killed by some of those machines. I've heard plenty of horror stories about things that happen in factories."

"I understand, Elica," Dagna smiled at Elica, looking for her approval. "Her life is a lot like mine. I know how much she wants to get away from her parents. If she had a job, she'd have money of her own. I want to have money of my own. That's why I am thinking of leaving school and getting a job at one of the factories. I don't want to spend my life depending on my parents for every little thing. It gives them too much power over me. If I had a job, I could get my own place. And then I could do everything I want to do."

"When are you turning sixteen?" Bernie asked.

"In three months," Dagna said.

"Well, don't you think sixteen is too young to be living on your own?" Bernie asked.

"Not at all. My sister left home at fourteen. We haven't seen her since," Dagna said.

"I'd love to be on my own. I hate my mother's constant watching eyes. She's always complaining about everything. She looks through my things and wants to know where I got this and where I got that," Elica said. "She wants to have control over everything in my life."

"And... what do you tell her?" Bernie asked, putting her uneaten pastry down on the grass.

"I tell her where I get my stuff and who I am seeing is none of her damn business."

Anna gasped.

"What?" Elica said in a challenging tone of voice, "What? Why are you so shocked?"

"I'm worried about you," Anna said. "What things is she talking about, and where are you getting them from?"

"She's talking about everything I have."

"You mean like that skirt, that sweater? All that makeup you're wearing. I know your mother didn't buy these things for you," Bernie said.

"I bought these things with money from babysitting," Elica said, then she glared at Bernie. "Not that it's any of your business, either."

"We've always told each other everything," Anna said. "Bernie and I want to help you."

Elica stood up. Then she glared at Anna and growled, "you don't have any idea what it's like to live my life. My parents are constantly fighting and scrounging for money. My father drinks up everything he earns. My mother is always crying, except when she slaps me around. It's easy for you to ask questions and be critical. You're a rich, spoiled, dirty Jew. Your parents give you everything. You always look perfect and pretty in your wool skirts and cashmere sweaters, but no one gives me those things, Anna. My parents expect me to finish school and then go to work in a factory and give them my money."

Anna let out a gasp. She was reeling. *A rich, spoiled, dirty Jew. I never thought I would hear Elica say that to me. She hates me now that we have grown up. Our friendship is really over. My mother saw this coming years ago when we were just young children. I never believed it would happen.*

"I have to go," Elica said, standing up.

"Wait. Please, let's talk about this." Bernie got up too. She tried to reach for Elica's hand. "Please don't go away angry."

"I just have to go. I have to get home." Elica didn't look at Anna, whose heart was breaking. She turned and walked away. Dagna stood up, took the last pastry out of the bag, and ran to catch up with Elica. Now Bernie and Anna were sitting on the blanket alone.

"I guess I am going home, too." Anna's voice cracked. She reached over and patted Bernie's shoulder. "I'm sorry I couldn't be of any help," Anna said, hiding her face from Bernie. She was fighting to hold back the tears.

"Are you all right?" Bernie asked.

Anna shrugged. "Sure. I'm fine."

"I know Elica hurt your feelings. She should never have said those things," Bernie said. "She's changing, and not for the better."

Anna nodded. She was afraid that if this conversation continued, she was going to break down and weep. "I'll see you soon," Anna said, and then she got up and left, leaving the empty bag from the pastries on the blanket.

CHAPTER TWENTY

Anna walked into her house and ran upstairs to her room. She needed to be alone. Elica had broken her heart today, and the shock and pain of it were still raw. Her parents were downstairs in the living room, and she could hear her parents having a heated discussion. She put her pillow over her head, trying hard to drown them out, but she heard them anyway.

"All of a sudden, you've been kicked out of the alpine club, even though you've been going skiing there for years. Isn't that enough evidence for you, Michael? Things are changing here in Austria. The Austrians seem to admire that new chancellor in Germany. They like his ideas, and because of him, the hatred of Jews is on the rise here in Vienna. Why don't we just sell the house and the factory? Let's make a new start. We can go to my brother Ari and his wife in New York, in America. He'll sponsor us. We can take the money from the sale of our house and the factory and open a factory there," Frau Levinstein begged.

"But all of our friends are here. Our family is here, Lil. We will be starting over from nothing if we go to America."

"Nu? So it would be so terrible to start over?" she said. "I am

82

worried. I just don't like the way things are going here. Let's just say I have a bad feeling."

"It will pass. You and I both know that wherever Jews have lived, there has always been this hatred for our people. My parents and grandparents lived through it. You and I made it through a pogrom in Russia. We'll make it through this too."

"But we left Russia, and we came here. Now it's time to leave here, Michael," Anna's mother said. "I'm scared."

Anna lay on top of her mattress. She pulled her pillow even tighter over her head. *Jews. I can't bear to hear one more word about how everyone hates Jews. Why couldn't I be born a shiksa? A little blonde shiksa with long blonde braids who everyone loves. A girl like Elica. Her family may be poor, but at least she can walk down the street knowing she is accepted. I hate being Jewish. I can't stand the way people feel about us, the way they think of us and look at us. The old myths make me sick to my stomach. How many times have I heard people talking loud enough for me to hear them on purpose, saying things like Jews make matzah out of the blood of Christian babies? Where do they get this nonsense, and how could they believe it? Whenever this happened, I didn't say anything to them. Instead, I ignored them because papa always said it was best to ignore them. I can't ignore Elica because I truly believed that Elica was my best friend, but when push came to shove, she called me a dirty Jew. She said it like it was some kind of fatal, contagious disease.*

I never knew she felt that way about me, and it hurt. It really hurts. I know now that our friendship is really over. I feel like a part of me died today, and the emptiness I feel now is so painful. So, I can understand how papa feels about going to America. He's trying to hold on to what we have here. But maybe mama is right. Perhaps we should go.

Then she thought about Daniel. She'd come to care for him. He was a good friend, and even if her feelings towards him weren't passionate, she could see herself married to him. They were both so similar it would be easy to live with him. However, if her family moved to America, it would be the end of any possible future between them. Anna sighed. *I don't know what is best. I have no idea.* She thought. Then there was a knock on the door of her room.

"Yes," Anna said, frustrated and a little impatient.

"Anna, can I bring you anything?" Frau Frey asked timidly.

"No, thank you," Anna said. But hearing Elica's mother's voice at that moment reminded Anna of how distinctive the class divide between herself and Elica truly was.

CHAPTER TWENTY-ONE

The following week, Anna returned from the library after an afternoon with Daniel to find Bernie in her room waiting for her.

"Bernie, it's good to see you," she said.

Bernie nodded, but her face was blotchy and red like she'd been crying. "I knew it would happen," Bernie said.

"What? What happened?"

"Elica and Dagna were arrested for shoplifting."

"When?"

"About a half hour ago."

"How did you find out?"

"Elica had the police call me and ask me to bring money to the station. Apparently, the shop owner has agreed not to press charges if she and Dagna can pay for the things they stole."

"Can't they just give the things back?"

"No, the only way the shop owner will even consider dropping the charges is if they pay for the things they took."

"How much money do you need?"

"A lot. Twenty marks."

"Twenty marks? You're right; that is a lot."

"The shop owner claims that Elica and Dagna were in her shop before, and when they left, lots of things were missing. She said she wanted to accuse them, but she wasn't sure. So she couldn't accuse them. But today, she caught Elica putting a sweater into her hand-bag. So she called for the police."

"Oh, no!"

"If you can loan me the money to help Elica, I'll pay you back. I swear to you, I will. I'll get a job and pay you every cent. I'm sure you must still be angry with Elica for the things she said, and if you can't forgive her, I understand. But, please, help me. Please, Anna, loan me the money. I just can't let Elica go to jail." Bernie was sobbing.

"I don't have that much money," Anna said. Then she hesitated for a moment. *Bernie is desperate, and although I am angry with Elica, I can't let Elica go to jail. I have to help her. But I don't have that much money, and I can't ask my parents for money. They would want to know what it was for. I know they would say they don't want to get involved. My mother would say that she always knew this would happen. She would say that she always knew that Elica was no good for me.* Anna shook her head and said, "I don't have the money."

"Can't you ask a friend? Can't you borrow it? I will do anything for you. I promise you will have it back."

Anna knew where her mother kept her *knipple,* her secret money stash that really wasn't a secret at all. Her mother had kept a *knipple* for as long as Anna could remember. Frau Levinstein received an allowance from her husband to run the house. He always made sure she had plenty because he knew she liked to keep the *knipple* for emergencies. So far, there had been no emergencies, and she'd only used that money from her secret stash to purchase surprise birthday gifts for her husband.

Anna began to reason with herself. *If Bernie can't get the money to pay me back, I could always get jobs babysitting. Or maybe I can help tutor other piano students. If I take the money, I'll have to replace it before papa's birthday. But that gives me until January. Plenty of time. I am still angry with Elica and feel I should hate her and not care what happens to her. But I just can't feel that way. We have been friends for too long for me to let her go to jail.*

"I'll get the money. I'll meet you at the police station in half an hour," Anna said, then she added, "do you think they are going to send a police car here to let Frau Frey know about Elica?"

"Hopefully not if we hurry."

"I'll hurry," Anna said.

After Bernie left, Anna checked the hallway between her bedroom and the bedroom her parents shared. The hall was empty. Anna knew it would be. Her mother was out at some charity meeting, and her father was at work. She knew Anselm would be in bed reading quietly, because that was where he could always be found. Until dinner time, the house would be quiet.

I have never stolen anything before in my life. I am about to steal from my parents. This is a sin. I know it is. Yet, there is nothing else I can do. I can't let Bernie down, and I can't allow Elica to go to jail. She thought as she opened the drawer where her mother kept her night clothes and her *knipple. Stealing is a sin.* These words were loud in her head.

I have no choice. If my mother ever finds out, she will forbid me to be friends with Elica. My mother had been waiting for something like this to happen so she could end the friendship. Even though Elica has changed, I have to believe she will come back to herself. I can't abandon her now. Not like this.

Anna's hands trembled as she took the small brown leather coin purse out of her mother's drawer. Inside, she found a thick stack of rolled-up bills. With a sick feeling deep in her stomach, she counted out twenty marks. Then she returned the rest to the purse and the purse to the drawer. *So long as I can put the money back in there before my father's birthday, my mother will never know. She never goes in there except to add money, and I don't think she counts it when she does or takes money out to buy something for him.*

As soon as Anna had the twenty marks tucked into her pocket, she looked out the doorway and checked the hallway, her heart filled with guilt. It was still empty. Her hands were trembling as she ran down the stairs, taking them two at a time, and grabbed her coat. Then, before Frau Frey could ask where she was going, Anna left the house. It was getting late, and soon it would be dark. She knew that if she didn't want to involve her parents, she must be sure to be home before dinner. So she ran all the way into town until she was in front of the police station. Out of breath, she stopped and looked at the large wooden door to the police station. In her mind's eye, she saw Elica sitting in a jail cell and was suddenly filled with overwhelming sympathy. *Poor Elica. She must be terrified. I hope the police aren't already on their way to my house to talk to Frau Frey.*

Anna squared her shoulders and walked into the police station. "Yes?" The officer at the desk said, "how can I help you?"

"I'm here to pay the money for Elica Frey?"

"And who are you?"

"I'm Anna Levinstein."

"Just a minute."

The front desk officer walked away. Anna looked around her. It was a dismal place painted gray and white with old wooden chairs.

A large police officer, who looked like a giant to Anna, came out from a back office and said, "You're here for Elica Frey?"

"Yes," Anna said breathlessly.

"All right. Come with me."

Anna followed the massive officer to another room where Dagna and Elica sat in a corner. Anna saw a pile of skirts and sweaters on the officer's desk, two tubes of lipstick, and a perfume bottle.

"It was her," Dagna said, pointing to Anna. "She told us to steal for her. She sells the stuff we steal and pays us for it."

Anna looked at Dagna. "Me? Are you crazy?" she said.

"Her name is Anna Levinstein. She's a Jew, and she's the one who we steal for. It's not Elica or me. She makes us do it. It's the only way we have of earning any money."

"I did not. That's not true. None of that is true. Dagna, stop lying."

"Oh yes, it is. It's true. I swear it," Dagna said. Then she turned to the officer. "Are you going to believe me, or are you going to believe a Jew?"

Just then, Bernie came walking swiftly to the room. "Sorry I am late, Anna; it took me a while to explain to my mother why I was leaving the house again without doing my homework."

Anna nodded. "It's all right. I understand."

"So, back to the problem at hand," the officer said, then he turned to Dagna. "You say that this girl here is a Jew, and that she is the reason you are stealing?"

"Yes, she's running a racket. She has people steal for her so she can sell the stuff."

"Wait a minute. What kind of lie are you telling now, Dagna?" Bernie said. "Anna has nothing to do with this. You are telling lies. I know because I went to Anna and asked her to come and pay for this stuff. She agreed because she wanted to help Elica. Anna's not guilty of anything except being a good friend."

Then there was some noise at the door. Anna heard her mother's voice, and she wished she could open the window and fly away like a bird before she had to face her parents. *I stole from my mother.* Anna thought, and the very idea of what she had done made her want to vomit.

Frau Frey was shaking as she stood in the harsh light of the police station. She looked small and helpless in her maid's uniform as she stood beside Anna's parents. Anna's father looked at Anna and shook his head. The look of disappointment on his face made her want to cry, and her mother's eyes were filled with anger. Anna's mother took Anna by the shoulders. "What would make you become involved in something like this?"

Anna shook her head. "It's difficult to explain," she said in a small voice.

The police officer cleared his throat, then he began to explain things to the Levinsteins and Frau Frey. "So, we have four girls and a bunch of stolen things. The merchant says that if she gets her money for this stolen merchandise, she will drop the charges. Anna Levinstein has declared that she is willing to pay the merchant. Is that correct?"

"Yes," Anna said. Her hand was shaking so badly when she took the twenty marks out of her handbag that she could hardly be still.

"Where did you get that?" Frau Levinstein's face fell open in shock. "You don't even have a part-time job?"

"She runs a stealing racket. I told you that," Dagna said to the officer.

"You are a good-for-nothing liar!" Bernie yelled at Dagna. Then she turned to the police officer. "That's not true. I swear it's not."

"I took it from you, Mama," Anna said as she looked down at her shoes, ashamed. "I was planning to babysit and pay you back."

"You see? Anna's a thief," Dagna said.

"I'm not, Mama. I would never have done this if I could have found another way. I feel so guilty about taking money from you, Mama. I feel awful," Anna said.

Then there was a commotion at the door as a heavy-set blonde woman came inside. "I'm Hilda Hofer. I was told that my daughter was here. Can you please direct me to her?" she said.

"She's right in there, Frau Hofer," a police officer said.

Frau Hofer whirled into the room like a giant tornado. She walked over to Dagna, and without a word, Dagna's mother slapped her daughter hard across the face. "What the hell did you do?" she said.

Dagna winced. "I didn't do nothin', Mama. I didn't. I promise you."

"Oh yeah, they just brought you here to the police station for no reason, just so you could interrupt my day. You're lucky they didn't come and get me out of the factory because if I would'a lost my job, you would be out singin' for your supper. You little ingrate."

"I didn't do it. I didn't do nothin' wrong."

"Yeah, I'll bet." Then she turned to the officers. "What happened here?"

Even the officers seemed intimidated by Dagna's mother.

The large looming officer sat behind the desk and explained the situation to Dagna's mother. When he finished, Dagna said, "This is all a lie. I swear it, mother. I swear it." Then she looked directly at the police officer and said in a shaky voice, "I told you, it wasn't me. It was her." She pointed at Anna. "She's a Jew, mom. You always said Jews were liars. Well, this one is lying right now."

"What are you doing palling around with a Jew, Dagna?" her mother said angrily. "Palling around with a Jew and getting into some kind of trouble. Do you realize that because I had to come here to this police station, I am going to be late for my second job? If I lose this job, we'll be hard-pressed to make the rent this month."

"I wasn't palling around with her. I never wanted her to be a part of our group. It was Bernie who insisted that we take her in, even though she's a Jew. And since Elica is Bernie's friend, Elica and I had to let the Jew be a part of our club."

"Bernie? What would your mother say if she knew?" Frau Hofer asked.

Bernie stood up straight. Anna had seen Bernie take this stance before, and it meant she was about to defend the righteous. In a firm and confident voice, Bernie said, "With all due respect, Frau Hofer, your daughter Dagna, is a liar. She's always been a liar. I never really liked her. She has always gotten Elica into trouble, and I want you to know that I would trust Anna before I would ever trust Dagna."

"You are one disrespectful young lady, aren't you? Well, just wait until I go to your home and speak with your mother. I'm sure she will be very unhappy that you are so friendly with a Jew. And as far as this stealing thing is concerned, I believe my daughter. Dagna would not lie to me." Then Dagna's mother turned to the officer. "So, what happens now? Do these lousy ungrateful children have to serve some time in jail? Or will it only be the Jew who serves time, or will my daughter have to face jail time, too, because of her association?"

"No, there will be no jail time. Anna Levinstein has paid for all the stolen merchandise. The merchant has agreed not to press charges. Therefore, they are all free to go. However, it would be a good idea for the parents to sit these girls down and make sure that they understand the weight of the crime they committed. A good, strong punishment is in order here."

"It certainly is," Anna's mother said.

"But she didn't steal anything. Anna wasn't involved in shop lifting at all." Bernie tried to defend Anna.

"No, I believe you, but Anna stole from me, and that is a sin. You know that, Anna."

"Yes, mother," Anna said, her head hanging low.

"Unless, of course, you would like your money back, Frau Levinstein. In that case, we would be forced to speak to the merchant and reevaluate the situation," the police officer said.

Anna's mother gave Anna a look of severe disapproval, and Anna's father shook his head, "No, officer, it's all right. They are just children, and children make mistakes. My only hope is that they will all learn from this and never do it again." He looked at Elica, who looked away, then he glanced at Dagna. "Next time, you girls might not be so lucky. I suggest you stop stealing before you end up in prison."

Elica looked scared, but Dagna looked angry.

"Now, let's go home," Herr Levinstein said. "Come, Anna."

They all left the police station without speaking to each other. Anna followed her parents to her father's automobile and climbed into the back seat. For a few moments, no one said a word. Then her father sighed. "I know you were trying to help your friend," he said, "and that's an admirable thing to do. However, you should never steal from me, your mother, or anyone else. Why didn't you come to us and ask us to help you? I would have given you the money."

"Papa," Anna said. Her voice was trembling, and she was ready to cry because she knew she had disappointed him. "Papa, I didn't want mama to forbid me to see Elica again."

Anna's mother began to speak in an angry, almost hysterical voice, "And what did you think would happen when I saw that the money was gone? What if I had accused Frau Frey? That would have been horrible. But she is the only other person who has access to my drawers. I would never, in my wildest dreams, have thought you would steal from me. So, I would have thought it was her."

Anna's mother stopped speaking for a moment, then took a long breath and began to speak in a calmer tone. "Anna, an innocent woman could have been wrongly accused of this. We would never have been able to look Frau Frey in the eyes if we had done that to her. We might have had to let her go, and she needs this job. You just have no idea of the terrible consequences that could have happened because of what you did. Now, I agree with your papa that you were trying to do a good thing by helping your friends. But I think you are too old now to continue this friendship with Elica. You are from two different worlds. Before you know it, she is going to be calling you a dirty Jew."

Anna's face turned white. *How did she know?*

Anna's mother didn't miss a beat. "That's how it happens. That's how it always happens. It happened to me when I was young. I was friends with a girl who lived in town. When the Cossacks were coming to our little village, I went to her house, trying to hide. She turned me in. My friend turned me in. Your papa rescued me, and thank God we were able to get out of Russia and come here to Austria. But the point of this story is that you can't trust the *goyim*. The *goyim* are different from us. They are raised to hate Jews. And sooner or later, that hate comes out. It's best that you stay with your own people from now on."

Anna felt the tears fall hot on her cheeks. She couldn't answer her mother. *I can't lie to my parents and say that Elica would never say anything bad about my being Jewish. After all, she already has. I would love to tell them how much I trust Bernie. I truly believe that Bernie will always stand up for what is right. But I know that no matter what I say to my mother, she will not believe me. The truth is, the money I paid to help Elica might have been my last hope at rekindling our once beautiful but lost friendship.*

There was no more conversation. When the family arrived at the house, Anna went upstairs to take a hot bath and go to bed.

CHAPTER TWENTY-TWO

Despite the relaxing bath, Anna hardly slept that night. She got up and got ready for school early, but when she left her room to go downstairs, she overheard her parents talking with Frau Frey.

"I don't see why you should have to leave us, Allis," Anna's father said. "Like I said at the police station, children make mistakes."

"Perhaps she's right, Michael. Perhaps it's for the best that she finds another position," Frau Levinstein said. "Allis, you have been a wonderful maid, and we love you like family, but I understand how you feel. I mean, the friendship between our daughters is not good for either of them. Now, of course, we will give you some money to help you get along until you find another position."

No! Frau Frey is quitting. She won't be here anymore. Anna thought. *If Frau Frey leaves, Elica and I will never be close again. Elica's mother needs this job, and Elica will blame me if she goes. Our friendship will really be over forever.*

"Yes, ma'am," Frau Frey said. "I appreciate the money."

"No, no, no," Herr Levinstein said gently, "this is unnecessary.

Didn't your husband become disabled last year? Hasn't he been out of work?" he asked Frau Frey.

"Yes, sir. He did."

"Well, that settles it. You can't leave. Of course, you must stay with us. In fact, I am going to give you a small raise. Perhaps it will help you to provide Elica with the things she needs." Then Herr Levinstein looked at his wife. "Is it all right with you, Lilian? It's a *mitzvah*, a blessing," he said pleadingly.

Frau Levinstein shook her head. Then, in a defeated voice, she said, "I don't know, Michael. I think it's best if Frau Frey looks for other employment. However, if you think it will be all right for her to stay, then it's all right with me. But I do believe that we should both make sure our daughters sever this friendship. They are older now, and their lifestyles are different. In my opinion, it's best that our daughters go their own way, at least for now. At least until they are older and can make better choices."

"Yes, ma'am," Frau Frey said. Anna could hear how relieved Elica's mother was. Anna was also relieved. She hid in the hallway when Frau Frey left her father's study and went into the kitchen. Then she listened as her parents talked.

"What am I ever going to do with you, Michael? You are too kind," her mother said.

"But that's why you love me, isn't it?" her father answered.

"It's one of the many reasons."

"You want to tell me the others, maybe?" he asked in a deep voice.

"Later tonight," she said.

He laughed. "By the way, how much money did Anna take from you?"

"About twenty marks."

"Here, let me give it back to you. For your secret *knipple*."

"How can my *knipple* be a secret if you know about it?" she asked flirtatiously. Anna had never heard her parents speak so lovingly to each other. It was a side of them she'd never seen before.

He laughed again. "It's our secret, my love," he said.

Anna marveled at their conversation. They seemed younger, somehow not like her parents, but like lovers in one of her romance novels. She had to smile.

My parents are still in love. It's hard to believe, but they are. She thought. *I am so glad that papa convinced mama to let Frau Frey continue working with us. I know my parents are going to forbid me to see Elica. But after time passes, my father will forgive, and he will convince my mother to forgive too. Maybe there still might be a way to salvage my friendship with Elica.*

CHAPTER TWENTY-THREE

Anna was right. That afternoon when she returned home from school and sat down at her desk to do her homework. Her father was at work, but her mother came to her room and knocked on the door.

"Anna. Can I come in?"

"Yes, Mama."

Her mother walked into the room and sat down on the bed. Anna put her pencil down and looked at her mother.

"Annaleh," her mother said gently, "I know you think I am being cruel when I tell you that I think you and Elica are too old to continue being friends. When you were babies, it didn't matter that you were Jewish, and she was a *shiksa*. But now, it does. She's running around with that low-class girl, the one with her at the police station. What's her name?"

"I don't know who you mean," Anna said.

"Yes, you do. The heavy-set girl with the small beady eyes. What was her name?"

"Dagna."

"Yes, that's right. Danga."

"No, I said Dagna, Mama."

"I'm sorry. Yes, Dagna." Lillian Levinstein sighed. "Oh, Anna. I know you are so much like your papa. You only see the good in people, and you forgive so easily. You'll do anything to help someone. I know you would never have stolen from me for something for yourself. Now, don't get me wrong. It's good to be kind and forgiving. But I worry for you. I don't want you to get hurt. And, right now, you are too young to know the difference between right and wrong. So, for now, your father and I feel it's best if you and Elica part ways."

"Mama. Please, reconsider. I would have found a way to pay back your money. I would have tutored younger children on the piano or babysat. It wasn't really stealing. It was more like borrowing."

Her mother shook her head. "No, Anna. You were borrowing without permission, and that's stealing. I am not as worried about the money as I am about your future. Your moral character."

"But what about Elica? What will happen if she and Dagna become best friends and I am not there to help her to do the right things?" Anna was desperately looking for some way to change her mother's mind.

"I'm sorry, my sweet little one. But you are too young, innocent, and naïve to befriend those girls."

"And Bernie?"

"Why not just let all of them go and find some new friends? Maybe some Jewish friends? Nu?"

"Bernie didn't do anything wrong."

"She wears her hair very short, like a boy and dresses in boy's clothes. I think she might have a problem. Something you are too young to understand."

"Again, you say I am too young. You think I am still a baby. But so many of my cousins got married when they were only a few years older than I am now. I'm almost sixteen. They were married by seventeen."

"You're a young sixteen, Anna. That's my fault. I kept you and your brother sheltered all of your lives. I wanted you to be safe.

Maybe it wasn't for the best; who knows? I don't know. But what I do know is that you are not to see Elica and her friends for a while. Do you understand me? Do you?" Her mother gripped her shoulders hard, but not hard enough to hurt her. Just hard enough to let her know she was not going to change her mind.

Anna had seen her mother like this before, and there was no doubt in her mind that whatever she said, her mother would not give in. She'd lost the argument. Her mother had won. Even crying would not help. There was a pain in her chest, and she felt as if her heart had been crushed. *I am defeated.* She thought.

Whenever Anna went into town, she looked for Elica or Bernie, but she never saw either one of them. Frau Frey had stayed on as the Levinstein's maid, but after the incident with the police, she distanced herself from Anna. Even so, Anna had to know how Elica was doing. So, she mustered up the courage to ask Frau Frey. But Frau Frey was cold. She refused to talk to Anna about her daughter. "Your mother prefers it this way, Anna. I don't want to upset her. I need this job. I hope you understand," Frau Frey said.

What could she do? Anna nodded and never asked again.

CHAPTER TWENTY-FOUR

1936

It took effort, but Anna tried to make new friends at school and piano classes. However, she never felt the same deep connection she had with her blood sisters. The blood sisters had been children together and knew each other very well, except for Dagna. When Dagna was not around, Anna felt she could tell her sisters anything.

The new friends Anna made were nice, but they were more like acquaintances. She received invitations and attended parties and picnics. She was a guest at her friends' piano recitals, even though Anna had excelled in her lessons and was now far more advanced at the piano. Consequently, her instructor had already moved her to a higher class. But even though she was trying to fit in with the other Jewish students, she could not deny the deep loneliness that seemed to always be with her. No matter what she did, Anna desperately missed Elica and Bernie.

Anna met Daniel at the library each week, and their friendship grew deeper. With Elica and Bernie missing from her life, Daniel became her best friend. The more time they spent together, the more they realized they shared many of the same interests. Aside from their love of books, they both loved animals and music. He had a wonderful gift for telling stories and often told her tales that made her laugh. Her favorites were tales about his experiences with his very strict and often rude violin instructor. Daniel was so good at imitating the old man that Anna found herself breathless from laughing. Finally, one day she turned to him and said, "I want to hear you play the violin."

"I would love to play for you. But where am I going to do this?" Daniel asked.

"I don't know," she admitted. "You know, I am a musician, too."

"Yes, you told me," he said.

"Well, I couldn't remember if I had mentioned it or not."

"I remember. You play piano, right?"

"Yes, that's right. I've been taking lessons since I was a very young child. My mother thinks every girl should play piano."

"I can't say I blame her. I think it's a beautiful instrument."

"Yes, it is," she admitted, "and I love to play."

"My parents had me studying the violin when I was three." He laughed.

Anna wasn't sure if he was serious or exaggerating. But when he went on to tell a story about his instructor, she began to laugh again.

Daniel brought his instrument with him when they met at the library the following week. That day, instead of discussing books, he played for her as they sat on the library steps. Anna almost cried because his music was so touching. When he played the violin, he was somehow different, serious, deep. This was a side of him she had not seen before. It intrigued her.

"That was so beautiful," she said when he finished.

"I'd love to teach you to play," he said. "Would you like that?"

"I'd like that very much."

And so, from that day on, they began to meet twice each week at the library and the park, where he gave her violin lessons.

Anna loved the way the violin sang to her. She'd always enjoyed the piano, but the straining notes of the violin sounded to her like a voice coming from the soul of a woman.

"You're a natural," he said.

"Not really."

"You are. It's like you have an innate understanding of the music. Not only do you play it with your fingers, but you seem to put your heart and soul into it. I would love to hear you play piano sometime."

"I couldn't possibly bring a piano to the park," she said jokingly.

"I'd love to see you try," he said.

They both laughed.

"If you're really serious about wanting to hear me play, you'd have to come over to my house," she said. "And that would mean meeting my parents."

"What would be so terrible about that?" he asked softly.

"Nothing, I guess."

"What do you mean?"

She shook her head and looked away from him. "It's just that we are getting older, and once my parents know I am keeping company with a boy, they will think that this is more than a friendship."

He looked away. "Yes. I suppose that would be the right thing to think."

"Oh?" she said. But she wasn't surprised. She knew Daniel was thinking of her as his girlfriend and maybe as his potential future bride. It was only natural that he felt that way. It was what was expected of them.

"Well," he cleared his throat. "I don't know if you realize it, but we have been seeing each other for over a year. I'm almost seventeen, and you know what that means."

"No, what does it mean? Why don't you tell me," she said, smiling but still not looking at him. She knew what he was going to say. She'd known for a while where their relationship was headed and liked him well enough. But she was still uncertain about her own abilities to be a wife and run a house and even have children.

"It means I should maybe be thinking about marriage."

"Marriage," she repeated the word. It felt so foreign in her mouth.

He nodded. "I have to admit, it scares me."

"Me too," she said softly.

He took her chin in his hand. Daniel had never touched her face before. It felt strange, exciting, dangerous even. Then he turned her face towards his and gently placed his lips on hers. It felt nice. She closed her eyes.

After they kissed, he seemed embarrassed. He looked down at the ground and said, "This may seem a little strange, but you have become my best friend. I look forward to the days we spend together. And, well..." He stammered. Then he cleared his throat. "If I am scared of getting married, and you are scared... Well." He coughed. "At least if we do decide to wed, we will be scared together. I mean, at least we will find our way together. Do you know what I mean?"

"Actually, I do," she said.

"Does that mean you are saying yes?"

Anna gasped. She wasn't aware that he was actually trying to propose. "I don't know. I am not sure," she said. Then she added, "Perhaps you should come over to my house and meet my parents and my brother. Then we can talk about this again. I can't accept your proposal without the approval of my parents."

"I understand," he said, "so when?"

"When?"

"Yes, when should I come to meet your parents?"

"Oh," she said as she let out a short, nervous laugh. "Would you like to come for *Shabbat* dinner this Friday night?"

"I'd have to bring my own parents. I don't know where I would tell them I was going otherwise."

"That sounds like a lot. Let's start with just my parents first, then we can meet yours later. What do you think?"

"I think that's a good idea. So, maybe not Shabbat, just yet."

"I agree," she said. "How about dinner on Thursday night?"

"Yes, that would be perfect."

"Six o'clock?"

"I'll be there," he said. Then he smiled at her and added. "I'll bring the violin. Perhaps we try a duet. Me on violin, you on the piano?"

She nodded. "Yes, perhaps we can."

CHAPTER TWENTY-FIVE

That night, as Anna and her family were having their evening meal, Anna told her parents about Daniel. "I hope it's all right that I invited him for dinner."

"Of course," her mother said, "we'd love to meet him." Then she smiled and added, "After all, you're getting close to that age, and he is a nice Jewish boy from a good family. What else could we ask for?"

Her father smiled at her. "Nu, so do you like him?"

"I do. He's very nice."

"How long do you know him?"

"A little over a year."

"You have been seeing a boy for such a long time, and we never knew anything about it?" her mother said, and when she did, Anna denoted a small degree of angst in her mother's voice.

"Please know that it has not been romantic between us. We are just friends." Choosing her words carefully, she went on, "I would see him in the library. Sometimes we would talk about the books we were reading. Then a few months ago, he played his violin for me as we sat on the library steps. Nothing inappropriate has happened, mother. Nothing bad. I've been a perfectly good girl."

Anna's mother's mouth fell open. "I can't believe you have hidden this from us for an entire year."

"Please don't worry. There were lots of people around, and we were never alone together or anything like that. I haven't told you because there was nothing to tell. We were just friends. We are still just friends."

Her father sighed. He reached over and patted her mother's hand. "It's all right, Lilian. She's growing up. Nothing inappropriate happened."

"Are you sure?" Lilian said. "Are you sure you didn't do anything you shouldn't have?" she asked Anna.

"Mother, please, I am sure. I promise you we have done nothing wrong."

"If Anna says nothing happened, I believe her," her father said.

"Do you think you'll marry him?" Anselm asked.

Anna turned to her brother and said, "Oh, I don't know. So far, we are just friends. I don't know what will happen in the future. Actually, the reason he is coming here for dinner is so that we can try to do a musical duet together. I'll play the piano; he'll play his violin."

"Well, that sounds good. If you have known this boy for a year, it's time we meet him," her father said to Anna. Then he turned to his wife, and in a gentle, understanding voice, he said, "Lil, ask Frau Frey to prepare something special. A brisket, perhaps."

"Yes, dear. I will do as you say," Anne's mother said.

CHAPTER TWENTY-SIX

I t was clear when he arrived at the Levinstein home Daniel came from a good family and had been raised by refined people. He wore a dark suit and carried a bunch of flowers and a bottle of fine red wine. When Anna introduced him to her parents, he shook her father's hand respectfully and told her mother that she had a lovely home.

But things had been going badly lately at the factory. And that day, Herr Levinstein experienced a problem at work. The workers were dissatisfied with their pay, their hours, and their working conditions. There were threatening rumors going around that the workers might be thinking about planning another rebellion like the one they'd had on that cold winter day in 1934. That terrible uprising had lasted for several terrifying days, and even now, Michael Levinstein got a chill when he remembered it. He had not only lost revenue, but he also felt he was in danger. After it was over, he'd been forced to fire several skilled employees. This also resulted in a loss of revenue due to the fact that he had to train new people.

That rebellion had failed, but it was a constant reminder of what could happen if the workers were permitted to get out of control.

That afternoon he'd had to endure an hour's worth of complaints from one worker who, he was quite certain, was an instigator. He would give in to a few of their demands. Not many, not enough to threaten his factory or his income, but enough to put out the fire that was burning in the hearts of these workers. As soon as the workers were appeased enough to settle down, he would fire everyone who had been involved in provoking the workers to think about rebelling.

Michael Levinstein had always thought of himself as a fair man. But after listening to all the grievances, he was beginning to question himself. He'd always tried to be available for his employees, relatable, and easy to talk to. At least, he'd thought he was. But that was not how this instigator saw him. For the first time in his life, Michael could see the unfairness of the class division, and it made him feel guilty. But if he wanted to continue giving his family the lifestyle they had come to know, he couldn't afford to increase wages. *If I am not strong, and the workers take control of my factory, it will ruin me.* He thought. He longed for camaraderie. He needed someone on the same level to discuss his dilemma with. Someone who would understand. Someone who would take his side. As they sat at the dining table, it was impossible for Michael to think of anything but his precious factory.

"Daniel, so, what does your father do for a living?" Michael asked.

"He owns a factory."

"I thought so. Just like me."

"Yes, sir."

"What do you feel about these communists and their ideas?"

"What do I feel?" Daniel asked.

"Yes, I was just wondering."

"Well," Daniel said. Then he took a deep breath. A smile came over his face. "My parents always told me never to discuss politics or religion."

"You can discuss it with me. I asked you."

"Are you sure you want to know my true feelings?" Daniel said.

"Don't tell me you're one of them? Are you a communist?" Michael asked.

"I suppose you could say that. My father says it's because he spoiled me. I grew up privileged. I'll admit it. I always had everything I wanted. So, now, I feel sorry for the workers who don't get what they deserve. I told my father that he should give the workers better pay and a safer work environment. If they felt like they were being treated properly, I'll wager that they would perform better. Therefore, I believe my father should welcome the ideas of the workers. I hope you won't hold that against me."

Anna eyed her father. Herr Levinstein put down his fork and knife. She could see that he hadn't been expecting this, and neither had she.

"I can understand how you feel, Daniel," her father said, "but if we give in to all these unreasonable demands of these ungrateful workers, our profits will suffer gravely. We may not even be able to pay all of our bills. The workers don't realize it, but the business owners take all the risk. We buy the materials, pay the workers, and rent or buy the workspace. We pay all the bills while the employees just come to work and collect their pay. If we didn't take these risks, these people would not have jobs, and then they would have no money at all."

"Yes, but the wealth should be more evenly distributed," Daniel said boldly. "I mean, the truth is that the workers are everything. They are the people who keep our factories alive, but they can hardly live on what we pay them. We must pay them fairly and give them better working conditions. I'm sorry. I know that this is not a popular opinion with men like you and my father. But it is fair."

"I see," Anna's father said. Anna glanced over at her father, and she could see he was getting angry.

Daniel continued, "I don't mean to be argumentative. I just think it would be the right thing to do. I tell my father the same thing all the time."

"Do you have any siblings?" Herr Levinstein asked.

"No, I am an only child. My father worries about what will happen when he dies. He talks about it all the time. But he's healthy and isn't going anywhere for a long time. However, he says he is afraid that if he leaves the factory to me, I will give away all the profits he has made over the years. But I think he's wrong. I believe that if I give more to the workers, they will work harder, and in the end, I will profit more by doing the right thing."

Michael Levinstein sighed and put down his wineglass. Then he spoke slowly, enunciating his every word. "I will try to be patient and explain this to you even though I am sure your father must have spoken to you about this. Do you know that there was a workers' uprising a few years ago?"

"Yes, my father's mentioned it to me."

"Well, then, you must already know that the business owners suffered a great loss of revenue due to the uprising. But more importantly, the workers, people who I thought I knew, people who had worked in my factory for years, became violent. These people, who I had thought of as loyal employees, changed in an instant. I no longer knew them. They became a threat to me and my family. This sort of thing must be stopped before it can gain momentum. It cannot be tolerated. Not even for a minute, or we will lose control and then... well... then anything can happen."

Anna frowned and shook her head because she knew her father. She had been so pleased when she first introduced Daniel, and she saw how quickly her parents were willing to accept him. But now that Daniel had spoken out about his communist leanings, she could see that there was a clear change in her father's expression when he looked at Daniel. He thought of Daniel as a fool, and he was repulsed by Daniel's way of thinking.

After dinner, Frau Frey began to clear the table. Frau Levinstein went up to her room, and Herr Levinstein went to his study. Anna told Daniel to follow her into the parlor. Anselm went with them.

As soon as they sat down, Anna asked Daniel, "Why didn't you ever tell me that you were a KPÖ supporter?"

"You never asked."

"Daniel, that's a serious thing to be. Are you a member of the KPÖ?"

"Well, I am not a member of the party or anything. I just like the ideas."

"My father is a successful businessman, and so is your father. I know how my father feels about the communists. I am sure your father feels the same way."

"My father hates anyone who questions his way of doing things, and he really hates the communists. But he's selfish. He thinks only of his own family. I can't be that way, Anna. I see that there are so many people in the world who don't even have their basic needs met. You and I are fortunate. We have never gone to bed hungry or spent a winter without heat. Shouldn't everyone have that same privilege?"

"Of course," she said.

"But they don't." He sighed. "There are children who die because their parents can't afford to pay for a doctor. Or they die of starvation or freeze to death. It's not right. It's not fair."

She couldn't help but agree with him.

A few awkward moments passed. No one spoke. Then Anna said, "Let's play some music. What do you think?"

"I'd love to."

When they played a duet with Daniel on the violin and Anna on the piano, Anselm was the only member of the Levinstein family who was there to listen. Neither of Anna's parents came into the parlor.

Anna could see that Anselm liked Daniel, and Daniel liked him.

But after Daniel left that evening, Anna went to her room. It was only ten minutes before Anna's mother knocked on Anna's bedroom door. Anna had just slipped on her nightgown, and she was about to hang up the dress she'd worn that night. But she stopped what she was doing and opened the door.

"Your father and I need to speak to you," her mother said firmly.

Anna felt sick, but she wasn't surprised. From the moment Daniel expressed his views on communism, she'd had the feeling that this conversation between herself and her parents was inevitable. Her father was a good, kind, and patient man. She had heard his story often. How he and her mother had come to Austria with nothing but the clothes on their backs. He had built his factory on his own sweat and blood. He worked hard, long hours to give his family a better life than they'd had in Russia. And he had done so. Anna knew her father adored her. He was indulgent and could often be convinced to forgive and forget. However, when it came to giving control of anything to his workers, he was unmovable. Daniel had struck a nerve, and Anna knew that her father was going to tell her that he didn't approve of her friendship with Daniel.

"All right," Anna said to her mother. She was trembling. The evening had not gone the way she had hoped it would. A trickle of sweat tickled her ribs as it made its way to her belly from under her breast.

"Come down to your papa's study. He's waiting for you. We'll talk there," her mother said coldly, and then she left.

Anna slipped on her robe and slippers and made her way downstairs. She walked into her father's study. It was a quiet room, dimly lit, with a thick ox-blood leather chair in the corner and a table in front of it. On the table was a bottle of whiskey. In the center of the room, there was a large mahogany desk which her father was sitting behind. Her mother sat quietly across from him. There was an open chair beside her mother. Anna knew it was for her. She sat down.

"This Daniel is a handsome boy," her father began. He picked up a pencil and taped it on the desk. Then he said, "And he is from a good family."

Anna nodded.

"He's Jewish. He has good manners, and he dresses well," her mother added.

"I can see why you would have been interested in him. However, he has very different political ideas than we do, Anna," her father said calmly.

"This was the first time we ever talked about this sort of thing, Papa," Anna said.

"You know how I feel about the KPÖ," her father said.

"Yes, Papa. I know," Anna said. Her hands were cold and trembling, but she was sweating, and a trickle of sweat ran down her brow. She didn't realize how much she liked Daniel until now, and she didn't want her parents to forbid her from seeing him again. And she was afraid that this conversation was headed in that direction. So, she grasped on to the only thing she could think of to say. "But I believe he will grow out of his fascination with communism. It is just that he has a very kind heart. He hates to see anyone suffering. He wants life to be fair."

"But life is not fair, Anna. In this world, you get what you work for. I made our lives the way they are. I am not willing to give away my profits. The communists are not good for us. They just are not," her father said.

"I know, Papa, and I agree with you. But Daniel is young and idealistic. Please don't hold this against him."

"I'm sorry, Anna. Your mother and I can see that you like him a great deal. But you are at the age when you should be starting to think about marriage. And because of Daniel's strong beliefs in this matter, we think it's best if you two don't continue seeing each other."

She looked down at the ground. *I knew this was going to happen.* Rage bubbled up inside her gut and came flying out in angry words. "Both of you take everything away from me. Everything and everyone that makes me happy. Oh yes, you give me plenty of material things. I have pretty clothes and piano lessons, and I even have some nice jewelry. But you took away Elica, and Bernie, my best friends, and now you want to take Daniel. Well," she said, seething, "I won't let you. I'll run away from here. I swear I will. Listen to me; I refuse to stop seeing him. I absolutely refuse."

"You will do as we say, young lady. Your parents know what's best for you." Her father slammed his fist down on the desk. His voice was firm.

"I won't. I won't listen to you anymore. I am tired of your demands on my life," she said as she tried to keep the tears from flowing down her cheeks. Her eyes burned, and she felt the sweat beading on her brow and under her arms. She wiped her forehead with the back of her hand.

"You are breaking one of the ten commandments," her mother said threateningly. "Honor thy father and thy mother—"

"I don't care. I don't care about your commandments. We aren't religious. We've never been religious. All of a sudden, you are leaning on religion because you can no longer control me. Well, I am not listening."

Her father took a long breath. He stood up and paced the room. Then he stopped to look out the window. When he turned back to look at Anna, his face was no longer red or angry. He had calmed down.

Then he said in a gentle but firm voice, "Annaleh, you have grown into a very beautiful girl. Now, I know you like this boy, Daniel. But you know your mother and I want what is best for you, and after tonight, I can see that Daniel is just not right for you. He has such controversial views on things that I am afraid he is going to find himself in a lot of trouble as he gets older.

"We are Jewish, whether we are religious or not. And the *goyim* are just looking for a reason to hate and punish us. It's been this way since the beginning of time. Mark my words, if Daniel continues down this path, he is going to get into trouble with the *goyim*, and that will be very bad for him and his family. I know this makes you unhappy. But I promise you that you will meet another boy who is more suited to you. We are your parents, and we love you. We only want what's best for you."

She softened. Her father always had a way of softening her. "But Papa, I know he won't ever join the communist party or anything. I know he won't ever work with them. His parents would never allow it. Please believe me; he is just an idealist. As he gets older, he'll change."

Her father shook his head. "I wish I could believe that. But you are too precious to me for me to allow you to put your safety in jeopardy by associating with a boy like him." He walked over to Anna and touched her cheek. "You'll see, you'll meet someone else. You'll forget."

"May I go to bed?" Anna asked. Her defiance had slipped away. She felt the tears coming, and she didn't want to cry. She knew that no matter what she said, she was not going to be able to change their minds.

"Of course. Go rest. You need your sleep; you have to get up for school tomorrow," her father said gently. Then he added, "I'm sorry. I wish I could give you what you want."

She nodded and left the room.

Lying in her bed, Anna felt the hot tears running off her cheeks and onto her pillow. She was sad and angry at the same time. She lay on her back and stared up at the ceiling. *There's no point in arguing with my parents. They have made up their minds, and they are so stubborn. Well, I am not going to give in to them. I have never wanted to deceive them. But they are always forcing me to. I will just continue to see Daniel behind their backs. And if we decide to marry, I'll run away. I am tired of them always trying to rule my entire life.*

Before Daniel left that night, he and Anna had made plans to meet at the library the following Wednesday. She had no intention of canceling those plans.

The week passed slowly. Anna spent a few afternoons practicing piano with Judith, and she spent another afternoon with Debra, writing a paper for class. She liked these girls, but the depth of the friendship she'd shared with Elica and Bernie was just not there. And now that her parents were against her relationship with Daniel, the loneliness he had helped to stifle was growing within her again.

On Wednesday, she met Daniel at the library. When she arrived, he was sitting at their usual table waiting for her. She looked at him sitting there, and a surge of anger came over her. *Why did he have to tell them all of that? Why did he feel he had to tell my father about his political beliefs? Couldn't he have kept all of that to himself?* Anna walked over to the table. Daniel looked up and smiled.

"Can we go outside? I need to speak to you," she said in a slightly angry voice.

"Sure," he said, not seeming to realize that he'd caused her so much trouble. "Look, I brought my violin."

She nodded, but she wanted to scream at him. He stood up and followed her outside, where they sat down on the library stairs.

"You seem upset about something," he said. "Is something wrong? Did something happen at school?"

"No. Nothing happened at school," Anna replied, finding it hard to believe that he was not even aware of what he'd done. "I can't believe you don't realize that what you said to my father the other night caused me a lot of problems."

"What did I do? What did I say?"

"You really don't know?"

"I don't know. What?"

"Oh, Daniel, you told him that you are a communist. You told him that you are on the side of the workers. He is a business owner. He, like your father, would lose a great deal of profit if the workers had their way and took over his factory."

"Should I be a liar? Would that be better? I am a communist, in a way. I don't belong to the party, but I think that its only right that the poor should be better cared for. They should be treated fairly. I feel sorry for the people who work for our parents. They work hard, and we, you and I, reap all the benefits. Yes, it's nice for us, but the truth is, it's not right. "

"Well, why did you feel the need to tell my papa this? He and my mother were livid. They want me to stop seeing you."

"And how about you? Do you think that it's fair the way the workers are treated?"

"Probably not, but I am really upset with you. Now, if I want to see you, I have to go behind my parents' backs. It makes life a lot harder."

"Oh," he said. "I really didn't realize that they would react that way. I mean, we were only having a conversation. I'm sorry. I forgot myself. I can get very passionate about this subject."

"Yes, we were having a conversation, and my parents were weighing and measuring every word. You were meeting them for the first time. Didn't you realize that they would be judging you?"

"I didn't, but you're right. I should have realized it. I probably should have kept my views to myself. I know how my own father feels about the KPÖ. I should have realized that your father would feel the same way," he said, then he added, "I am so sorry. I've ruined everything."

They were both silent for several moments. Then, in a small voice, Daniel asked, "Is this goodbye? Please don't tell me that this is the end of us. Let me talk to your parents. I'll tell them I am sorry. I'll tell them whatever you want me to tell them."

She stared at the ground, and for a long moment, she didn't speak. Then she said, "Oh, Daniel. You don't understand. It's too late. It's best you don't talk to them." Clearing her throat, she added, "But I don't want to say goodbye. You're my best friend."

"So, we'll continue the way we have been? Meeting once a week at the library and once a week at the park?"

"Yes. It will be harder now that they don't approve. They will be watching me more closely, but this is our only option. It's all we can do."

He took her hand. "You are my best friend, too," he said. "I am a stupid boy. I talk too much."

She nodded. "Sometimes, you do. I have to agree."

CHAPTER TWENTY-SEVEN

Over the next few months, Daniel and Anna met. They talked and explored their views on everything from world politics to religion. Then one afternoon, Daniel finally grew bold enough to put his arms around her and kiss her passionately. From then on, they kissed goodbye each time they saw each other.

Then a few weeks later, when they were playing the violin at the park, as he was showing her a cord on the violin, his hand brushed across her breast. Then their eyes met. It felt nice. Too nice. Anna looked away.

"I'm sorry," He said, taking the violin and holding it to his chest. "That was accidental."

She didn't answer. Her face was flushed. She was embarrassed.

Clumsily, he handed her the violin. Then cleared his throat and said, "Why don't you try that piece again?"

She nodded and began to play. The uncomfortable moment passed. But that night, when Anna was alone in her bed, she thought of how delicious it felt when he touched her. And she was ashamed.

On an autumn afternoon, Anna and Daniel left the library. They were headed towards the soda shop. When they turned the corner, they found themselves face to face with Elica and Dagna. Daniel didn't realize what had happened, but Anna tensed up. There was no way to avoid this confrontation. They were standing face to face. Elica looked away first.

"Hello," Anna said timidly. "It's been a long time since I last saw you."

Elica nodded. "Yes, the last time was that horrible night at the police station." She cleared her throat. "Anna, I wanted to thank you for what you did. If it hadn't been for you, Dagna and I would have gone to jail."

"I didn't want you to go to jail. But I could not believe you let Dagna accuse me of those horrible things. That I was running a racket. If it hadn't been for Bernie, I don't know what would've happened." Anna was consumed with anger. Then she saw Elica's eyes get glassy like she might begin to cry, so Anna took a deep breath. "But I thought I might see you around over these last few months. But... I haven't seen you at all, anywhere."

"I didn't know what to do. I wanted to come over to your house so many times to apologize, to explain... but my mother forbade me to see you. She threatened me that your parents would fire her if I went to your house. So, I stayed away," Elica said. Her voice was trembling.

Anna nodded. She knew that Elica was telling the truth. "But you could have come by my school."

"Yes, but I was afraid. My family needs my mother's income. I didn't know what to do. Besides, you could have come by my school, too."

"That's true," Anna said. "I am as guilty as you are of avoiding the situation. I didn't know what to do either."

There were a few moments of silence. Elica was looking down at the ground, and Dagna was glaring at Anna. Then Anna, without a word, reached out and put her arms around Elica and hugged her.

Anna and Elica hugged tightly.

"Why don't you two girls join us for a soda? It's on me," Daniel said, and he smiled.

"Sure," Dagna answered.

"Yes?" Anna asked Elica cautiously. "Will you join us?"

"Yes," Elica answered.

Daniel got a table, and they all placed their orders. "Have you seen Bernie?" Anna asked.

"No, not since that night," Elica said.

"I don't miss her," Dagna said. "She is obviously a lesbian, a pervert, who had her eyes on Elica."

"I miss her," Anna said. "I miss her all the time."

"You haven't seen her either?" Elica asked.

"No, she hasn't come by. But it's not all her fault. I haven't gone searching for her either."

"We should get together again," Elica said. "We would have to keep the meeting secret from our families, of course."

Daniel laughed. "It seems that Anna has to keep everyone she knows a secret from her parents."

Anna was offended that he'd shared his feelings about her family with Dagna and Elica. He hardly knew them. She glanced over at him and gave him an angry stare.

"I'm sorry. I probably should keep my mouth shut," Daniel said.

"No, please don't. If we have to keep secrets from the adults, that's one thing. But if we keep secrets from each other, that means that we can never really rekindle our friendship," Elica said.

Just hearing those words come out of Elica's mouth made Anna feel warm inside. She missed her friend. Missed her desperately. "I would love to rekindle our friendship."

Dagna's eyes darted from Elica to Anna and then to Daniel, but she didn't say a word.

"Let's try and find Bernie," Anna said.

"I can find her easily at school," Elica said. "I'll invite her to a meeting. When and where?"

"The spot? Next week?"

"Perfect. I am sure Bernie will come if I ask her," Elica said.

The sodas arrived. Daniel thanked the waitress.

"Let's set an exact date. How about next Monday after school? We can meet at the spot. I'll tell my parents I am working on a project, and I have to stay late," Anna said.

"All right with me," Elica said.

"I'll be there," Dagna sulked.

"I should be going. I have to get home," Anna said. "It's getting dark."

"All right. See you Monday," Elica said.

CHAPTER TWENTY-EIGHT

Daniel walked Anna towards her home. As they strolled along, he asked, "So, where do you tell your parents you are going when you and I meet?"

She laughed, "The library, of course. It's not really a lie, right?"

He nodded, "Right."

"And the park. That's not a lie either, right? I mean, I don't tell them you are going to be there. I just say I am going for a walk in the park. It's not a lie, right?"

"Right, it's their own fault. They have forced me to lie by forbidding me to see you..."

"I will do something to win their favor. You'll see," Daniel said.

"I don't think it's such a good idea. I think maybe it's best if you stay away."

"I'll stay away for now. Let's give them some time, and then we'll discuss this again," Daniel said.

They were only a few houses away from Anna's house. "You'd better leave me here," she said, "just in case my mother happens to look out the window."

"Until we meet again," he said, "parting is such sweet sorrow."

She laughed.

He laughed too. Then he turned and walked back in the direction from which they'd come.

CHAPTER TWENTY-NINE

Anna was surprised by how nervous she was as she walked towards their special spot to meet Elica and Bernie. Of course, Dagna would be there, but she had to admit she really didn't care about her. They had never really been friends. But Elica had been her best friend, and Bernie had always been a close second. It had been a long time since they'd spent a day chatting and telling secrets, and she wondered if things would be the same or if they had all grown up and grown apart. Only time will tell.

When Anna arrived, the other girls were already sitting in a circle under the same tree they'd sat under on that night when they'd become blood sisters. The only difference was that now, they were no longer children. It was easy to see that they were on the brink of becoming women. For a moment, Anna stopped and just watched them. Her stomach flip-flopped like a fish that had been caught and longed to get back into the water. *Everything is so different now. If only we could go back to the way things were when we were children.*

Standing there watching Elica, Bernie, and Dagna, Anna's entire being ached for the days when she felt so close to Elica and Bernie. Those days when the meetings of the blood sisters were the most precious moments of her life. With a bittersweet smile, she remembered how she would run out the door of her house and race to the park, eager to share her most intimate secrets with her dearest friends. But these girls who she was looking at were different. They resembled her childhood friends, but they were not the same. They were more guarded than the girls she had once shared the deepest of bonds with. There were still traces of the children they had once been.

Elica's deep blue eyes and blonde hair were still as striking, if not more so. Bernie's slender, tall, athletic build was the same. When she moved, she was still incredibly graceful. They were the same girls, yet they were different. Then there was Dagna. Anna had to admit, she never really knew Dagna at all. She didn't like her, and so she had never taken the time to really get to know her. *We are not children anymore.* Anna steeled herself. *I believe things will go one of two ways in this meeting today. We will either find a new way to bond as adults, or we will leave the park in an hour or so and realize that we have grown up and become nothing more than strangers.*

The whole thing—the prospect of facing the fact that her childhood and her childhood friends were gone — made her anxious. Anna considered leaving the park and running home before they saw her running away. These feelings were so uncomfortable. Yet, she walked forward and approached the other three blood sisters.

"Hello, it's good to see you," Bernie said.

Elica didn't say a word. She just stood up and gave Anna a hug.

Anna felt a hot tear run down her cheek. Then she looked at Elica, who was crying too. "I've missed you," Anna said.

"I've missed you too."

Without another word, Anna knew that the bond between her and her blood sisters was as strong as it had ever been. They were not children anymore, but the pact they'd made was still strong. And they were still blood sisters.

CHAPTER THIRTY

Anna was filled with mixed emotions. It was wonderful to be reconnected with Elica and Bernie. But at the same time, she felt guilty for lying to her parents. It seemed that she was lying to them about everything these days, and she truly wished she could just tell them the truth. However, she knew they would not accept the fact that she was seeing Elica and Bernie again or the fact that she had not given up on her friendship with Daniel. If she wanted to continue these friendships, she was forced to lie. Anna was meeting her girlfriends after school one day each week and meeting with Daniel two days a week. In order to do this, she had to tell elaborate lies to her parents. She found she was always making up stories as to where she had been and what had been detaining her.

When winter came, it was too cold to meet at the park, so the girls met once a week at Bernie's house. Her mother was at work, and that meant there was no one home and no one to ask any questions.

During the cold winter, Anna continued to meet Daniel at the library, but now they no longer met at the park. Instead, they went to the library twice a week, where they found a quiet corner where they could whisper.

If Anna could describe winter with a color, that color would be gray, even though the snow was white and the icicles that hung from the trees were crystal clear. In Anna's mind, winter was gray, and it seemed to last forever. She hated the cold and the days when the ground was icy. This usually occurs the day after a snowstorm if the temperature drops. And ice made walking outside challenging.

One afternoon when Anna arrived at the library, Daniel was waiting for her with a big grin. She walked over to him, and in a whisper, he told her that his mother had become president of the sisterhood at the synagogue where his family attended. This meant, he said, that she would not be home until five o'clock each day.

"I thought you weren't religious," Anna said.

"We're not. But my mother has always been involved with charities in the synagogue. It occupies her time."

"My mother is involved in charities, too," Anna sighed.

"So, the reason I told you about my mother's being president was that now you can come to my house for violin lessons. No one will be home. Just our maid, and the maid and I are good friends. She won't say a word to my parents."

"All right," she said softly. She felt unsure. Nice girls did not go to boys' homes when there was no one there to chaperone. But then again, nice girls didn't lie to their parents either.

Anna knew that her parents would be appalled if they found out that she was not only seeing Daniel but was now planning on going to his house when no one was there to chaperone. *If I want to continue my violin lessons, we have no other choice but to go to his house. It's too cold to go to the park, and we certainly can't play the violin in the library.* She rationalized. And So, that Wednesday, they met at the library, and Daniel escorted Anna back to his home.

When Daniel opened the door and Anna entered his house, she gasped. Daniel's home was spectacular. It was even prettier and larger than her own. "Your home is beautiful," she said.

He just smiled. "Would you like some refreshments?" he asked as he took her coat and hung it next to his own on the coat rack.

"Oh no, thank you," she said.

"So, let's get back to our violin lessons, yes?" he asked coyly.

"Yes," she said firmly, "I've missed playing."

"Well, follow me," he said.

Anna followed Daniel into the study. It was all dark wood. Built into the wood were bookshelves lined with beautiful leather-bound books. "Have a seat," Daniel said.

Anna sat down.

Daniel walked over to a shelf where there were two violin cases. He brought them back to Anna and handed her one. "I got this for you," he said.

"You got me a violin?" she asked.

"I did," he said. "It's used. But it's a good one. I checked it out."

"You didn't have to do that," she said.

"It will make learning easier for you. You can practice at home."

She laughed a little. "And what will I tell my parents? Where will I tell them that I got a violin?"

"Babysitting money?"

"I'd have to babysit for ten years to be able to afford this."

They both laughed.

"But thank you, Daniel. This was so sweet of you. And I will find a way to practice. I promise. Even if it's not at home. I'll practice at school in the music room."

He smiled at her. "Look at it. It's a very pretty instrument."

She took the violin, made of polished blonde wood, out of its case. "Oh, it is beautiful. Thank you." She gasped.

Daniel took the violin out of Anna's hands and placed it on the floor. Then he began to kiss her. His kisses felt even more forbidden than before and maybe even more passionate. *We are alone in his house; anything can happen.* She thought. Anna was nervous. He eased his hand up the side of Anna's body and fondled her breast. Her heart was beating wildly. She wanted to allow him to go further, but she couldn't. *This is wrong.* She thought as she gently pushed his hand away.

"I don't think this is a good idea," she said. "I don't feel right about coming here and being alone in the house with you. My parents would be disappointed if they knew. And the truth is, Daniel, I already feel like I am drowning in lies."

"Anna, you are taking this much too seriously. I only meant to be affectionate with you. We've kissed before."

She didn't know why, but suddenly she felt like crying. "I should go home now."

"No, please don't go. Please stay for dinner. I would love for you to meet my parents. I promise I won't try that again."

"I can't. I can't stay. I have to go. What would I tell my mother? She would be worried if I didn't come home. I really should leave now."

"Let me walk you home."

"No need. I can get home on my own."

"Please. Let me escort you. I didn't mean it. Forgive me," Daniel said. His face looked so forlorn that she nodded.

"All right. You can walk me home. But I have to go right now."

"Whatever you say," he said. Then he took their coats off of the coat rack and helped her to slip hers on.

They walked to Anna's house in silence. When they were only a few houses away, Daniel said, "I'm sorry. I really am. I didn't mean to offend you."

"I know," she said. There were so many things she wanted to say, but she was feeling guilty and upset. She couldn't organize her thoughts well enough to say anything, so she walked away, leaving Daniel standing alone as the snow fell.

The following week, when she went to the library to meet Daniel, he was not there. She sat at the table in the back where they sat each week and waited, but he did not come. Anna tried to read, but she couldn't concentrate on the book. Instead, she watched the hands of the large round wall clock in front of her. When the clock struck five pm, Anna realized he was not coming. With a heavy heart, she put on her coat and left the library to walk home.

As she walked home, the chill seemed to penetrate even deeper through her coat. Anna's heart ached, and she felt betrayed. *If that was all he wanted from me, then I don't need him.* She told herself, but the truth was she was deeply hurt.

Everyone was busy when Anna got home, and she was glad. She could easily slip into her room unnoticed. Her room was her sanctuary. She closed the door and reached for one of her novels. Her hands trembled as she opened the book. She tried to read, but she couldn't. Her heart was broken. So, she closed the book and wept.

CHAPTER THIRTY-ONE

Anna thought that she would hear from Daniel. *Perhaps he has some excuse for not showing up; maybe he was sick. Maybe one of his parents was sick.* She tried to rationalize. But Daniel made no attempt to contact Anna, and she felt lost. If nothing else, they had been best friends, and it hurt to be betrayed by a best friend. Anna had to admit, she was glad that at least she had rekindled her relationship with Elica and Bernie before she and Daniel had parted ways. The next time she and her blood sisters met, she told them about Daniel and what had happened. It was just like it was when they were children. She felt she could tell them anything. Anything at all.

"And all he wanted was to try to feel me up," Anna said. "I was so hurt, I didn't know what to do or say. And to make matters worse, I know that if my parents ever found out, they would ask me what I expected to happen when I went to a boy's house to be alone with him without a chaperone."

"You didn't think he was going to act that way. You thought you were going to learn the violin," Bernie said reassuringly. "You were innocent."

Elica looked away.

"Boys can be like that," Dagna said. "I've had to let plenty of boys feel me up. It's nothing. Once you let them do it, they stick around and keep taking you out."

Anna shrugged. "I don't know. All I can say is, it just didn't feel right."

"It wasn't exactly all his fault, you know," Dagna said, "boys are made different than girls. I overheard my mother say that when she was talking to one of her friends. She said men need sex. Women need men."

"What the hell does that mean?" Bernie said.

"It means that it wasn't his fault," Dagna said, as if she was sure what she had said was an absolute truth.

"I think it was his fault," Bernie said. "He had no right to act that way towards Anna and expect her to do what he wanted her to do. Then when she didn't give him what he wanted, he stood her up? What kind of fellow is that? A louse. That's what I say."

"Well, no need to think too much about it now; he's gone for good," Anna said.

"You didn't lose anything of great value," Bernie said to Anna. Then Anna saw Bernie cast a quick glance at Elica and then look away. "If he really cared about you, Anna, he'd wait forever if he had to."

Anna nodded, but she felt the loss very deeply.

CHAPTER THIRTY-TWO

February 1937

I t was a cold winter afternoon. A few weeks after Anna had told her blood sisters about the incident with Daniel, Elica was leaving the general store when she saw Daniel coming out of the bakery. She was sure it was him. As she walked quickly, she looked away, trying not to make eye contact with him. Then Daniel pulled his scarf tighter around his neck as he walked over to Elica and said, "I remember you. Aren't you Elica? Anna's friend?"

Elica nodded. She was shivering from the cold.

"You probably forgot my name. I'm Daniel."

"I remember you," she said as she looked at him. He was handsome in his long black wool coat and red and black wool scarf. His hair was combed perfectly, and it shone in the sunlight, glistening from the cream he used to style it. His eyes were dark and so deep she felt herself getting lost in them. He wore a gold watch that she knew, just by looking at it, was expensive. And the gold ring on his pinky finger had a red stone in the center. Elica was fairly certain it was a ruby.

"You're trembling," he said, his voice soft and deep. "Say, it's certainly cold out here. I have an idea. Why don't we go into the café and I'll buy you a cup of hot coffee? Then maybe you can tell me how your friend Anna is doing. I haven't seen her in a while."

"All right," Elica said tentatively. He made her nervous. She knew how much Anna cared for him, and she could see why. *He is terribly charming and so attractive. The best thing I can do is to tell him I have to go; I must get home. But the very thought of a hot cup of coffee in a warm restaurant is very appealing. Perhaps this meeting with Daniel need not be a betrayal to Anna. Maybe I could help them get back together. Maybe spending time with Daniel could be good for Anna.*

Daniel opened the door to a small coffee shop, and Elica followed him inside. Immediately, the warmth from the heater caressed her face. He helped her to take off her coat, and when he did, she was suddenly ashamed. *My coat is so old, and the sleeves are frayed. I am sure he has noticed how worn it is.* She thought, but Daniel just smiled at her. He didn't seem to pay any attention to the old coat. He hung it on a hook on the wall. Then he took off his own coat, hat, scarf, and gloves, which he placed on the hook beside hers. He pulled out a chair for her, and she sat down. He took a seat across from her and looked directly at her. She had to admit to herself that sitting across from this very attractive, dark-eyed boy made her heart flutter.

"What would you like?" he asked.

"A coffee," she answered softly.

"How about a pastry too?"

Her eyes lit up. She couldn't resist. It was so rare that she had pastries. "Yes, please."

"I'll order for us." He smiled.

She watched him. He was so handsome and confident in his impeccably clean white cashmere sweater and black wool pants as he motioned for the waiter, who came immediately. "The lady will have a coffee, and so will I. Will you please bring the pastry cart so we can make some selections?"

The waiter nodded. Daniel smiled at Elica.

The hot steaming ersatz coffee arrived quickly. Elica took a sip, and it warmed her up inside. Then the waiter brought a dessert cart. Elica had never had the opportunity to make such a wonderful selection, and she was having difficulty deciding. "I want them all," she said, laughing. Forgetting to be intimidated.

"Chose as many as you'd like," Daniel said.

Elica would have been happy to have one of each. However, she chose two, a piece of strudel and a slice of cake.

After they both made their selections, the waiter served them and then left them. Once they were alone, Daniel asked, "Have you seen Anna lately?"

"I see her sometimes," Elica answered.

"How is she?"

"She's fine," Elica said.

"Does she talk about me often?"

"Not really," Elica lied. She wanted to believe that Anna was over Daniel because she found him attractive.

"Do you think she still thinks about me?" he asked.

"I don't know."

After the first time Anna told her blood sisters about what had happened with her and Daniel, she hardly mentioned him again. Elica wanted to believe that Anna was over him, but she knew in her heart that it wasn't true. After all, sitting across from this boy and looking at his handsome face, Elica knew that if she were in Anna's place, she would not let him go so easily. *Not only is he handsome, but he is also such a gentleman, not coarse like the other boys I've been going out with.*

"So, she never talks about me at all?" Daniel asked again. He was fishing, and Elica knew this. She knew he wanted to hear something more encouraging.

"No. Anna never mentions you." Elica knew what she said was cruel, but she didn't want to talk about Anna.

Daniel looked at Elica, and she could see that he was sad, and suddenly she was sorry she'd been so harsh. "But she doesn't talk about any boys at all. I mean, I don't think she's seeing anyone else."

He nodded. "I made a mistake," he admitted. "I guess I made more than one mistake."

"What do you mean, a mistake?"

"Well, I should have shown up on the day that she and I were supposed to meet at the library, but I didn't. I was stupid. I was angry, and I acted like an idiot. And not just that, I was a damn fool to tell her father I am for the workers, and politically, I have communist leanings. I should have known better. After all, her father is just like my own father. A rich businessman who doesn't give a damn about the poor. I should have kept my mouth shut, but I wasn't thinking. You see, I can't help it. I hate the unfairness of it all. I hate to see the workers sweat and struggle and hardly make a living wage, not to mention the terrible working conditions. Even so, it was the first time I met her father, and I should have kept my mouth shut." He sighed. "I suppose I made quite a mess of things, and now there is no going back. I don't know how I am ever going to do this, but I am going to have to find a way to get over Anna. It seems she's over me."

Elica looked into his dark eyes and felt her heart beat faster. She had plenty of experience with boys and knew how to make a boy forget anything and everything. In a soft, breathy voice, she said, "I can help you."

He looked into her eyes. She could see that he was puzzled at first.

"I know just what to do," she said softly and winked. Then she saw a wave of understanding come over his face, which broke into a smile.

"And just how do you propose to do that?"

"Leave it to me."

CHAPTER THIRTY-THREE

After Elica and Daniel finished their pastries and coffee, they walked outside. "How far do you live from here?" he asked. "Not far at all," she said.

"I'll walk you home."

It was very cold. Elica was shivering as they walked side by side. "You're very handsome. But I suppose you hear that all the time," she said boldly. She was beginning to understand that although he was more polished than the boys she'd dated, deep inside, he wanted the same thing.

He laughed, embarrassed.

"No, I mean it. You are. And you're so mature. You're not like the boys at my school. Or even the older fellows I have gone out with. I suppose what I am trying to say is that you are refined."

"Refined?" he asked, then he laughed a little. "My mother would love to hear me described that way."

Elica laughed, "I mean it. You are. You have a special way about you. I think you might call it suave." Then she laughed again, even harder. "I sound like a fool. I think it's time I stopped talking."

"No, please go on. I love the compliments. Even if the words you're using hardly fit me," Daniel said. Now he was laughing too. They were both laughing so hard that they stopped walking. He turned to her. She looked up at him. They stopped laughing. Daniel bent down to kiss her. Elica rose to meet him. Their lips brushed softly, and then they gazed into each other's eyes. Without saying another word, they kissed again. This time, he put his arms around her and held her tight to him. Elica no longer felt the cold. She melted into his arms.

"Would you like to come to my house?" he asked. "My parents aren't home. It would be just you and I."

She trembled. "Yes."

They walked silently, arm in arm. Elica knew what was going to happen when they were alone. This was not her first time. Not by a long shot. There had been other boys her own age, and then when she grew tired of them, she had been intimate with older boys who she'd met. Boys in their early twenties who worked at one of the local factories. But she had to admit Daniel was different. *I wonder if it's because he's a Jew. I mean, that makes him different, doesn't it?* She thought. *But it's more than that. When he looks into my eyes, I feel like he is looking into my soul. I feel like I am bound to him, tied to him by an invisible rope that I never want to break free of. His smile makes all of my problems seem small, and I long to feel his kisses on my neck. Yes, he is different.*

When they arrived at Daniel's house, Daniel called out to let the maid know that he was home and was going to his room. He also said that he was not to be disturbed. When Elica heard him speaking to the maid, she thought of Anna and her mother, Anna's maid, and the thought made her cringe. She forced herself to put those thoughts out of her mind as she entered Daniel's room. He quietly closed the door behind her. Then, without a word, he took her into his arms and kissed her passionately. From that moment on, Elica did not think about Anna or her mother being a maid or anything; everything else was outside of Daniel's room.

They made love. He was clumsy and a bit inexperienced. Elica could see that, but their lovemaking was more intense for her than it had ever been with anyone else. Afterward, as she lay in his arms and he held her tightly, she wondered what it might be like to live in a house like this. What it might be like to have a maid and to be the wife of a very successful man.

CHAPTER THIRTY-FOUR

D aniel had promised that he would be outside of Elica's school when she was released the following day. When the bell rang, telling the students that school was out for the day, Elica practically ran outside. Daniel wasn't there. She made a hundred excuses for him as she stood on the snow-covered stairs outside her school for an hour, shivering and waiting until she finally walked home. *Something had to have happened. He wouldn't just not show up. There had to have been some kind of emergency.* She told herself over and over. *Perhaps he will come tomorrow.* But he didn't and didn't come the next day either. By the end of the week, she was certain that he was not ever coming again. Her heart was broken. She felt used and broken. Dagna saw Elica standing outside and went over to her. "What are you waiting for?"

"Nothing. I was just trying to remember something about my homework," Elica lied, not wanting to tell anyone how bad she was feeling.

"Are you ready to go home?" Dagna asked.

"Yes, sure," Elica said.

They walked home together. As they walked, Dagna was talking about some movie actress, but Elica wasn't listening. When they arrived at Elica's apartment, Dagna asked, "Can I come in for a while?"

"Not today. I have too much homework," Elica lied. She longed to be alone.

"Since when did you care about your homework?"

"Since today," Elica said curtly. Then she turned and walked into the apartment building, leaving Dagna standing outside on the sidewalk.

The apartment was quiet and dark when Elica walked inside. There was a faint odor of sauerkraut permeating the air. Her father was asleep in his room. She could hear him snoring softly. The heat in her building was not working well, and she felt the cold penetrate her clothes even as she slipped off her coat and hung it on a hook by the door. Hugging her arms against the chill, she walked slowly to her room, where she tossed her schoolbooks down on the floor and threw herself on her bed, and began to weep. *I thought Daniel cared for me, but it turns out he was just using me. He really cares for Anna. I mean nothing to him.*

And even though she knew he was gone and their sexual encounter had not had the same effect on him as it had on her, she still looked for him every day when she walked outside at the end of her school day. And every day, he was not there.

Elica was heartbroken. This boy was different. He was everything she wanted. He was wealthy, refined, handsome, and charming. When she could not have him, she no longer wanted to be bothered by the other boys. She stopped dating. Elica had never had such strong feelings for anyone before, and she couldn't bring herself to date just for the sake of fun anymore. Since she'd made love with Daniel, sex was no longer just a pastime. It now had deep meaning for her.

Her parents were too busy and too tired to notice how sad and heartsick she was. Elica desperately needed someone to lean on. So, she turned to the only people she had ever really trusted, her blood sisters. Even if she could never tell them that she thought she might be in love with Daniel because of Anna's relationship with him, she knew that spending time with them would help her to forget. And if she ever did decide she needed to talk to them about her feelings for Daniel, as long as she didn't use Daniel's name, they would listen to her, advise her, and help her get through this.

CHAPTER THIRTY-FIVE

Finally, the cruel winter was over. The icy chill had given way to a brisk and refreshing wind. The ground had melted. Little buds of grass were springing up, and tiny flower blooms peaked their heads out of the ground and turned their faces to the sun. Life was reemerging. On a lovely spring day, Anna met with Elica, Bernie, and Dagna in the park for a picnic. They each brought a dish. The sun was out, and the sky was as crystal blue as blue topaz. Taking a deep breath, Anna could smell the sweet fragrance of flowers, lemon balm, and lavender. The tiny flower blooms made the park appear more like a garden than a wooded trail.

The local boys were playing ball and showing off for the girls. Elica was smiling at the boys who were looking her way as she pinned her braids up.

Bernie spread out an old gray blanket, and the girls sat down. Anna began to lay out the food. Elica and Bernie helped. It was easy to see that Dagna and Elica were bursting with excitement about something. Once they were all settled and the food had been passed around, Elica smiled broadly and said, "Dagna and I have something exciting to tell you both."

Bernie cast a worried glance at Anna, but she didn't say anything.

"Tell us," Anna said, trying to sound enthusiastic. She, too, was a little concerned that Elica and Dagna might be doing something that could get them into trouble again.

Elica smiled, and once again, Anna was reminded of just how pretty Elica truly was. Then Elica winked and said, "Listen to this." She paused for a moment to create even more excitement. Everyone was silent. Then Elica continued, "Dagna and I are going to Berlin this summer. We have jobs working as babysitters for two families."

"Berlin?" Bernie said. "Why would you be going to Berlin?"

"I just told you. We have jobs," Elica said proudly. "We are going to earn money and see a new city."

"So, let me understand this correctly. You two have jobs babysitting?" Bernie said with a little sarcasm in her voice.

"Well, yes, we have jobs where we will be living with families who will pay us a small salary. We get a place to stay while we are in Berlin, and meanwhile, we help them out. In my case, it's with their children. Dagna is going to be helping an old man who can't take care of himself," Elica said.

Bernie looked lost. "So, you'll be gone all summer." Bernie cleared her throat. "Elica, you mean we won't see you all summer then?"

"Not unless you get a job in Berlin too!" Elica said excitedly. "There are plenty of jobs like the ones Dagna got for her and me. Maybe you could get one, Bernie. Maybe both you and Anna could come to Berlin. It would be so much fun. We would be far away from our families, so they wouldn't always be asking us questions. We would earn some money so we could buy the things we want. I think it would be the greatest summer of our lives."

Bernie shrugged. "I suppose I could go to Germany; my mother wouldn't care so long as I sent her some of my pay. What about you, Anna?"

Anna shook her head. She felt bad already. If the three of them went to Berlin, she would be left out and alone in Vienna for the summer. "My parents would never go for it."

Elica nodded. "I hoped you could go, but I really didn't think your parents would allow it."

Dagna had a smirk on her face that made Anna want to slap her.

"Well, hold on a minute. I have an idea," Bernie said. "How about if you asked your parents to send you to some special school in Berlin for your piano lessons? They'd go for that, wouldn't they? I mean, they are always wanting you to practice."

Anna's eyes lit up. "Bernie, you're brilliant. You just might be on to something. I will ask the music teacher at my school if she knows of any programs that are taking place this summer in Berlin. And, if she can help me get into one."

Dagna gave Bernie a look of disgust. "She doesn't need to come with us. We're going to have to work while she is studying her precious piano," she said.

"I'd like it if Anna could come with us; whether she is studying or working wouldn't matter much to me. I would just like for all of us to be together on our day off," Bernie said to Dagna. Then she turned to Anna. "Talk to your teacher and see what you can find out."

"I will," Anna said.

Elica, Dagna, and Bernie walked over to watch the boys play ball. Anna began to cover the food. Then she sat down under a tree with a book and began to read. Oliver left the game and walked over to speak to her. He wasn't the young boy with a crush on Anna, who had flirted with her in the park anymore. At seventeen, he'd grown into a handsome young man. He smiled at her and said, "I saw you over here."

Not knowing what to say, she just nodded.

"Any chance I could bother you for a glass of water?"

"Of course. Let me get you one," Anna said. She poured the water from a jug into a glass and handed it to him. He drank it greedily.

"You look beautiful today. But then again, you always do," Oliver said.

She giggled. "Thanks."

"Do you remember when we were children, and I said that someday I was going to marry you?"

"I do remember that."

"Well, I still mean it." He leaned over and kissed her. She felt her face grow hot and red with embarrassment. "You'll see. Someday I won't be just some boy, you know. I'll be important to you. I'll have meaning in your life."

"Oh, Oliver," she said, looking away embarrassed, "would you like some more water?"

CHAPTER THIRTY-SIX

The girls returned to help Anna finish cleaning, and when they arrived, Oliver shyly walked away.

Elica managed to smile; "He grew up to be so handsome," she said, but she couldn't meet Anna's eyes. Whenever she looked at Anna, she was reminded of how she had betrayed her with Daniel. Her lips were trembling. But she didn't say a word.

"Well, I had best be getting home," Anna said. "I'll let you girls know what my teacher suggests."

The four blood sisters put away the food and folded the blanket. Then they separated. Anna walked towards the Jewish part of town, and the other three headed home to the same neighborhood.

Elica walked slowly with Bernie beside her and Dagna on her heels. Dagna was loud and animated as she was telling Bernie something, but Elica wasn't listening. Her thoughts were of Daniel. She felt guilty for what had happened between them the last time they were together because she wasn't sure that Anna was over him. Even though Anna rarely mentioned Daniel, when she did speak of him, Elica could see that Anna still cared for him. But things between Elica and Daniel had escalated so quickly.

Elica had to admit to herself that she was surprised by how attracted to him she was, and she knew that she had been responsible for what happened between them. She'd been taken in by his earnest good looks, then she'd listened in awe when he spoke of how he wanted to help the poor. How he was willing to make sacrifices in order to make sure that those who had been born less fortunate than himself could live a better life. He came from wealth, but he seemed to understand what her life had been like. And when he became passionate about his ideas, his deep soulful eyes set her heart twirling. Memories of that day when they had made love came flooding back to her. In her mind's eye, she saw two of them sitting in his home, which, to her, seemed like a castle. Elica couldn't say what came over her, but she leaned over and kissed him. Then she put his hand on her breast. This was nothing she had not done before, yet it was different with Daniel. The sensations were so intense that she felt she was losing her mind. The kissing grew even more passionate, and before she knew it, her skirt was lifted, and his hands were exploring every part of her. She didn't stop him. She couldn't. The more he touched her, the more she wanted. Then, when he was inside of her, she felt her body explode. It wasn't until later that night, when she was at home in her bed trying to sleep, that she closed her eyes and thought of Anna. Guilt engulfed her like a tidal wave, and she was sorry for what she'd done. However, when he disappeared after that day, she forgot her guilt. The feelings she had for him were intensified, and she no longer cared about anything but winning him back.

And now, As she was walking home with Dagna and Bernie, it seemed all she could think of was Daniel. That day, after they'd made love, he had walked her home in silence. When they arrived at her apartment, they'd said goodbye without looking into each other's eyes. She knew he felt guilty, too. But he'd promised to come to her school the following afternoon and had not shown up. *How could he do that to me? I thought he had feelings for me. Ever since we made love, I can't think of anything but him. I shouldn't be so upset; It wasn't as if he was the first boy I ever had sex with. But I really wish he could be the last.* She wished she could just forget him, but it was not that easy. Elica waited and hoped he would call or drop by, but he didn't. That was why she had been so eager to go to Berlin that summer. She wanted to escape from her feelings for Daniel. She thought that if she could go away, she might not think of him as often, and maybe it would be easy to forget him altogether.

And then they were standing in front of her home.

"Are you all right?" Bernie asked Elica.

"Yes, I'm fine," Elica said, snapping back into the present moment at the mention of her name.

"You seem so distracted."

"I am just tired," she said. "I babysat for the Schmidts last night, and their boys are a handful."

"Well, try to get some rest."

Elica nodded. "Yes, I will. Of course, that will be after I get done with all the chores my parents expect of me."

"It will be good to get away from our families and all the responsibilities they put on us," Dagna said.

"Don't you think our employers are going to have plenty of work for us to do? They aren't going to pay us for nothing. You can be sure of that," Bernie said.

"I suppose you're right," Dagna said. "Still, I can't wait to get away from my mother." Then she sighed, "And by the way, why did you invite Anna? She won't be working like the rest of us if she comes. She'll be studying music. Doesn't it get to you sometimes that she is so privileged? We have to work. But she gets to study."

"Sometimes it bothers me," Elica said. "Sometimes I feel angry, and I ask myself, why is it so easy for her and hard for us?"

"Elica! Anna is our friend. She happens to have been born to a wealthy family, but she is a good person and a good friend to us," Bernie said.

"She is a spoiled Jew," Dagna said.

"Dagna!" Bernie said angrily.

"You know I am right," Dagna said indignantly.

"I don't know that you're right. Anna has always been kind to all of us, you included. Although I have no idea why she is so nice to you. You've always treated her horribly. But no matter, Anna has always proved to be a good friend," Bernie said.

"Yes, it may be so, but Dagna's right. She's not like us. She's not one of us. Not really. The Jews stay with their own," Elica said, and she was thinking of Daniel. *I am not a Jew, and that's probably why he abandoned me. For all of his fancy talk, no matter what he wanted, I'll bet his family would never permit him to have a serious relationship with me.*

"I never thought I would hear you talk that way about Anna," Bernie said, looking directly at Elica.

"Well, sometimes it gets to me. Think about it, Bernie. Think about how it makes me feel that my mother is Anna's family's maid. My mother cleans her house and washes her clothes while I have to go inside our small apartment and wash a whole big bucket of laundry. It's not fair. It hurts," Elica said. Then she turned and walked into the apartment building where she lived.

CHAPTER THIRTY-SEVEN

Anna sat outside under the large oak tree in her backyard and thought about Daniel. *I miss him; I miss talking to him, and I feel like I have lost a dear friend. Even if we are not going to be more, I wish we could maintain that friendship. But I don't think he wants that. I know he felt rejected when I said no to his advances, but what did he expect? He knows me. He knows that I have never done anything like that before, and I have no intentions of doing it until I get married. I like him so much, but I couldn't honestly say I am in love with him. But none of this matters because I haven't seen or heard from him, and that should be enough to tell me that he has no interest in talking to me anymore.* She sighed. A feeling of melancholy came over her. Reaching down, she plucked a dandelion and held it up to the sun. Then she made a wish. *I wish that somehow, I could go with my friends to Berlin. I wish I could get away from here for a while. I need to forget Daniel, and it would be good to have some time away from my parents. Besides, if Elica and Bernie are gone all summer, I am going to be just miserable. All I want is to be happy again.*

The following day, when she went to school, she asked one of her music instructors if he knew of any programs in Berlin that summer.

He said he didn't. On her way home, she stopped by the home of her private piano teacher and asked her if she knew of any programs. Her instructor shook her head. "I'm sorry. I don't know of anything in Berlin right now. However, I could increase your lessons with me over the summer if you'd like. I have some extra time available."

"Thank you, but I wanted to get away and take a little holiday from Vienna, just for a while."

Three weeks passed. There had been no meetings with the blood sisters. And Anna felt defeated and sad as she walked home from school. It was a beautiful day. The sun was bright, and the trees had begun to blossom. Soon school would be out, and summer would arrive. The beauty of spring all around her was lost on Anna. She wasn't seeing any of it. Her head was down, and her shoulders were slumped. *It's probably best that I am not going on some big music program.* She thought. *If I was, it would only further alienate my friends. They are going to be working. So if I was studying, it would only make me look even more spoiled. But it's going to be terrible to be here all summer without my friends or Daniel.*

"Anna," a voice called to her from across the street.

Upon hearing her name, Anna looked up. It was Bernie. "Hello," Anna called back, and she waved.

Bernie ran across the street. "Did you ask your teachers about Berlin?"

"Yes, I tried both my teachers, the one in school and the one who gives me private lessons. But neither of them knew of anything. So, I guess I can't go with all of you."

"Nonsense," Bernie said, winking at Anna. Then she gently elbowed Anna and whispered, "I have an idea."

"What is it?"

"How about this? Can you steal a piece of letterhead paper from school?"

"I think so."

"Good. Get the paper, then you and I can type up a letter from your music instructor to your parents telling them about a program that we made up taking place this summer in Berlin. We'll say that he thinks it is important for you to attend. What do you think?"

"I think it's a great idea. But where will I stay?"

"I figured that there might not be any piano programs in Berlin this summer. So, I took it upon myself to find you a job like the ones the rest of us have. If you take it, you'll have a place to stay and a little money too."

Anna stopped in her tracks. She let out a laugh. "Have I ever told you that I think you're a genius?"

"You haven't," Bernie said, "but it's nice to hear. Even if it's not true."

"It is true."

They both giggled.

"How soon can you get your pretty little hands on a piece of letterhead paper from your school?"

"Tomorrow," Anna said.

"Perfect. Then come over to my apartment on your way home."

"Do you have a typewriter?"

"Yes, my mother has an old one," Bernie said.

"How did you find these jobs?"

"It was easy. The jobs are posted on the bulletin board outside the office at my school."

"So, you have a job for sure?"

"I do, and so do you if you want it. After Elica said she was going, I sent a letter to a lady whose name was on that bulletin board. I told her that I had a friend who wanted to come to Berlin and work, too. I asked her if she had any friends who needed a nanny. She wrote to me yesterday and said she would hire me and she did have a friend. It's a young woman who is married to an older man. It is her first marriage and his second. He has an older son who is attending the university. The older boy is from his first wife. You won't have to be bothered with the older one. It's the two young boys she needs a nanny for. They are nine-year-old twins. She admits in her letter that they are a holy terror, but I know you can handle them."

"I hope so. I don't have any experience with children."

"It's easy. You just have to outsmart them." Bernie winked. "I have faith in you."

"I wish I had as much faith in myself. By the way, how did you know I wouldn't be able to find a music program?"

"I didn't know for sure, but I wrote just in case. And it sure is a good thing that I did."

"Yes, thank you for going through all of this trouble for me. It was very kind of you," Anna said sincerely, but she thought, *I don't know how I am going to convince my parents to allow me to go. And even if they do, I hope I can handle a job like this. I've never worked with children. The scariest part of all of this is that their own mother admits that they're difficult children. Oy Vey. Am I getting myself into a mess? Probably, but I really do want to go. I want to be with my friends this summer, and it would be better if I worked as a nanny, just like they are, rather than studying. Then we would all be equals, and they wouldn't look at me like I was a spoiled child.* She sighed. *I'll find a way to make this work.*

"You are a blood sister. I want you to come with us to Berlin. It won't be the same unless you are a part of this adventure," Bernie said, smiling. "So, here's what we'll do. Tomorrow you'll come to my apartment on your way home from school with a piece of letterhead paper?"

"All right, I will," Anna said excitedly. She was also a little nervous.

"My mother won't be home from work yet, so we can work on this together without worrying about her asking questions."

"Sounds good."

"All right, then I'll see you tomorrow," Bernie said. "I've got to get home. I have a lot of homework." She winked and giggled. Anna giggled too. Then Bernie turned and sprinted across the street; within moments, she was gone.

CHAPTER THIRTY-EIGHT

It wasn't difficult for Anna to acquire a piece of letterhead paper. All she had to do was go into the office in the morning when the staff was very busy and pretend she had a question about volunteering to tutor students the following year. The flustered secretary got up to look through a file cabinet to retrieve the papers concerning tutoring. When she turned around, Anna reached across her desk and took a few pieces of the school's letterhead paper, which she stuffed between her books. Then, before the secretary returned, she grabbed an envelope.

"All right, my dear, I think this is everything you will need." She handed Anna a pile of papers. "Just fill these out, return them to my office, and I'm sure you will be selected as one of the tutors next year. I checked your file, and as far as I can see, you have good marks and are considered a good student," the middle-aged woman said, smiling kindly. She had a round, chubby face, bright blue eyes, and light brown hair. Anna felt a pang of guilt for having taken the papers from her desk. *I have become such a bad girl. But it's the only way I can live my life without my parents restricting me from everything.* She rationalized.

"Thank you," Anna said. She took the papers and left. *Maybe I will tutor next year. Not for the money. In fact, I could offer my services for free in order to be of help to another student. Maybe if I help someone else, Hashem will forgive me for all the terrible things I have done.*

The bell rang, and Anna ran to her classroom. She slipped inside just as the teacher was arranging her books and papers on her desk. Anna took her seat quickly.

"Good morning, class," her teacher said and began a lecture, but Anna wasn't listening. She was too excited about the possibility of getting away for an entire summer with her friends. *Is it really possible that I'm going to Berlin this summer with Bernie and Elica?* She thought.

That afternoon, Bernie was waiting when Anna arrived at Bernie's apartment.

"I've got some lemon cookies. The woman I babysit for gave them to me. Do you want one?" Bernie asked.

"No, thanks," Anna said.

"Were you able to get the letterhead paper?"

"Yes, I have some papers right here."

"Good. Come and sit down." Bernie ushered Anna to a table with an old black typewriter. "It's not the best typewriter, but we'll make it work," Bernie said, smiling.

Bernie sat in front of the typewriter, and Anna plopped beside her. "I just want you to know that I really appreciate this," Anna said gratefully.

"I know," Bernie said, then she glanced at Anna and winked. "We made a pact that day, when we mixed our blood, to always help each other."

Anna smiled. "And you know that if you ever need me, I will help you, too."

"Of course, I know it. I will never forget what you did for Elica and Dagna when they stole that stuff from that store. That day, you proved to me that you are a true sister."

"Thank you for believing in me," Anna said.

"All right," Bernie said, changing the subject, "So, here we go."

Bernie carefully rolled the paper into the typewriter. Then she began to type with one finger.

Dear Herr and Frau Levinstein…

The 'E' and 'A' typebars stuck each time they were pressed, but Bernie manually pulled them back down and continued to type. Then halfway through the letter, the ribbon spool came undone, and Bernie got ink all over her fingers as she carefully put it back in place. Then, to make matters worse, she forgot that she had ink on her hands and accidentally smeared it on the paper she was typing. So, she was forced to scrub her hands and then start the entire letter all over again. Finally, after two grueling hours, the letter was finished.

Anna held it up and read it. "It looks very authentic," she admitted, nodding her head.

"It does, doesn't it?" Bernie said proudly.

Anna bit her lower lip. She was filled with emotion. "I can't tell you how much this means to me," she said.

"You don't have to. I know. And I know how hard things have been for you being different than the rest of us."

"You mean being Jewish?"

"Yes, I do," Bernie said.

"But you don't resent me for being Jewish, do you?"

"No, I don't, and I don't resent you for being rich. You've always been a good friend. You never judged any of us for the things we did, and when Elica needed your help, you were there to help."

"As I would be for you," Anna said honestly.

"And that's why I am there for you, too. I always will be. Now, let's write another letter. This time we'll write to the woman who is going to hire you for the summer. We'll tell her you have lots of babysitting experience and you are so looking forward to working for her."

"All right," Anna said, "but it's kind of a lie, Bernie. I have very little experience babysitting."

"But you do have some, don't you?"

Anna shook her head and laughed, "Yes, I do have some."

"So, it's not a lie. We won't say 'lots.' We'll just say you have plenty of experience babysitting. The term 'plenty' is relative, right?"

"Yes, I suppose so." Anna laughed.

"All right. We won't need to use the letterhead for this. Let's save the rest of the letterhead paper in case we need it in the future for some reason. My mother keeps plain paper right over here," Bernie said. Then she got up and took some paper off a shelf. She rolled it into the typewriter and began to write.

        Dear Frau Fischer…

"Do you suppose we should tell her I am Jewish?" Anna asked.

"No, I don't want to hurt your feelings, but I don't think we should. From what I hear in Germany, they've passed this strange law that non-Jews are not permitted to hire Jews to work for them," Bernie said, "so I think the best thing to do is to forge papers for you that say you are a Christian. Is that okay with you?"

"Sure. Why not? I've been lying so much to my parents lately; what's one more lie?"

"Do you feel bad about it?" Bernie asked as she looked at Anna.

"Of course I do. I don't want to be ashamed to be Jewish, but I feel like everyone hates us, even Elica."

"I don't think she really does. I think she's just jealous because she sees you as having a better life, and Dagna doesn't help matters."

"Dagna is mean. No matter what I do, she will never like me," Anna said.

"But the best part about that is, it doesn't matter. I like you, and so does Elica, even if she is a little envious."

"I wish I could just be proud to be Jewish, and no one would think anything about it. But it's not like that. Everyone seems to hate the Jews."

"Not everyone, Anna."

"I know, not you. But most people who aren't Jewish."

"People hate what they don't know," Bernie said. "They need someone or something to blame their troubles on. Don't worry about it. Everything will be all right."

"And I feel guilty about lying to my parents about why I am going to Berlin. But they force me to lie. They have taken everything away from me, my best friends, the fellow I was seeing. Everything. If I want to have any kind of life, I have to lie."

Bernie nodded. Then she patted Anna on the shoulder, "Well, don't worry about it because they'll never find out. And on our days off, we'll see all of Berlin together. That will be so much fun!"

CHAPTER THIRTY-NINE

When Elica returned home from school to find Daniel waiting for her outside her apartment building, she was elated. He had a bunch of flowers in his hand and looked at her sheepishly. "How have you been?"

"All right," she said.

He handed her the bouquet. "These are for you."

"Thank you," she said. Her heart was pounding. She couldn't believe Daniel had finally come back. All of her prayers had finally been answered, and her wish had come true. She wanted to jump into his arms, but she dared not. There was an awkward silence. Then Elica said, "I am so glad you came. But I have to ask you why it took you so long to come around and see me?"

Daniel cleared his throat. "I knew you were going to ask me that. The truth is, I felt guilty. I felt like I took advantage of you. I didn't want to do that. But things got out of hand that day we were together, you know?"

She nodded. *Daniel is apologizing for making love to me. That means he doesn't want to continue our relationship. He has come to say he's sorry and goodbye.* Her heart ached as she held back the tears.

He continued, "I mean, we were swept up in the moment and—"

"I know," she said, looking away from him so he could not see the disappointment on her face.

"But, Elica, I have to tell you that I really like you. I mean, I really like you," he said. "And I don't want to stop seeing you just because we come from different backgrounds."

"I don't either," Elica said, surprised by this wonderful, good news. She was about to cry, but now her tears would be tears of joy. She liked him so much, and she thought that he was about to be gone from her life forever. But now here he was, standing in front of her, and he was telling her that he liked her too.

"How do you feel about me being Jewish?"

She shrugged, "I don't know. Does it matter?" she asked, then cleared her throat. "How do you feel about me being poor?"

"I don't care," he said. "I like you for who you are."

"I feel the same way about you," she admitted, "but what about our parents?"

"I don't care what they say or do," he said.

"And what about Anna?" she asked.

"Anna..." He said softly and trailed off.

"She is one of my best friends, and I feel guilty about you and me."

He looked away. "Anna and I had a good friendship. But things never advanced beyond that. It was more of a childhood crush. What you and I have is different."

She felt her heart open and pull him inside. She wanted to put her arms around him and kiss him on the street. He was saying all the things she had dreamed he would say. "I can't tell her about this," she breathed.

"Then don't."

"But there is something you should know. I am going to Berlin to work for the summer. Anna and two of my other friends might join me. I'll be leaving in two weeks."

"You're leaving?"

"Yes, but just for the summer," she said.

"So, we'll make the most of these two weeks." He smiled and touched her cheek. "But I must admit, I'm surprised that Anna's parents are allowing her to go to Berlin to work."

"I'm not sure if she's going yet. But from what my friend Bernie says, Anna's parents think she's going on some kind of music program."

He nodded. "It doesn't matter. It's really none of my business. My main concern is you."

She felt her heart swell. She wanted to throw her arms around him.

"And I will really miss you," he said. "So, how about we go out for dinner tonight and make the most of the time we have until you go?"

"Out for dinner? You mean to a restaurant?"

"Yes, I would like to take you to a nice restaurant."

"I've never been to a nice restaurant for dinner before."

"So, you'll go with me?"

"Yes, of course, I'll go."

"I'll be here at seven. Can I knock on the door, or will you be outside waiting for me?"

"I'll meet you in town in front of the candy store. Would that be all right?" she asked.

"Of course," he said. "Whatever is best for you."

CHAPTER FORTY

Elica carefully packed the best dress she owned into her handbag. Then she told her parents she was going to Bernie's apartment to study. Her mother nodded. "Will you be home for dinner?"

"No, I'll eat at Bernie's house. We have a school project to finish."

"All right." Her mother was always tired these days, as was her father. They were getting older, and hard work was taking its toll on them. When Elica looked at her mother, who was slender to the point of being skinny, bent with a slight hump in her upper back and deep lines around her eyes, she found it easier to justify dating Anna's boyfriend. After all, her mother worked for Anna's family. She'd given the Levinstein's the best years of her life. Instead of paying attention to Elica, her mother was busy caring for Anna's needs. *So, why shouldn't I take what is being offered to me? I'm sure Anna thought nothing of taking my mother's time and youth. I know she got paid, and she needed the job. But why should Anna have all the good things? It's not fair. Now it's my turn. Daniel likes me, not her, and I refuse to feel guilty about it.*

CHAPTER FORTY-ONE

D aniel was waiting when Elica arrived. "You look beautiful," he said.

She smiled.

"I know of this lovely steakhouse that I think you will enjoy," he said. "It's not far from here. Do you like steak?"

"Why yes, of course," Elica said. She couldn't remember the last time she'd eaten meat as they walked in silence for several blocks. It was a crisp spring night. Elica had curled her long white blonde hair, and it was dancing in the wind.

At the restaurant, the maître d', a tall thin man with a thin mustache, looked at Daniel suspiciously. "We don't serve Jews," he said.

"I am not Jewish," Daniel answered.

Daniel's answer seemed to satisfy the man, and he led Elica and Daniel to a table in the corner. Daniel pulled out the chair for Elica, and she sat down.

"Does that ever bother you?" she asked.

"You mean when people say bad things about Jews like that?" he asked.

She nodded.

"It makes me feel lousy, but what can I do? I find the best thing to do is to just ignore them."

"I'm sorry that people treat you like that. It's not right, and I don't like it," Elica said.

He smiled at her. "It's all right. It's not your fault, after all."

Her hands were trembling as she read the menu. "I don't know what to order," she finally admitted. "This is the first time I have ever been in a restaurant like this. It's so lovely."

"Well, don't you worry about what to order. Just let me order for you. Is there anything you don't like?"

She smiled and shook her head. "No, I'll eat whatever you choose," she said as she put the menu down. A few moments passed, then Elica said, "Daniel, I was so hurt when you didn't show up that day. You were supposed to meet me after school."

He sighed. His shoulders dropped. "The truth is, I was scared. I had never felt this way about anyone before, and it scared the hell out of me."

"Why?"

"For so many reasons," he said, then he hesitated and looked down. After several silent moments, he looked up and stared directly into her eyes. "One of the biggest reasons, of course, is the fact that I am Jewish, and my parents won't approve of us. And the other reason is... well, it's scary to feel like you might be falling for someone."

She laughed a nervous laugh. "Yes, it is a little scary. It makes you feel vulnerable. I feel the same way. But it hurt my feelings when you disappeared."

"I know. I shouldn't have done that, but I panicked. Can you forgive me?"

She nodded. "Yes, of course I do."

He reached across the table and took her hand. Bringing it to his lips, he kissed it softly.

She smiled. "I am so happy that you came back."

After they finished their dinner, he walked her home. "Can I see you again?"

"Of course," she said.

"Tomorrow?"

"Yes, after school."

"I'll wait outside your school for you."

"Don't you have to go to school?"

"I skip school all the time."

She shook her head. "You shouldn't do that."

"I shouldn't, but I do," he said with a wink.

CHAPTER FORTY-TWO

The following day, as soon as the final school bell rang, Elica walked quickly outside. She was terrified that Daniel might not show up again. But there he was. Daniel was standing against the fence, watching the door and waiting for her. When he saw her, his face lit up. Daniel smiled broadly, and her heart beat faster. *He's so handsome, and he's here waiting for me.* She thought. Then she smiled at him shyly. He walked forward to meet her.

"Let's go back to my house," he said, his voice husky. "I want to play you a song on my violin. I composed it for you."

"You wrote a song for me?" she asked, blushing with surprise.

"I did," he admitted. "When I tried to stay away from you, it seemed that you were all I could think about. And when I am overcome with emotion, I write music."

Her breath caught in her throat. "Really? I can't believe you wrote a song for me," she said. Her voice was barely a whisper.

"Yes, really," he admitted, "and it scared the heck out of me."

"It scared the heck out of you to write a song?"

"Yes, I told you, my feelings for you really scare me."

"I know. That's what you keep saying. And I am afraid it's because I am from a poor family and not Jewish."

He nodded. "I must admit that's part of it. We come from different worlds, but I truly believe in the equality of the classes, and I don't adhere to religion. I know my parents will give us a rough time," he said. Then he took her books out of her hands and carried them in one arm. He slipped his other arm through hers as they walked together. "There's more to it than just that. If it were just a fight with my parents, I could cope. But I thought about what you said yesterday, and I realized that I just never felt so damn vulnerable." He shook his head.

"I don't know what to say," she said. "I'm sure you've dated other girls. I know you were dating Anna—"

"Anna," he said softly. "Yes, I was dating her, and I like her. She's a nice girl, but I never felt this way about her, or anyone else, for that matter. Do you know what I mean?"

These were the words she longed to hear, and he'd said them verbatim as if he were reading her mind. She stopped and looked into his eyes. "Yes, I know what you mean because I, too, have dated other people, but no one has ever affected me the way you do." She stopped and turned to look at him. "I wept when you didn't show up after we made love."

He touched her face. "I'm so sorry. I never meant to hurt you."

"But you did," she whispered.

"I know. I can be thoughtless sometimes. I don't mean to be. But when I am confused or frightened, I run away. It's a fault of mine. Please forgive me."

She melted like ice on the sidewalk on a summer day. "I already have."

When they arrived at Daniel's home, he led her into the study. It opened up to a library with shelves of books. "This is really my father's study, but he's at work, and I can play for you here," he said.

She glanced around at the heavy brown leather furniture and the brown wood desk and sighed. "It's such a lovely room."

He smiled and took his violin down from the shelf. Then he played for Elica. She let the music move slowly into her heart and soul. It was so tender that she found that when he'd finished, she was crying. He put the violin on top of its case and stood up. Then he walked over to her and took her into his arms. His embrace was warm and safe. She had yearned for him for so long that when he kissed her, she wanted him as much as he wanted her. Falling into his arms, he laid her down on the large, overstuffed sofa, and they made love.

After they'd finished, he whispered, "Someday, I would like to marry you."

Her breath caught in her throat. She realized she wanted the same thing. It would be like a dream come true to be married to this handsome boy, to live in an opulent house like this. She would feel like a queen. A smile crossed her face. It would be wonderful to have all these lovely things. She could see herself shopping for beautiful clothes and having dinner parties. Several moments passed as she imagined what it would be like to be as wealthy as Anna. When she thought of Anna, a wave of guilt came over her. Now she might be Daniel's wife...

"Elica, you haven't answered me. You haven't told me if you want this too or not," Daniel said. His voice was trembling.

"I'm sorry. I know I haven't."

"So, will you marry me someday?"

"Yes. I will. Of course, I will," Elica said. *Why should I worry about Anna? I don't know how I will ever tell her. But she has always had everything. It's my turn now.*

He pulled her to him and kissed her again. Passion filled her, and she forgot about Anna. They made love again.

"So, when do you want to get married?" she asked him as she stood up to get dressed.

"I don't know when," he said earnestly. "I have to finish school, and then I suppose I'll have to take over my father's business. He'll have me work under him for a while before he gives me any kind of a real job."

"So, next year?"

"I don't know," he said, a little annoyed by her questions. "I can't give you a time or date, but someday."

"I should get home," she said, not hiding the disappointment in her voice. *Daniel was just daydreaming, and I took him seriously. I believed him.*

"I want you to meet my parents someday soon. I want to tell them I am going to marry you. When are you graduating?"

"Next year," she said.

"My father will be hard on you."

"I don't see why we can't get married now. I will work while you finish school so we can pay our bills. I don't need to finish school," Elica said earnestly. Her voice was cracking. *Please marry me. I love you and want to marry you before you get scared again and change your mind.*

"Let's just wait," he said. Tiny beads of sweat had formed on his forehead. "I am not quite ready. Besides, you are going to Berlin. We'll talk about it when you return. That is, if you still want to go."

She wanted to go. This would be the first time she was away from home, and she and her friends would be on their own in a big, exciting city. But she didn't want to lose him. "I have to go," she said softly. "I promised my friends. Besides, the lady who hired me is counting on me."

"That will be all right. You'll take some time away to think things through. I'll have some time too. We'll stay in touch by letter."

"You make it all sound so simple." She smiled.

"It will be." His voice exuded confidence

Daniel is used to getting everything he wants. He likes the idea of marrying me, but he isn't really serious. He just likes to daydream. She thought resentfully. *He can afford to daydream. In fact, sometimes I think all he does is daydream, but I am forced to be practical.*

He caressed her hand for a few moments.

"I really should go. It's getting late," Elica said.

"Stay for dinner. I want my parents to meet you."

"Don't you want to talk to them and tell them a little about me first? Give them a little warning?" she asked.

He laughed. "My father needs to be shocked out of his comfortable, oblivious state. Besides, given a little time, they will learn to love you. Stay?"

My family will be worried when I don't come home for dinner, but Daniel wants me to stay. I want this marriage. I want him and life with him more than anything. It would be like a dream come true. I have to stay. My father might beat me when I get home for not leaving a note telling them where I am and for making them worry, but it will be worth it. "All right. I'll stay," she said, "but I need to fix my hair and tidy myself up a bit before I meet your family."

"Of course, but you're gorgeous right now, just as you are," he said. Then he smiled and added, "The bathroom is right down the hall."

CHAPTER FORTY-THREE

Elica pulled herself together as best she could. She braided her long wheat-colored hair and straightened her worn clothes. *I wish I had something nicer to wear.* She thought. *His mother will see immediately that I am from a poor family.* She sighed. There was nothing she could do to make herself look any better than she did. So, she returned to the study to find Daniel playing his violin. When she walked into the room, he stopped and smiled at her. "You are so pretty. I think I may have told you that once or twice before." He smiled, and his smile lit up the room.

"I hope I can make your parents like me."

"I don't care what they say," he said. "I like you."

Daniel played a few more songs for Elica, then they heard two female voices in the kitchen. He whispered, "My mother's home. She's talking to our maid."

Elica felt her stomach twist. "I'm nervous," she admitted.

He smiled. "It will be all right."

Fifteen minutes later, they heard a door slam. "That's my father. He always slams the door," Daniel said.

"I'm really scared," she said honestly. "I am not Jewish and am from a poor family—"

"It's all right. My father and I fight all the time about my political beliefs. He might get angry, but he should expect nothing less from me."

I hope I am more to Daniel than just a way of rebelling against his parents. She thought. The very idea made her uncomfortable, so she put it out of her mind.

"Ready?" Daniel said cheerfully.

"For what?"

"Let's go into the living room. I'll introduce you to my family. Who knows, maybe they will become your family very soon."

She smiled, but her lips were trembling. *I want this. I want this boy, and I want this life. So, I have to be brave and meet his parents with confidence.*

Daniel took Elica's hand and led her to the living room. His father was upstairs in the bedroom getting ready for dinner, and his mother was in the kitchen speaking softly to the maid. They heard the whispering but could not make out what was being said. Then Daniel's mother walked through the living room. She was an elegant, tall, and slender woman. Her hair was perfectly styled in a neat twist. She wore a cashmere camel-colored dress. Elica watched Daniel's mother move about the kitchen. She was so graceful. Elica held her breath.

"Mother," Daniel said, "I would like you to meet someone."

His mother turned to face him. "Yes?" she said, looking at Elica and not even trying to hide the shock on her face.

"This is Elica Frey," Daniel said proudly.

His mother stared at Elica. "Hello."

"She will be staying for dinner."

"I see," his mother said, a little confused. Then she smiled, "Of course. Daniel, please get ready for dinner. We will be eating soon."

Then, without another word to Elica, Daniel's mother turned and walked upstairs. Once she was gone, Elica whispered to Daniel,

"Maybe you should have told them something about me before you brought me here. Your mother looked very surprised. She didn't look too happy."

"I'm sure she was quite surprised. I can't wait to see my father's face."

Elica looked at Daniel. He was smiling, but she was uneasy.

"Let's go and wait in the study," he said. "Marta will let us know when dinner is served."

"Marta is your maid?"

"Yes," he said.

She thought of her mother as she followed him. *My mother is a maid, but if I marry Daniel, I could be the mistress of this house one day or of another one just like it. This has been my dream since I was a child, playing with Anna and her expensive toys. Now, it's within my grasp. So, why am I so terrified? I am afraid that Daniel is just using me to upset his father and that he is not serious about the marriage. After all, he keeps on saying 'someday.'*

CHAPTER FORTY-FOUR

Marta announced that dinner was served. Daniel took Elica's hand. "Come on. You're about to meet my father, the most obnoxious man on earth. He thinks his money can solve anything and everything."

"Well, this certainly sounds inviting. I just can't wait to meet your father," Elica said sarcastically. "What happens if he hates me?"

"Don't worry about him. Let me handle him. My goodness, your hand is so cold!" he said as he led Elica into the dining room.

Herr Goldenberg sat at the head of the table with his wife beside him. He looked up when Daniel and Elica entered.

"Father, this is Elica," Daniel said.

"Hello, Elica," Daniel's father said. He was courteous, but not warm.

Daniel pulled out a chair for Elica and went into the kitchen. Elica heard him say, "Please set another place at the table. I have a guest tonight."

"Yes, Daniel," Marta responded.

An older woman with thinning hair caught in a knot at the nape of her neck came walking out of the kitchen quickly. Within a few moments, she'd arranged a place setting in front of Elica, who whispered, "Thank you."

Marta nodded, then she began serving the food.

No one spoke, and the silence made Elica uncomfortable. She wriggled in her chair.

Once everyone had been served, they began eating. Then Daniel said, "I brought Elica here tonight because I have a wonderful surprise for you."

Herr Goldenberg looked up. There was a deep wrinkle between his eyebrows. "Oh?" he said.

"Yes," Daniel said, and Elica detected a slight arrogance in Daniel's tone. "I've asked Elica to marry me."

Daniel's mother's mouth flew open, but she quickly regained control of her emotions and sat silently, waiting for her husband to respond. Daniel's father put his fork down slowly. Then he shook his head. "Are you Jewish?" he asked Elica in a calm, matter-of-fact tone of voice.

"No," she answered softly.

"I see." Daniel's father looked directly at him. "You will not marry this girl." Then he turned to Elica, "Forgive my son. He cannot keep his promise to you."

"Oh, yes, I will. I am sick and tired of you constantly trying to control me. I am graduating, and haven't you said I am ready to marry?"

"Yes, I have. But you are ready to marry a girl who is right for you, not a *shiksa*."

Elica felt her throat tighten. She wanted to get up and run out of the room and out of that house, but she couldn't. She felt glued to the chair.

"We love each other, and you have nothing to say about it," Daniel said.

"Oh, don't I?" his father scoffed, and it seemed to Elica that Daniel and his father fought often. "We'll see about that."

"Yes, we will," Daniel said defiantly.

"Young lady," Herr Goldenberg turned to Elica, who couldn't eat a bite. She was afraid if she tried, she might choke.

"What do you plan to do for a living?" Daniel's father asked.

"I was going to go to work at one of the factories in town after I finish school. Or maybe I could be a nanny."

Daniel's father smiled condescendingly. "Yes, and that will certainly provide enough money for the lifestyle you are used to, won't it, Daniel? It will take her a week to earn the amount of money you spend on a single sweater."

"I don't expect my wife to support me, father."

"Oh, don't you? Don't forget Daniel, I know you. You've never worked a day in your life. What exactly do you plan to do for work?"

"I'll give violin lessons."

His father let out a laugh. "And you and your young wife will live in some dump of an apartment. Do you know why? Because if you marry this girl, I plan to cut you off completely. The two of you will be on your own. I won't give you a cent."

"Do you really think I need your money?" Daniel asked.

"I know you do." His father looked at Daniel and sneered. "You just don't realize how much you need it. You've always had the finest of everything. You don't know any other way of life. Now this young lady you brought here for dinner seems nice enough. But quite frankly, she is not for you, and if you marry her, you will divorce in a year. I promise you that. You, my dear son, are in for a rude awakening when you try to live out those idealistic fantasies of yours."

Elica stared down at her food, then studied the hand-painted pink roses around the perimeter of the China plate. She wished she had magical powers so she could make herself disappear.

"These are not fantasies, father. The future of the world lies in a redistribution of wealth. It's coming. You mark my words. You won't be able to look down on people like Elica's family. They will be our equals.

"So, you think," Daniel's father roared. "It is you who should open your eyes. It is you, Daniel, who should take more notice of what is going on in the world. Jews must stick together. We are hated, and that hatred is growing stronger by the day—"

"Yes, and that's because of people like you. Rich men who make non-Jews feel like they are beneath them."

"I don't feel they are beneath me, Daniel. I feel they are different. There is nothing wrong with being different, but marriage is a difficult proposition. And when you marry, it is more than just physical attraction. More than just what happens between the sheets," he said.

Elica felt her face grow red with embarrassment. It seemed as if Daniel's father knew what she and Daniel had been doing earlier that afternoon. She looked away from Daniel's father in shame. Still, he ignored her and went on talking. "Marriage," Daniel's father said, and then he cleared his throat, "marriage is not so much about physical attraction as it is about understanding each other's way of life. Understanding and sharing a culture. Like eating the same foods and celebrating the same holidays. Do you know what I mean by that, son?"

"No, I don't," Daniel said defiantly. "I don't at all."

"If you were to marry this young lady, you would find that you and she have more differences than things that you share in common. The passion driving you would disappear within a few years, leaving you with nothing but perhaps a child who would be the ultimate victim of a bad choice."

"How dare you call her a bad choice, father!"

"Besides, I believe that in these tumultuous times, when there is so much hatred towards our people, it is important that we stick together."

"Yes, Daniel. I agree with your father," Daniel's mother said. "What happened to that nice Jewish girl you told us about? The one you were seeing. I believe her name was Anna."

Elica looked down at the table; she couldn't meet anyone's eyes. She was feeling dizzy and a little sick to her stomach.

"I disagree with you about Jews sticking together. The more we stick together, the more we are ostracized. We should integrate ourselves into the world rather than stay separate and only marry our own. Anna and I broke up. It's over between us, and like it or not, I plan to marry Elica."

"And when do you plan to do this?"

"As soon as I can," Daniel said.

Elica was looking down at her plate. The food was good, but she couldn't eat. Everything she put into her mouth stuck in her throat. Daniel's father was staring at her, but she could not meet his eyes. Regardless of what he had just said, she was hoping Daniel was serious about getting married soon. Earlier, when they discussed marriage, he had been elusive about giving her a date. He had only been willing to commit to someday. Now she was hoping that Daniel's anger towards his father would drive him to commit to a date.

Daniel's father had lost his calm. His face was red with anger. His fists were clenched. He stared at his son as if he could shoot daggers out of his eyes and said, "If you defy me and marry her, I promise you that you will struggle with her. You will work from morning until night, and still, you will live in poverty and squalor. I won't help you, son, and your mother won't either. I will not allow her to, and when I die, I won't leave the two of you a penny. Mark my words; you will live to regret it if you go against my will."

"I don't need you, father. I don't need you or your money."

"We'll see about that, Daniel."

"Let's go," Daniel said to Elica, throwing his napkin on the table as he stood up. Elica was trembling so hard that she almost collapsed when she stood up, but Daniel walked over to her and took her hand. Then he led her out of the room. "Come on, we'll go to a restaurant and have dinner."

She wanted to go home. It was late, and her parents were going to be furious with her, but she dared not tell him that. He was all fired up from his fight with his father. "I'll get your books," he said. "Wait here."

Elica stood by the door, waiting for Daniel to return. Her hands were so cold, and she felt so afraid. Daniel's father hated her. It was easy to see that. She thought about Marta and her mother and the things Daniel's father had said. Tears threatened to fall from her eyes.

If I marry him, I won't have this lifestyle. I won't have any money, and he doesn't know how to work. He's been pampered all of his life and has never had to do anything for himself. I'll bet his violin lessons cost more each month than my parents' apartment. He's spoiled like Anna, but worse. She's grateful and kind, at least. But he hates his parents and resents the fact that he's always been given everything he wants. I don't see why he is so angry. I wish I had grown up with a family like his. He can't imagine how hard it is for working people. He thinks he can cope, but he can't. I wonder how he will respond when we can't afford the lifestyle he's used to. I am worried. I am afraid that even if he commits to marrying me, it won't be everything I hoped it would be. I am afraid it won't be because he loves me; it will be because he wants to show his father that he doesn't have to obey him. In a way, I'm glad I'm leaving for Berlin for a while. It will give me time to think things over.

Elica was surprised. Her parents were not upset when she arrived home late that evening. She told them that she was working on a project for school with Bernie. Her parents were too overwhelmed with their own problems to care. The rent was late, and they didn't have the money to pay the landlord because her father had needed to see a doctor recently. So when she told them that she would be coming home late from school for a while because she had to finish the project with Bernie, they didn't ask her any questions. Her father had gone back to work and had been working extra hours. Each night he returned in terrible pain, hardly able to stand up, his back aching so badly. Her mother had been overwhelmed. She was busy baking each night for a special event that Anna's mother was hosting.

Every day after school, Daniel was outside waiting for Elica. They went for sodas, walked back to his house, and made love before his parents got home. She could see the difference between them that Daniel's father was talking about. Still, it was that difference that she found so attractive. She was charmed by his impeccable manners and the tender passion of his lovemaking. Elica adored him, but she was haunted by his father's words and always afraid of how difficult marriage to Daniel would be because his parents didn't approve. He didn't have any skills to help him find work. When she thought of him working in a factory with his soft hands, she couldn't lie to herself. She was certain that he would be unable to do the job. And quite frankly, she couldn't imagine how they would get by financially. But the more difficult things seemed, the more attracted to each other they became.

CHAPTER FORTY-FIVE

The Jewish families in Austria were aware of the growing hatred of Jews in Germany since the appointing of the new chancellor, Adolf Hitler. Many people felt certain that Germany was planning to take over Austria. To make matters worse, there were a lot of Austrians who were ready to welcome the German chancellor as the leader of their country. Life became difficult for Jews in Austria. Many shops refused to sell to Jewish clientele, and many of the Levinstein family's close friends lost their jobs and even their businesses. Although her father tried to keep a brave face, Anna could see that her father was starting to worry.

His brow was deeply wrinkled, and there were dark purple circles under his eyes. Anna overheard him tell her mother that the workers in his factory were growing bolder with their demands. He tried to meet their demands, but they were becoming more and more unreasonable. One night as she lay in bed trying to sleep, Anna heard her father tell her mother that two of his employees asked for more money. When he told them that he had recently given them a raise and could not afford to do so again, they called him "dirty Jew" and

"Jewish swine." He fired them, but he told his wife that he feared that things were going to get worse before they got better.

Anna's parents were consumed with the political climate in Vienna. Then they were forced to face a recent bout of illness that left Anselm weaker than ever. So, when Anna told her parents about her trip to Berlin that summer, they were so distracted that they agreed to allow her to go even without taking the time to contact her musical instructor in school to ask for additional information.

Anna was elated. For the first time in her young life, she was to be on her own, away from her controlling parents. Anna was worried about her brother, but it was hard to feel bad for him. She was too excited about visiting a new country while being surrounded by her best friends, Elica and Bernie.

One afternoon after school, the blood sisters met at Bernie's house to discuss their plans for the summer. Bernie was thrilled when Anna told them all that her parents said she could go with them to Berlin. Elica tried to smile, but she didn't speak. She was very quiet. In fact, Elica didn't say much these days, and Anna wondered if Dagna had poisoned Elica's mind. Dagna was the only one of the girls who had any interest in politics. The others were too busy looking at fashion and movie star magazines, but Dagna had no interest in these things. She was consumed with the progress Germany was making under the direction of the new chancellor.

A week later, when the girls met at the park, Dagna was in a wonderful mood. She was excited as she explained that she had officially joined the political party that Adolf Hitler belonged to. It was called the National socialist German workers' party, and she was quite taken with its ideology.

"They hate Jewish people," Bernie said. "I read a little bit about them recently," her tone reflecting the disgust she felt. "Why would you join a group like that?"

"I think Germany is going to annex Austria, and I want to be a part of the new Austria," Dagna said proudly.

"I don't like the way you feel about Jews," Elica said. She was nervously picking at her nail.

Dagna looked at Elica. "I didn't think you liked them either."

"Well, whatever gave you that impression," Elica snapped.

"I just thought that you felt they were rich and spoiled."

"Stop all of this, you two. Anna is here with us. Have you ever thought about her feelings?" Bernie asked.

"I'm going home," Elica said, standing up. Then turning to Anna and without meeting her eyes, Elica added, "I'm sorry if I ever hurt your feelings."

"Don't go," Dagna said.

But Elica was already walking away.

"Dagna, when you and Elica got into trouble, it was Anna who risked getting into trouble herself so she could help you. I know you must remember. Don't you?"

"Yes, but it wasn't me she was helping. It was Elica. If I had gotten caught stealing by myself, do you think she would have helped me?"

Bernie didn't answer.

Anna glared at Dagna for a moment. Then she said, "I would have helped you, Dagna."

Dagna huffed, then she stood up. "I'm going home," she said, and she left.

"Come on, Anna, let's go home," Bernie said.

"Do you think that if Germany takes over Austria, my family will have anything to worry about?" Anna asked Bernie as they walked home.

"No. Unfortunately, there has always been hatred for the Jews. I don't think this will be any different. Nothing really bad will come of it. I mean, of course, it's bad when people say mean things, but I think that's all that will happen even if Germany does take over."

"But what if they find out I am Jewish when we are working in Berlin? It's illegal for a Jew to work for a non-Jewish family."

"That's why we forged papers for you that say you aren't Jewish. Don't worry, you'll be safe in Berlin. No one in Berlin will know."

"I wish people didn't hate Jews," Anna admitted.

"So do I," Bernie said. "But since we can't do anything to change it, we'll just go around it. Right? Your papers say you are a Lutheran. Like me."

"Right," Anna said. "Are you nervous about going to work in Berlin? I've never been out of Austria before."

"I am a little nervous. I've never been out of Vienna, either. But, I am excited too."

"I hope I can handle the children. Twin boys might be a handful."

"They might, but I have faith in you. You'll win them over," Bernie said, patting Anna's shoulder. "You are smart, Anna, and you're very compassionate. I think you will do just fine."

CHAPTER FORTY-SIX

Two days before Anna was to leave for Berlin, she was going over everything she'd packed when there was a knock on the door to her room. She opened it, expecting her mother or Frau Frey, but it was her father.

"Annaleh," he said softly, "may I come in?"

"Of course, Papa."

He walked in and sat down on the chair next to her desk. Then he looked at her with deep concern. "You should never feel you have to lie to me," he said solemnly.

"What do you mean?" she said, clearing her throat nervously.

Anna glanced at her father quickly without meeting his eyes.

Herr Levinstein shook his head. "You don't trust me? You don't trust your papa?"

"I don't know what you mean."

"I left the factory, and I went to see your music instructor this morning. I wanted to see if you needed anything special for this trip you are making to Berlin." He let out a long sigh. "You are not going on a musical study program at all, are you?"

She put her head in her hands. Then she took a long breath and looked up at him for a moment. His head was bent. In the light from the overhead bulb, she could see his scalp shining through the thin hair that no longer covered his head completely. As she watched him, her heart ached. He looked so small and almost helpless. "No, I am not going to Berlin for a musical program. I am sorry I lied to you, Papa, but I really want to go, and I was afraid you wouldn't allow it."

He let out a long breath. Then in a soft voice, he said, "Nu, so where are you going? And what are you going to be doing? Just tell me the truth."

She felt the tears well up in her eyes. Once she told him the truth, she was certain that there would be no chance he would allow her to go. This dream would be smashed before she'd even finished packing. And she had gotten so close; it was only two days until she was to leave. Her mind raced, but she knew she must tell him the truth. She couldn't make up another lie. *I have to tell him the truth and let the cards fall where they may. I will not lie to him again. Not to my papa.* Not to the old man who sat there vulnerable, awaiting her answer. "I know you don't like Elica and Bernie, but we are all going to Berlin for the summer, where we will be working as nannies. This is a program from their school. I am to live with a very wealthy family who has nine-year-old twin boys. I will be in charge of watching the boys and taking care of them."

"I see," he said softly.

There were several moments of silence. Anna felt her palms sweating. She sat down on her bed beside her suitcase. "Please, Papa, can I go? I really want to go. I lied to you because I was afraid if I told you the truth, you would forbid—"

"Berlin?" He interrupted.

"Yes, but only for the summer."

"There is a lot of hatred towards the Jewish people in Berlin right now. It could be very dangerous."

"But I have false papers. No one will know I am Jewish."

"Where did you get false papers? Nu? What is with you?"

Anna looked away. "Bernie and I forged papers. I am sure no one would take the time to look deeply at my papers. Besides, we did a good job, and no one will care about one young girl like me."

"Anna, Anna. So, you are ashamed to be a Jew?"

"No, Papa, I am not ashamed, but this program was not for Jewish girls. I just wanted to spend the summer with my friends. I wanted to see what it was like to earn my own money."

"You don't have enough? I don't give you enough pretty clothes and things a girl your age would want?"

"It's not that. I just wanted to see what it was like to stand on my own two feet. I wanted to have a job and earn money. I wanted to see my friends once a week and go shopping with the money I earned myself. The family I work for is responsible for my wellbeing. They will feed me, and I will stay at their home. I am promised my own room. This is all part of the program. I didn't do this to hurt you or mama; I just wanted to be a part of the group instead of always being the outsider. Please try to understand." Tears fell from her eyes and ran down her cheeks. She wiped them away.

"Hmm..." he said, running his tongue over his teeth. There was a deep crease between his brows, which indicated to Anna that her father was thinking. She did not speak. Instead, she waited. It was several moments before her father sighed, then he looked into her eyes, and in his gaze, she thought she could see how deeply he loved her. A wave of guilt came over her. "I'm sorry, Papa," she said, her voice cracking.

He nodded. "I know you are. I know sometimes your mama and I are maybe a little bit too strict with you, but it's only because we love you, Annaleh. You're our baby girl."

Anna was crying now.

"All right, all right, now don't cry," he said, putting his arm around her shoulder. She lay her head on his chest. Then he said, "Well, your mama doesn't know the truth, and that's good because she would absolutely forbid you to do this. Believe me, I am nervous about it. However, I think it's only for a few months. Perhaps it will be all right. Perhaps it will even do you good."

"You mean I can go?" She was elated. She hugged him tightly. "Oh, Papa, thank you so much. I don't want to hurt you or mama ever, but I really want to go. I want to go more than anything."

"Your mother and I only want what is best for you. I have been feeling bad because I know you liked that boy who you brought home; I believe Daniel was his name. But he was not good for you. He is an idealist, and that could get him into trouble. Being a Jew, it could even get him killed. I would never want to hurt you, but that's why I had to put a stop to your relationship with him. I didn't want you to get caught up in things that might hurt you."

"I understand, Papa," she said, but when he mentioned Daniel, it felt like someone had driven an ice pick through her heart.

"And as far as your girlfriends are concerned, your mother and I discouraged your friendship with them, not only because they are not Jewish. It is mostly because Elica and that other one, Dagna, I think her name is, got into trouble by stealing."

"Yes, her name is Dagna. She and I are not really friends. Elica was very young when that happened. She has grown up so much since then. She's learned her lesson; she doesn't steal anymore."

"Yes, well, I am assuming you never stopped seeing them, even when your mother and I forbid it."

She looked at the ground and shook her head. "I tried. I really did. But Elica is my best friend. I missed her so much. And Bernie never did anything wrong. Elica and Bernie mean a lot to me. Please try to understand, Papa."

His eyes met hers. The wrinkle was still deep between his brow, but Anna could see his love for her shining in his eyes. "All right. You'll go to Berlin. I'll give you some money. On your days off, you'll call me and let me know you're all right. Nu?"

"Yes, Papa. I will. I promise. I'll call you every week and let you know how I am doing."

"And if anything goes wrong, I want you to come right home. You must promise me."

"I promise you, Papa."

"I hope I don't live to regret this," he said, patting her shoulder.

"You won't. I promise you, you won't. Thank you, Papa. Thank you."

CHAPTER FORTY-SEVEN

The day finally arrived for the girls to leave Vienna for Berlin. Dagna, Elica, and Bernie went to the train station together. They took an earlier train. Anna was to travel alone because her mother still did not know the truth about where she was going. Both of her parents accompanied her to the train station. They kissed her goodbye as she boarded, and her father put a wad of bills into her hand. "Here is money, so you can call me, and a little extra in case you need anything." Her mother was standing close and listening, so her father added, "I know you are staying in a dormitory at the music academy, and all your needs should be met. But take this money just in case of an emergency." Herr Levinstein winked at Anna.

"Thank you, Papa," Anna said, taking the money. She knew he mentioned the dormitory so that her mother would not suspect the truth.

Anna felt grown up in her dark blue travel suit and matching low-heeled pumps as she climbed the stairs and boarded the train. When she turned back and waved at her parents, they both looked proud and a little worried at the same time.

The train whistle blew. Anna sat down in her seat and waved at her parents through the window.

They waved back.

Then the train made a chugging sound. Anna's parents were waving. She waved too, but she felt a pang of guilt. *I lied to my mother.* She thought.

As the train pulled away from the station, Anna had mixed emotions. She was thrilled to be going on an adventure in a new city. The idea filled her with excitement. Yet, she was terrified. She had been adored and coddled, perhaps to the point of being overprotected, all of her life. She'd hated it. For so long, she had yearned for independence. But being sheltered was all she knew. Now she was alone on a train that was on its way to a new city. An hour passed, and she stared out the window as the train made its way through fields where cows and horses stood grazing. Everything was unfamiliar, and the newness of it made her heart thump faster in her chest. *I wonder what it's going to be like. I wonder what is in store for me.*

Anna tried to sleep to pass the time, but she couldn't. She tried to read, but she was unable to concentrate. Elica's mother, Frau Frey, Anna's maid, had packed her lunch that day. When she handed it to Anna, she looked at Anna suspiciously. Anna thought that Frau Frey probably suspected she was going to Berlin with Elica because they were both leaving for the same destination on the same day. Anna was sure that Frau Frey knew Elica was going to work in Berlin, but she didn't know if Frau Frey knew she would be working too. Or, if Frau Frey believed the story she'd told her mother about the music academy. It didn't matter because Frau Frey didn't ask Anna anything or say a word to her parents. And for this, she was grateful. Anna opened the bag of food Frau Frey had packed and picked a cheese sandwich, but when she took a bite, she realized she was too nervous to eat. So, she wrapped the sandwich back up and put it away. *Perhaps I'll eat it later.*

CHAPTER FORTY-EIGHT

When Anna arrived in Berlin, Elica, Dagna, and Bernie were sitting on a bench in the train station waiting for her. It felt so good to see them. She ran to them and hugged Elica and then Bernie. Bernie helped Anna to retrieve her suitcase. Then the girls, each of them carrying a small valise, walked outside the station, where they sat down on a bench to wait for their employers to pick them up. This had all been arranged with their respective employers by mail over the past month.

"You should have seen it. When the three of us got off the train, two young fellows almost got into a fight trying to help Elica with her suitcase," Dagna said.

"Oh?" Anna said, "I'm not surprised."

"Yes. These two fellows came running to help her. They were practically falling all over themselves, trying to make an impression on her. Elica is so pretty," Dagna said proudly. It was as if Dagna took pride in Elica's looks, as if she were living vicariously through Elica. This made no sense to Anna, but she smiled.

"Well, of course, we all know that Elica is gorgeous," Anna said, smiling.

"Yes, you certainly are," Bernie said, and Anna thought she could hear a small bit of yearning in Bernie's voice.

Elica giggled nervously.

"So, who won?" Anna asked Dagna.

"What? I don't know what you mean?" Dagna said.

"Who won? Which one of the fellows was given the opportunity to carry Elica's suitcase?"

"Oh, she wouldn't let either one of them help her," Dagna said. "I would have. But she just walked away from them. It must be nice to have boys chase you like that."

"I didn't want to get involved with strangers," Elica murmured. "Besides, my suitcase is very light. I didn't have much to bring."

The girls were silent for a moment, looking around at their new surroundings. Then Dagna asked, "Is anyone else starving?"

"Not me. I'm sick to my stomach with nerves," Elica said.

"Me too," said Anna.

"I'm all right," Bernie said.

"If you're hungry, I have a cheese sandwich," Anna said to Dagna.

"Well, if you're offering."

"Of course," Anna said, handing Dagna the lunch Elica's mother had packed for her.

"I finished my lunch a half hour into the train ride," Dagna said. Then she turned to Anna. "Thanks, this was nice of you."

"Sure." Anna smiled.

Dagna unwrapped the sandwich and took a bite. "It's good," she said, her mouth full of bread and cheese.

Anna smiled. "I'm glad you are enjoying it."

There was a moment of silence. "I thought you hated me," Dagna said.

"I never hated you, Dagna. I don't hate anyone. I just wonder sometimes why you hate me."

"It's not that I hate you. But, it's just not right for Jews and non-Jews to be friends. That's all. I was raised to believe we should all stay amongst our own people."

"Well, we are friends. Blood sisters," Bernie said, smiling. "Besides, as long as we are in Berlin, Anna is Lutheran."

"Not really," Dagna said.

"Of course, she is," Bernie said, "and because we made a pact to be blood sisters forever, we should take care of each other, right?"

"Right," Anna said.

"Right?" Bernie spoke to Elica.

"Yes, right."

"Dagna?"

"Right."

"So, we all agree," Bernie said.

There were a few moments of silence. Then Elica said, "I can't believe we are actually here in Germany, in Berlin."

"I'm excited and nervous, too," Dagna said. "We are going to be earning our own money. We'll be able to go into town and buy whatever we like without our parents trying to take every cent we earn."

"Yes, that will be wonderful," Elica said.

"I'm going to save my money. I don't need much to be happy. Instead, I want to travel after we get out of school. Maybe go to Italy," Bernie said.

"By yourself?" Elica asked.

"Unless you want to go with me?"

"I... I don't know," Elica said as she thought of Daniel. She hoped that they would marry as soon as she returned to Austria. She didn't care that she would be unable to finish her last year of school. He was a year older, and he would be graduating. And she felt that his education was more important than hers. But when Bernie mentioned traveling, the idea sounded like fun, and she wondered what it would be like to travel with Daniel. *He is rich, and we could stay at the finest hotels and eat the most extravagant food.*

"Why not? If you save your money, we can go anywhere. We can see the world together," Bernie said. "I want to see the world."

They had all made previous arrangements with their employers to have Saturdays as their days off. And they were also given a few hours off on Sunday morning to go to church if they chose to.

"What are your employers like?" Dagna asked the others.

Bernie spoke first. "Mine are a young couple. The wife is very ill, but they are both still working at factories. They can't really afford my salary, but they need me badly. You see, they have a little girl, four years old, who I am caring for while they are at work." Bernie turned to Anna. "What are yours like?"

"My employers are wealthy. They have twin boys, nine years old," Anna said. "The wife told me that this is the husband's second marriage. She sent me pictures of her and the twins. She is young and very pretty. He was in the picture, too. He is older than her by quite a few years. I would say she is in her early twenties, and he looks like he is nearing fifty. She told me that he and his first wife divorced, and that they had a son. Their son is at the University of Berlin. But he isn't coming home for the summer, so I don't suppose I'll meet him."

"What about you, Elica?" Bernie asked.

"Mine are wealthy too. They have a little five-year-old girl and a six-year-old boy," Elica said. "That's all I really know about them."

"What about you, Dagna?"

"My employers need me to care for the husband's father. He is old and very ill. The couple doesn't have any children, but they are both working. And the wife told me her husband's father would need me to prepare meals for him and do light housekeeping. I think it should be rather easy," Dagna said. "He's in bed most of the time, or at least that's what I gather from the letters I've received."

A black automobile pulled up to where they sat. A man in a dark suit got out. "I'm here to pick up Anna Baumgartner," he said. "I'm Peter, the driver of the Fischer family."

"I'm Anna," Anna said as she stood up.

"She lied about her name?" Dagna whispered to Bernie. "Her last name is Levinstein, not Baumgartner."

"Be quiet. I told you that while we are here in Berlin, Anna is not

Jewish. Anna and I had to make up a fake name and fake papers so she could get this job."

The driver opened the door to the car, and Anna got in. "I'll meet you, girls, at this same bench on Saturday morning?"

"Yes," Bernie said. "We'll all meet right here at nine am."

"Perfect." Anna smiled, but her lip was quivering with nerves.

Anna got into the car. The driver closed the door and then got into the front seat, and they were off on the way to the Fischers' home.

CHAPTER FORTY-NINE

They drove for about a half hour before the driver turned on to a winding road covered with shady trees. As they slowly went up the path to the house, Anna felt a little sick to her stomach with nerves. She had never worked before. Anna wondered if this was what it felt like to be Frau Frey, the woman who had nurtured her since she was a child. It felt very strange to Anna to be a servant, but the truth was she had never thought of Frau Frey as a servant. Anna had always thought of her as a second mother. But now, she was going to be a nanny to two boys, and she wasn't sure what they would think of her. *I don't know how to act. I don't know what to say. The only thing I can do is try to act like Frau Frey, and hopefully, I will be able to do that.*

The house was a sprawling brick mansion set back from the road, sheltered by tall oak trees. The grounds were covered in an array of colorful and well-groomed flowering bushes. Anna had grown up in a lovely home, but it did not compare in opulence to this one. As they drove up the winding road toward the house, Anna took a long breath. Never before had she considered how people must feel when they came to her home to apply for work. She'd seen them come and go over the years; window washers, gardeners, drivers, and cooks. The only person who had been working for her family for as long as Anna could remember was Frau Frey. It was strangely enlightening to be coming to this home as a nanny. Her mouth was dry with the nervousness and fear of saying the wrong thing. She was very uncomfortable, but it helped her to better understand why Elica sometimes lashed out at her with jealousy.

The driver stopped the car. Then he got out and opened her door. "We're here. This is the house," he said cheerfully. "Go to the door. Frau Schneider is the maid's name. She will be waiting for you. Don't look so scared. She is very kind. She'll help you get situated. And by the way, my name is August. If you should need anything while you are here, just ask me." He smiled at her. His teeth were a bit uneven, but he had a warm and lovely smile.

Anna had been too lost in thought to really look at him before, but now she realized he was young, perhaps twenty or twenty-one, and actually quite handsome. "Thank you," she murmured.

He winked, "Of course. And really, I can't stress this enough. You don't need to be afraid. The Fischers are very nice people. They will be fair to you as long as you do a good job."

"Does my fear show that much?" she asked.

"Yes, it sure does." He smiled, and his eyes twinkled. "Like I said, you'll be just fine."

"And the boys?"

"They're holy terrors until you get to know them. Once you get to know them, you'll realize they are just young boys being boys." He smiled. "And once you realize that, you'll adore them." He winked. "Now, chin up and go on inside." He pointed to the door and winked. "I promise you are going to do just fine."

CHAPTER FIFTY

Anna used the brass knocker to knock on the large, heavy wooden door. Then she stood outside and waited. It seemed like a long time. Anna considered knocking again, but just as she was about to lift the knocker, a heavy-set woman with a little too much rouge on her cheeks, sporting chin-length curly gray hair, opened the door. She wore a black and white maid's uniform, just like the one Frau Frey wore.

"You must be Anna," the woman said warmly.

"Yes, I am."

"Well, good. I'm so glad you're here. Come on in." She smiled, and Anna noticed she had deep dimples. She had to be in her late fifties, but when she smiled, she looked much younger. "I'm Eva Schneider, and I'm the maid here. Follow me, and I'll show you your room."

Anna walked into the house. The white marble floor against the dark, elegant wood furnishings was breathtaking. Her heels clicked as she followed Frau Schneider up a winding staircase to the second floor and down a short corridor to a small but brightly lit room. "This will be your room for the summer," Frau Schneider said.

It was a cheery room with a bed made of the same mahogany wood as the rest of the furniture in the house. The bedspread was yellow with white flowers, and it matched the curtain that covered the small window. There was a short wooden dresser with three drawers and a small closet where she could hang her clothes.

"Thank you," Anna said. "When will I meet the rest of the family?"

"This afternoon, when Herr Fischer returns home from work. The boys will be home from their last day of school by then, too. It's too bad you won't be meeting Wolfgang, the husband's older son. He's at the university and won't be home for the summer. But he's a very nice boy."

Anna smiled.

"So, there is a bathroom right down the hall. Just go out of your room and turn left; you can't miss it." She smiled. "I'm sure you will want to freshen up after traveling all day."

"Yes, ma'am, I do," Anna said.

"Well, good. You have some time to yourself, so you can get some rest too. I'll knock on your door when the family is ready to meet you."

"Thank you," Anna said.

CHAPTER FIFTY-ONE

At six o'clock, Frau Schneider knocked on the door to Anna's room.

Anna had washed up, and although she'd laid down on the bed, which was comfortable, she hadn't slept. She had changed into a clean, pastel pink dress. Anna opened the door. "Come in," she said to the maid.

"You look very nice," Frau Schneider said. "Everyone is in the living room waiting to meet you."

"Thank you," Anna said.

"Follow me. You'll meet the family, then you and I will have dinner in the kitchen."

Anna nodded and followed Frau Schneider downstairs, where the family was waiting for them. Frau Fischer was smiling when she saw Anna. She had an arm around each of the twins. They were charming little boys who looked very much like their mother. Anna thought Frau Fischer was probably in her early twenties. She was quite pretty with long wavy golden hair and bright eyes.

Herr Fischer was seated on the sofa. He gave Anna a quick smile but didn't say anything. He was quiet, and he appeared distinguished as he smoked his pipe. His thick hair was salt and pepper, but he was handsome despite his age. The room smelled of pipe smoke. It was a lovely blend, and Anna found that she didn't mind it at all.

"I'm Elsa Fischer. This is my husband and our twin boys," she said. "And you must be Anna?"

"Yes, ma'am."

"This is Klaus, and this is Gynther. As you can see, they are twins. Sometimes they can be a handful, but they have promised me that they are going to be good this summer. Haven't you boys?"

"Yes, mother," Gynther said, but Klaus gave a twisted smile, and Anna felt her stomach drop. *He's going to be trouble.* She thought.

"Well, it's late, and I am sure you are quite hungry, so go into the kitchen and have some dinner. Tomorrow morning, you will start work."

"Thank you, ma'am. It was nice to meet all of you," Anna said.

CHAPTER FIFTY-TWO

Early on Saturday morning, Anna's day off, she walked to the train station, where she saw Bernie, Elica, and Dagna awaiting her arrival. When the girls saw her, Bernie and Elica waved. Then all three girls stood up and walked toward Anna.

"Are you ready to go into town?" Bernie asked. "We're going to see Berlin today."

"I'm ready and excited," Anna said.

They linked arms and walked towards the city. As they entered the shopping area where they planned to spend the day, Anna saw flags with swastikas hanging from the buildings. There were signs on walls that said, "Jews Forbidden." Anna didn't say anything, but she felt her skin crawl. The girls walked past a newsstand, and Anna caught a glimpse of a newspaper with a caricature of a Jewish man with a large nose on the front. The headline read: "Protect your children from the dangerous claws of the Jew."

Anna glanced at her friends to see if they had noticed the newspapers. Elica was not aware. She wasn't paying attention. Instead, she was staring into the shop windows, tempted by all the beautiful dresses, the newest designs, and the finest fabrics. Anna wasn't surprised; she knew how much Elica loved fashion and how much she coveted garments of high quality. But when Anna looked at Dagna, the look on Dagna's face sent a chill through her. Dagna looked directly at Anna; she was suppressing a sly, wicked smile.

Bernie's expression was one of serious concern, and Anna knew by looking at her that Bernie had noticed the newspapers, too. Then Bernie gave Anna a smile of confidence. She patted Anna's arm and said, "Well, I'll tell all of you about my employer now. I'm working for a poor family. It's a young couple. The wife is very ill. They have a child. A very sweet four-year-old girl. She's my responsibility. Now, nobody knows this, but I'll tell you because you are my blood sisters: the wife is Jewish."

"You're working for a Jew?" Dagna said. "I believe that's illegal here in Germany."

"I know it is, but no one needs to find out," Bernie said, glaring at Dagna. "I chose to take this job."

"Why would you do that? I know there were plenty of jobs on the bulletin board. Why would you choose this one? Did you know they were Jews?"

"I didn't know at the time, but it wouldn't have made any difference to me. I took it because the wife is sick and needs me."

"She's a Jew," Dagna said. "You shouldn't have anything to do with Jews."

"Stop it, Dagna. Anna is Jewish, and I'm sure you are hurting her feelings when you talk like this."

"I don't mean to, but the fact is that although Anna is nice and all, she's a Jew, and she shouldn't even be here with us." Dagna snorted. "We could get in trouble if anyone finds out she's Jewish, and we are friends with her."

"But no one is going to find out. Isn't that right, Dagna? Anna has papers that say she is a gentile, and that should be sufficient as long as nobody makes trouble. Do you understand me, Dagna?" Bernie said menacingly.

"Of course, I was just making you aware of the dangers of being friends with someone who is Jewish. That's all," Dagna said.

Elica didn't say a word. She couldn't look at Anna because she felt guilty about stealing Daniel. She hadn't looked directly into Anna's eyes since they arrived in Berlin. Elica was afraid that somehow if Anna could look into her eyes, she would know what Elica had done. The summer was not what Elica had hoped it would be. She had hoped it would give her time to think and decide what to do about Daniel. But she found she couldn't think anything through. All she knew was that she missed Daniel terribly. She missed his gentle touch and the kind words he said to her. Every time Dagna said something derogatory about Jews, she wanted to slap her, to defend him. But she couldn't. So, she said nothing.

"Well, no matter what you think or feel, make sure you don't forget that while we are here in Berlin, Anna is not Anna Levinstein. She is Anna Baumgartner, a Christian girl just like the three of us. Do you understand me, Dagna?" Bernie's voice was filled with warning.

"I understand, but do you think it's right to lie?" Dagna said.

Bernie let out a laugh. "You lie all the time. You steal too. Who are you to pass judgment on anyone? You better remember what I told you. You better make sure that you never tell anyone that Anna is Jewish while we are here in Berlin. And if I hear you told anyone the truth, you'll have me to contend with."

Dagna looked away from Bernie. "I wouldn't do that. Not to you," she said, annoyed.

"My employers asked me if I was going to go to church this morning. I said yes, but of course, as you know, we didn't go. Do you think our employers will expect us to go to church?" Elica asked.

"They might. But we can do as we wish. Remember, they are our employers, not our teachers or our parents," Bernie said. "Now, here is a phone number where you girls can reach me in case of any kind of emergency." She handed them each a piece of paper. "Call me if you need me. And please get phone numbers if you can. So, we can all have a way to stay in touch in case we need each other during the week while we are working."

"Great idea," Anna said. "I can give you girls my employer's phone number. I have it."

"Yes, so can I," Elica said.

"Me too," Dagna added.

"Good, let's go get some coffee and pastry for breakfast, and we can all exchange numbers," Bernie said.

CHAPTER FIFTY-THREE

They crossed the street and headed to a small café. "By the way, Anna, have you spoken to that boy you were dating?" Dagna asked.

"Which boy?" Anna asked, but she knew who Dagna was referring to and why Dagna was asking. It was Dagna's quiet little way of trying to upset her by bringing Daniel up. Anna had already told the girls that she and Daniel were broken up.

"You mean Daniel?" Anna said.

"I think that was his name."

Elica's head whipped around. She glanced at Dagna, then quickly looked away and bit her lower lip. She stared down at the ground, hiding her expression.

"No, I haven't heard from him in a long time. I thought I told all of you that I think Daniel and I are over."

"Do you miss him?" Dagna asked.

"Sometimes. I liked him very much. But he wanted something I wasn't prepared to give him," Anna said in a matter-of-fact tone.

"You mean sex?" Dagna asked.

"Yes, he wanted that," Anna said.

"I know all about sex; believe me, all boys want that. It's the only way to keep them coming back because if you don't give it to them, somebody else will," Dagna said in a tone that made her sound worldly and grown up. "I've done it. Have you?" she asked Bernie as she cast her eyes at Bernie skeptically.

Anna cringed inside. *I am sure that Dagna knows that Bernie is a lesbian. I think deep down, we all know it. So why the hell is she trying to make Bernie feel uneasy?*

Bernie laughed a nervous and uncomfortable laugh, but she didn't answer Dagna's question. Then they were at the door of the restaurant.

"And I just so happen to know that you have done it, Elica. You have, haven't you?" Dagna said as she opened the door.

Elica coughed, embarrassed. All of them knew that Elica had been sexually promiscuous. Elica looked straight ahead. She didn't answer Dagna's question. She also wouldn't look Anna in the eyes. So, she focused on the open tables in the restaurant. "Let's sit down. I'm starving," Elica said.

"All right, I won't ask any more questions. I can see all of you are too shy to talk about it. I don't know why. It's only natural," Dagna said, shrugging her shoulders.

The hostess smiled at them.

"A table for four," Anna said to the hostess.

"Follow me."

CHAPTER FIFTY-FOUR

"What is the family who you work for like?" Dagna asked Elica.

"They are all right. They are nice to me, even if they do treat me like a servant."

"Well, what did you expect them to treat you like? A long-lost relative?" Dagna sneered. "We are servants to them."

"I don't know what I was expecting. I expected them to treat me the way Anna's parents treat my mom," Elica said.

"Anna's family has known your mother since you were a baby. Of course, they treat her differently than our employers treat us," Bernie said. "After all these years of working for Anna's parents, your mother is like family to them."

Anna's face was red. She hated this conversation. Everything that was being said made the gap between her and her friends seem wider. *How I long to close this gap. How I long for Elica to see me as an equal and not as the daughter of her mother's employer.* She reached over and touched Elica's shoulder, and Elica looked at Anna for a moment. "You are like a sister to me," Anna said.

Elica looked away. "Yes, I suppose that's true. We were best friends when we were just children. We've known each other for a very long time," she murmured.

"So, what's your employer like?" Bernie asked Anna.

"They are an impressive couple. The husband is older, but very handsome. The wife is young and beautiful. I don't know what the husband does for work or if he inherited his money, but they are very wealthy. Much more so than my parents. They don't speak to me very much. They are busy with their own lives, but the twin boys, Klaus and Gynther, who just turned nine, are under my charge. They aren't easy children.

"Both of them are very smart, and they take great pleasure in outsmarting me, but I am working on winning them over. I must admit that Klaus is a brat. He is always beating up his brother. Although they are twins, Klaus is stronger, and somehow he seems healthier than Gynther. When they play fight or even get into a real fight, I always worry that Klaus will really hurt Gynther. I try to stop them from fighting, but sometimes it's impossible." Anna sighed.

"Are they Jews?" Dagna asked.

"Of course not." Bernie gave Dagna a look of disdain. "Why do you need to bring that up all the time?"

Dagna ignored the question. Instead, she smiled and said, "Oh yes, that's right. They can't be Jewish and employ an Aryan girl. It's against the law. Of course, Bernie thinks she's above the law. Don't you, Bernie? I can't believe you would stay at this job working for a Jew. Once you found out the wife was Jewish, you should have turned them in for trying to employ an Aryan. But you didn't, and that's just like you. Oh yes, I almost forgot that Anna is pretending to be Aryan."

"Stop it, Dagna, or I'll punch you in the nose," Bernie said. "I have had it with you and this constant reference to Anna's being Jewish. What difference does it make? None. She is our friend, and you need to leave her alone. Stop trying to make her life miserable already. You have no right to treat her like this. I am about to get angry with you—"

"All right, don't make this into more than it is," Dagna said. "Really, Bernie, it was an honest mistake. Stop getting on your high horse already. We all know you're a Jew lover."

Bernie pushed Dagna, but she was solid and didn't move. So Bernie pushed her harder. This time, Dagna was thrown off her balance and almost fell.

"Please stop this," Elica said. "Can't we just enjoy a decent day off together without all of this arguing?"

Dagna looked at Elica. "Sorry. I really am. I didn't mean to offend anyone. Bernie just takes everything so seriously," she said softly. Then she said, "The family I work for makes me feel like a servant too."

"I must admit, when we came here to Berlin, I was expecting my employers to treat me the way Anna's parents treat my mother," Elica said again.

Anna felt her face grow hot and turn beet red again. *I am quite tired of this conversation.* She thought. Then she said, "Elica, that's because your mother has always been a part of our family. You have always been like a sister to me."

"Sort of, but not really. Not when things came down to it," Dagna said. Her voice was sweet, sickeningly sweet, but the undertone was ugly. "However, no disrespect, Anna; I recall something about your parents not approving of the friendship between you and Elica. I don't know if it had anything to do with you being Jewish or not—"

"Dagna, I warned you," Bernie said. "Today could be the day I make you sorry for getting on my nerves."

"I'm just talking to Anna. I haven't said anything wrong. I haven't lied. Her parents didn't like that she was paling around with Elica because they wanted her to make friends with other Jews. You know it's true, Bernie. So, there's no reason to get all huffy."

"Maybe Anna's parents don't approve of the friendship between her and Elica because of that incident when you and Elica were caught stealing. Did you ever think that might just be the reason?" Bernie said.

"Whatever our parents think or say doesn't matter. Let's let all of this go. It's not important. We are friends. Blood sisters forever. Isn't that right?" Anna said.

Elica nodded. "Yes," she said, her voice a little above a whisper, but she did not look up. She stared at the ground. She could not meet Anna's eyes.

"Blood sisters forever," Bernie said, then she patted Anna's shoulder.

"Sure, we're blood sisters." Dagna snorted.

Bernie changed the subject. She told the others how much she missed them during the week. Elica and Anna both agreed.

Then the food arrived. Dagna ate a thick slice of brown bread as she told the others about her current employer. She worked for an old man who demanded a great deal of her attention. "He's not sick. He's just demanding. His son is wealthy, and he pays for me to be his companion. This should be easy, but it's not. He will not leave me alone for a second. He demands that I prepare elaborate meals, which I must feed to him with a spoon, even though he is quite capable of feeding himself. And he demands that his clothes be cleaned and pressed each day. When I finally retire to my room, he still calls after me. He won't let me rest. Even though my day is over, he wants me to read to him. I'll be quite honest; I can't stand him."

"That's a shame," Bernie said with a small smile. "Maybe you should take a moment to consider the good thing you are doing. He sounds like he is lonely and just wants a companion. Being kind is a virtue."

"Some virtue. I'm exhausted," Dagna said.

"And what about you, Bernie? What are your employers like?" Anna asked.

Bernie explained that her employers were a young couple who could hardly afford her services and had only paid her half of her weekly salary. "I know I could change jobs, even now, and earn more money, but I can't leave them because they desperately need me. The husband and wife work long hours at a factory and have a physically disabled child. I care for the child when they are at work. The wife is not well either, so she really needs my help. They are trying so hard to survive, and I feel sorry for the wife, the husband, and the child. I must admit I am a little disappointed that they were unable to pay me this week, and I am a little worried that they will continue to be short. But what can I do? As a decent person, I can't just leave them when I know how they are struggling. It would be wrong to be so selfish."

"The family I work for expects me to clean. They have a maid, but they expect me to help her and care for their two very snotty little children, a six-year-old boy and a five-year-old girl," Elica said. "I feel a strange sense of loneliness working for them. Just wait until you hear this gossip. The permanent maid told me that the husband was having an affair. She explained that the wife is a socialite who is too busy planning events to notice.

"But I can't imagine any woman wanting him. You should see him; he is repulsive, fat, and always sweating. I believe it's true because he is even lecherous with me. When I walk by him, he tries to grab my buttocks or my thigh," Elica said, shaking her head, then she stood up suddenly. "Excuse me, girls, I'll be right back. I have to go to the toilet," she said.

Even though Bernie, Elica, and Dagna were disappointed with their jobs, which were not all they had hoped they would be when they left home to come to Berlin, it was still exciting to be on their own.

Elica returned, and they finished eating. The food was delicious, and perhaps even more so because they'd worked hard to pay for it. Once they finished, they left the restaurant to walk through town. They couldn't wait to see the sights and go shopping.

CHAPTER FIFTY-FIVE

The four girls walked down the street together. Elica and Dagna eyed the dresses in the windows of the dress shops. "Oh, look at these dresses," Elica said breathlessly. "Let's go inside."

They walked inside one of the shops but found that the garments were priced higher than they expected. Still, Elica and Dagna tried them on. They were excited and giggling until Dagna split one of the seams on a green silk frock and the owner of the shop, hearing the seam split, demanded that they purchase something or leave. Since they could not afford the dresses, they left in a huff. They went into a few more dress shops. Bernie and Anna watched as Elica and Dagna tried on dress after dress. Elica frowned at herself in the mirror. "I don't look good in any of these," she complained. "I look fat."

"You look beautiful," Bernie said.

"You really do," Anna added.

As the afternoon sun began to set, the girls split up and headed back to the homes of their respective employers.

Elica went to her room as soon as she returned from her afternoon with her friends. She had to run to the bathroom in the restaurant and vomited after lunch. She hid it from the other girls, but now she was starving. This vomiting started happening almost every time she ate. Dinner would not be served for a few hours, so there was nothing she could do but wait. Nervously, she locked the door to her room and immediately checked her panties. *Still no blood. I'm pregnant. I know it.* She thought, and a wave of fear spread over her.

Daniel had written to her once, declaring his love and telling her how much he had missed her. But she was afraid that if she told him that she was pregnant, he would run away. Elica was still afraid that he was only wild about her because she was everything that was forbidden to him. And she was afraid that he was using her to rebel against his parents. Her feelings for him were not based on rebellion at all. She didn't relish the fact that her parents would be angry when she told them that she was pregnant and about her feelings for Daniel, who was Jewish. But her love for him was so deep and intense that it was almost painful. She yearned for his love. *I long to be his wife. To wake up every morning in his arms, wash his clothes and prepare his meals.* She wrapped her arms around herself and wept. *Why can't I be Anna? If I were born to her parents, I'd be Jewish and wealthy, and Daniel's family would accept me without question. They might even be happy that I am pregnant. The real question is, would Daniel still love me if his parents accepted me, or is his attraction to me based on the fact that I am from a poor family and gentile too? I believe his fascination with communism is only to get a rise out of his father. His father is very overbearing, and Daniel wants to show him that he can't be controlled. But what if that is the only reason he loves me? Because I don't care about what anyone says, I truly love him. I love everything he is, and I feel so guilty for what I have done as far as Anna is concerned.*

I don't know if she still cares for him, but I know Anna would think it was wrong to do what I did, and she would be right. Still, I can't help my feelings. This love affair between Daniel and I might end my friendship with Anna forever and maybe Bernie. Because Bernie, who is always so fair about everything, will take Anna's side. Dagna doesn't care about what is right or wrong, so I know she will be the only person who will stand by me. And my parents, oh, they will be livid. I know they will throw me out when they find out that I am having a baby out of wedlock. They will be even more outraged when they discover that the father is Jewish. And worse yet, Daniel, the father of my child, is the boyfriend of the daughter of my mother's employer. My mother might lose her job because of this. My father will definitely beat me. He will beat me to within an inch of my life. Oh, what am I to do? What am I ever to do?

Elica stood up and looked in the mirror. She turned to the side. So far, there was no trace of a baby bump, but her skin, which had always been good, had started to break out into pimples. Today, she could see that a small red bump had begun to form on her chin. This made her feel ugly. Elica moved closer to the mirror and studied her face. She always had a good complexion: peaches and cream. In fact, she'd always relied on her beauty, but now she was worried that it would not be enough. Terrified, she felt the tears well up in her eyes, and she began to weep. *Crying isn't going to help.* She thought as she wiped the tears from her cheeks with the back of her hand. *I must be brave.* She took a deep breath, sat at the little desk in the corner of her room, and began writing. Her hands were trembling as she wrote,

Dearest Daniel...

Weighing each word carefully, she wrote him a letter telling him she loved him and that she was pregnant. But then she thought of how repulsed he would be when he read this needy and grasping letter. She imagined him shaking his head. She could see his eyes, and in them, she was sure that she could see that he no longer cared for her. *The greatest part of my charm with men has always been my aloofness. I have never declared my love for any man, nor have I ever chased anyone. Now that I am really in love, I am afraid that all of my charms will be wiped away, leaving me bare and exposed. And Daniel will see the poor and pathetic girl that I really am.*

She tore up the letter. Then she put her head in her hands and wept.

CHAPTER FIFTY-SIX

When Dagna returned home from her afternoon off, she slipped into her room as quietly as she could. She longed for some time to just relax, but that was impossible in this house, and she hoped that the old man hadn't heard her come in.

Dagna hated the old man. If she wasn't afraid of being arrested, she would have poisoned him. He demanded all of her time and attention. In fact, he even woke her up early sometimes to bring him something he wanted. *He never leaves me alone, not for a minute. How could one old person need so much attention? He is always hungry. And if I don't come right away, when he says he has to go to the toilet, he messes himself and his bed, and I have to clean him up. I'd love to just let him lie there in it for a while. I'd like to punish him for thinking he is so clever. Damn, but I hate him. I got the worst job of all my friends.*

"Dagna!" the old man called out from his room.

He heard me come in. He's probably been waiting all afternoon. The old bastard.

"Will you please bring me a hot water bottle? My legs are cramping. They've been cramping all day, Dagna. You were out for so long, and I have been in such terrible pain."

She tried to pretend not to hear him. *It's my day off, but still, he is bothering me. I am going to ignore him.* She put her hands over her ears and lay down on her bed.

He persisted. "Dagna! Dagna, do you hear me? I need you. I need a hot water bottle, and I haven't eaten today. The sandwich you left for me didn't taste right. I need something to eat."

What else could he possibly need? He always needs something.

"Dagna!" he screamed out her name. "Answer me. Dagna. I need something to eat, and I need a hot water bottle. I need them now!"

Finally, she got up and went into his room. "I heard you," she said, annoyed, "but I have to boil the water. I'll be back as soon as it's ready."

"It's about time you answered. I don't know why it took you so long to hear me," the old man said. She didn't answer him. There was no tone of gratitude in his voice, just a slight edge of anger.

She left his room and walked into the kitchen, where she put a kettle of water up to boil. Then she sat down and waited. *At least I have a few minutes to read while this water is heating up. Even five minutes away from him is better than nothing. Being here in Berlin is almost worse than being at home, and that old man is the reason. If I had found a better job, this would have been a nice summer. This man is a misery.*

CHAPTER FIFTY-SEVEN

The little girl Bernie watched was waiting in the window for her return. When she saw Bernie coming up the walk to the apartment building, she began to wave. Bernie saw her and waved back. She had already fallen in love with the clever little four-year-old Ingrid, who was in her charge. Ingrid, although she was not a pretty girl, was a bright child, and she truly adored Bernie. She was a quick learner, and whatever Bernie tried to teach her, she did her best to understand.

When Bernie walked into the apartment, Ingrid ran into her arms. Bernie scooped her up and hugged her. "I missed you," Bernie said.

"You did?" Ingrid smiled.

"Of course. Did you miss me?"

"So much. I waited by the window all day," Ingrid said. "My *mutti* tried to get me to come away from the window, but as soon as she fell asleep, I came right back. I really did miss you, Bernie."

"Well, I'm here now, and guess what?"

"What?" Ingrid asked curiously.

"I brought you a sweet bun."

"You did!" Ingrid said excitedly.

"I did!" Bernie smiled. "However, it's very close to dinnertime. So, you can't have it until after dinner."

"Please?"

"Ingrid, your mother would be angry with me if I spoiled your dinner. Please be a good girl and wait?"

"All right." The child conceded.

She was so agreeable that just being with her warmed Bernie's heart. "Shall we go into my room, and I'll read you a story?"

"Yes, please."

Bernie and Ingrid had established a routine from the first day Bernie arrived. Each morning, after Ingrid's parents left for work, Bernie would give Ingrid her breakfast, followed by a quick bath, and then the two of them would go to the nearby park, where they played for hours. Then they would return for lunch, after which Bernie read Ingrid a story as she put the child down for her nap. While Ingrid napped, Bernie straightened up the apartment and usually put up a light soup or stew for dinner.

Bernie found that she enjoyed playing mother. This confused her because she didn't ever want to marry a man, and she was certain that it was not destined for her to ever have a child. In fact, because of the way she felt about men and how she was more attracted to women, she had come to believe that she was going to be forced to go far away from everyone she knew and loved in order to keep them safe from that knowledge. So much shame surrounded her secret.

She decided it was best if her mother never found out that she had what she felt were unnatural feelings toward other women. Bernie had never had a romantic relationship of any kind, man or woman, and she doubted she ever would. *I will live a lonely life, but I will travel and see the world.* The only romantic interest she'd ever had was towards Elica, and the love she felt for Elica existed only in her mind. She knew Elica did not feel the same. *I could never tell Elica how I felt about her. She would run away from me, and I would never see her again. No, I would rather take her friendship in bits and pieces than lose her forever.*

That was why she had planned to run away after she had saved some money from working this summer. She thought she might go to Italy. But now that she had worked with Ingrid, Bernie realized that she loved children, or at least she adored this one. Bernie thought of how much she would love to have a home and a child, but she knew she could not have a relationship with a man. It was then that she decided she would take the trip she had been dreaming of. *When the summer is over and I go back home, I'll make arrangements to go to Italy as soon as possible. I'll have to take some time off from school, but I don't care. It will be worth it to fulfill this dream.*

CHAPTER FIFTY-EIGHT

Anna went to her room two days after her day off to find that Klaus had stolen her hairbrush again. He didn't need it; he didn't even want it. He just enjoyed watching her search for it. She knew he'd taken it because when she ran downstairs to ask him where it was, he stared giggling. Anna looked at him with absolute frustration. He was sitting on the sofa with his brother beside him.

"My hairbrush is missing again," Anna said as calmly as she could. "I know you have taken it."

"I didn't. I didn't take it last time either," Klaus said, then he started laughing. He elbowed Gynther and Gynther started laughing too.

"I know you think this is funny, but—"

"Boys, I have a surprise for you. Now I know you were planning to go to the lake to go swimming today, but there has been a change of plans." Their mother breezed into the room in a lovely gray silk dress, her blonde hair perfectly styled in waves around her face.

She really is lovely, Anna thought.

"We can't go swimming?" Gynther asked.

"Well, you can," their mother said, then she winked, "but I do have some exciting news, and once you hear it, you might just want to change your plans."

"Tell us what it is, *mutti*," Klaus said.

"Your brother, Wolfgang, has come home for a visit. He is here right now! But he is only staying for the weekend. So, hurry and go upstairs. Get cleaned up because he has brought someone home with him who he wants you to meet."

"Ulf is here!" Klaus said, his voice was filled with excitement.

"Ulf?" Anna asked.

"That's their nickname for Wolfgang," Frau Fischer said, turning to Anna. "You'll meet him too. He's such a nice young man."

"Here." Klaus handed Anna her hairbrush. He'd lost interest in the game of torturing Anna. He was now consumed with the excitement of seeing his older brother.

"Thank you," Anna said as she let out a sigh. *Klaus is impossible to control, especially when he is bored. Well, maybe he will behave while his older brother is here, and that will give me a weekend off from putting up with his antics.*

Anna turned and walked towards the stairs to her room.

"Fräulein."

She heard a male voice call to her. Anna turned around quickly.

"You must be Fräulein Anna, my brothers' nanny for the summer, are you not?"

She nodded, staring at him. "Yes, I am," she stammered, taken aback by his appearance. Anna had never thought about the boys' older brother, and she had certainly not expected him to be so handsome. He was tall, with a strong muscular build. His hair was golden blond. And his jaw was strong, as were his high cheekbones. His eyes were deep blue, the shade of dark sapphires. A smile came over Anna's face.

"I'm Wolfgang; I'm the boys' half-brother. My friends call me Ulf." He smiled. Then shyly, he added, "You can call me Ulf if you like."

"It's nice to meet you, Ulf." Anna felt her heartbeat quicken. *Am I crazy, or is he looking me over from head to toe? Is it possible that a college boy would be interested in me? And such a handsome one too. I'm probably just imagining it.*

"I'm sure my stepmother must have told you about me. I've been away at the university, but every so often, I get homesick. That's when I come back for a short visit. I know it's hard to believe, but I actually miss my two wild little monster brothers." He laughed, then his face broke into a flirtatious smile, and he said, "And now that I have met you, I am even happier that I came."

Anna felt herself blush. She was at a loss for words. Trying to think of something to say, she cleared her throat. "Well, it's very nice to meet you."

"Are you going to university next year?"

"No, I don't graduate for another year."

"But would you like to go?"

"Yes, actually I would."

"Really? And what would you study?"

"Music. I love music. I play piano and a little violin too. I hope it's not too bold of me to ask, but what are you studying?"

"Of course, it's not too bold. You can ask me anything," Ulf said, and his eyes locked on hers.

Anna felt a warm heat travel over her entire body, but before he could answer, a young woman fluttered into the room. She was as slender as a young blade of grass and as graceful as a dancer. Her hair was shiny, like liquid gold. She wore a skirt and blouse that fit her perfectly. *I can see that her clothes are of good quality.* Anna thought. The pretty young woman ignored Anna as if she were not even there and walked over to Ulf, locking her arm through his. "Ulf darling, what are you doing in here talking to your brother's nanny? We have a lunch date with Trudy and Werner in a half hour, and you're not ready."

"Yes, my dear," he said, a half-smile coming over his face, "I know."

"I realize you don't like Werner, but you promised me you would be civil. You said you would at least have lunch with my friends. Now, come on and get ready, so we aren't late. It's rude to be late."

"I'd like you to meet someone," he said. His pretty friend stared at him, giving him a look of disgust, but he ignored her and went on, "This is Anna. She's here from Austria for the summer. She takes care of my brothers."

"I see," the pretty girl said. Then she straightened her back and gave Anna a wicked smile. "It's nice to meet you, Anna. I'm Matilda, Wolfgang's fiancée." Anna noticed Matilda put her emphasis on the word fiancée.

"Her name is Matilda, but our friends call her Mattie," Wolfgang said.

"Yes, that's correct. However, this is the nanny, Ulf, not our friend," Matilda reminded him. Then she turned to Anna, who was mortified, and said, "You can call me Matilda. Or better yet, just call me Fräulein Weber."

"Yes, ma'am," Anna said, trying to sound the way that Frau Frey sounded when she spoke to her parents.

"Now, come on, Ulf. I am becoming annoyed with you. I can see that you are just wasting time because you don't want to get ready to visit with my friends."

"Excuse us, please," Ulf said.

Anna wasn't sure, but she thought she saw something in his eyes that indicated that he wished he could spend more time with her. Just then, Klaus and Gynther came out from eavesdropping behind the corner.

"I don't like her," Klaus said. "I don't want my brother to marry her."

"We don't really know her," Gynther said, "we only met her for a minute."

"He brought her here to meet all of us. I don't want him to marry her," Klaus said again, and he folded his arms over his chest.

"Well, why don't you boys go to your room and put on your swimsuits. That is, if you still want to go to the lake?"

"I want to go," Gynther said.

"Yes, me too," Klaus admitted.

"Then go on, get into your suits."

The boys went to their room.

Anna ran up the stairs to her room to put her hairbrush back in the drawer where she kept it. She slipped on her swimsuit. Then she sat down on her bed. *I am confused. Ulf is engaged. Yet, I am certain, at least I think I am, that he was flirting with me. I mean, I don't have a lot of experience with boys, but it felt like he was flirting. I could have imagined it. Or maybe he's one of those fellows that is just a flirt. Maybe he flirts with everyone. What if he is one of those boys who always chases women and has trouble being faithful? If that is the case, I wouldn't want anything to do with him. Look at me going on and on. I don't know anything about this boy. I'm just daydreaming. Besides, he'll only be here for the weekend. That's not very long. So, while he's here, I should probably stay far away from him if I can. I don't want to get into any trouble with Frau Fischer.*

Earlier that morning, before she knew that Wolfgang was coming home, Anna had promised to take the boys to the lake, which was just down the road. She had received permission from their mother after she explained that she was a strong swimmer and that she would be diligent in watching out for them. The cook had already packed a basket lunch for the three of them to take.

Anna looked in the mirror at herself. She was skinny, and her breasts were small. *I am not pretty like his fiancée. I am really nothing to look at.* She thought. *And his fiancée was so rude to me. I never realized what it was like to be the hired help in someone's home. I hope I never made Frau Frey feel the way Matilda made me feel this afternoon. Mattie, or should I say Fräulein Weber. Ha.* She scoffed out loud.

She slipped a shapeless dress over her head to cover her swimsuit. Then she left her room, stopped at the bathroom, and took several towels and an old blanket. *Oh well, I am here to work and visit with my friends on my day off. I shouldn't let anything that girl says to me upset me.* Anna thought as she began to walk down the stairs to the kitchen to pick up the picnic basket. The boys were waiting in the living room for her. They were wearing their swimsuits.

"I'm excited to be going to the lake. Our mother never let us go alone," Gynther said.

"But we could. You see, I can swim," Klaus bragged.

"He's not that good of a swimmer, and I'm glad we are going, and I am also glad Anna is a good swimmer, so we don't have to worry about drowning," Gynther said.

"You're such an idiot," Klaus said, slapping the back of Gynther's head. "He says I'm not a good swimmer, which is not true. But you know what? He can't swim at all."

"Well, let's all be careful. I can swim, but you boys need to mind me. Now, you promised you would do as I say if I took you to the lake. Do you both remember that promise? Because unless you are going to mind me, I cannot take you near the water."

"Yes, of course," Gynther said.

"Yes," Klaus said reluctantly, hating to give in.

"All right then. Who would like to carry our basket?"

"I'll carry it," Gynther said.

"Sissy," Klaus said. "You're always trying to kiss up to anyone in charge, aren't you?"

"Shut your mouth, Klaus," Gynther said.

"Alright, now listen to me, boys. You said you want to go swimming, and I agreed to take you. I have had enough of your bickering, and I will not tolerate you two fighting. If you can't behave properly, this will be our last outing to the lake. Do you understand me?"

"Yes," they both said in unison as they hung their heads.

Then Gynther assured Anna, "We'll be good. Please, can we go?"

"All right then. If you say you will be good, I am going to believe you. But if there is even one incident where either of you doesn't behave, I will not take you on an outing like this again. Now, let's go."

The boys followed Anna down to the lake. When they arrived,

there were a few groups of people scattered around. Anna set the basket of food down on the ground and then spread out the blanket.

The sun blazed like a bright yellow beacon. Tiny diamonds reflected upon the water. It was early in the summer, yet there was already a promise of hot, lazy afternoons. The boys pulled off their shirts and ran into the water. Anna sat down on the blanket and watched them.

"Don't go in too deep," she called out. She was well aware of how fearless children could be, and she knew how excited they got around the water. So, she kept her eyes fixed on them until she was shocked to see Ulf and Mattie come walking toward the lake. Anna felt ugly and childish next to Mattie, who wore a red bathing suit and matching lipstick and looked like a movie star. Anna's hair was in a ponytail, but in spite of the wind, Mattie's hair was still perfectly coiffed in waves. Anna looked down at her sensible black bathing suit and groaned. She wished she could hide under a rock. *I don't know how I could ever have thought that Ulf was actually attracted to me. He was just being nice. I wanted to believe it was something more, but just look at his fiancée. She is gorgeous, and I am frumpy and plain. I hate myself. I wish I were beautiful like Mattie.*

Anna had no idea what Ulf and Mattie were talking about, but when Mattie laughed, the sound of her laughter carried like the song of a bird.

Ulf shook out a blanket Mattie had been carrying, and as he did, he turned. And that was when he saw Anna. Their eyes met. She felt her face turn hot, and she knew she was blushing. A big smile broke out over his handsome face. "Anna!" he called out. "Why don't you come over here and join us?"

Anna wanted to go over there to spend more time with him, but she was intimidated by Mattie, who she knew looked down on her. The idea of being subjected to Mattie's snide remarks left Anna cold.

"I can't," Anna called out. "I'm watching your brothers."

Ulf didn't have a chance to answer her because, just then, another young couple walked over to him and Mattie. They sat down on the blanket. Ulf was distracted by the man who seemed to have asked him something. Anna could not hear their conversation, but she could see that Ulf was busy talking to the other couple. So as not to look as if she were a puppy hungry for Ulf's attention, Anna turned her body around so her back was to Ulf and her eyes were on the twins.

The boys were playing rough in the water, and Anna didn't like the look of it, but they were boys after all, and it seemed they hadn't gone out where the water was too deep. So, she just kept her eyes on them. Then there seemed to be a struggle. Anna stood up to see better. And then...

"Help!" Gynther screamed, "Help. Anna, help."

Anna was already on her feet. She'd sensed some sort of danger, yet she didn't know why. She ran to the water and began to swim over to the boys.

"Klaus' foot is caught in the branches. He can't stand up, and he's being sucked under the water," Gynther said.

"Get on land. I'll help him." Anna took charge.

"Please don't let my brother drown. Please, Anna."

"Do as I say. Get on land!"

Gynther did as she said.

Anna held Klaus' head above the water. It was difficult because she had to tread water to stay afloat. She knew she must try to free his foot, but each time she tried, his head slipped under again. He was gasping for air and swallowing water. Anna was terrified. She didn't think she could free him. She tried again and failed again. Not knowing what else to do, she held his head above the water and began to pray. Tears were running down her face. She didn't know what to do next.

Anna hadn't seen him coming, but suddenly Ulf was at her side.

"Can you hold him up and tread water too?"

"Yes, I think so," Anna said.

"I'll be back in a second. I am going to get my pocketknife so I can cut away the branches," Ulf said.

"All right," Anna said, thanking God that Ulf had seen them.

Ulf swam away. It was getting difficult for Anna to keep treading water while holding Klaus' head above the water, but she managed. Although it was only a few moments, it seemed like forever before Ulf returned. He went under the water and cut the branches away, freeing his brother's foot. Klaus was coughing and shaking as Ulf held him by his head, and then, swimming, he brought him to shore. Anna swam quickly behind them.

Ulf lay Klaus down on the blanket. He was coughing. *But he's alive.* Anna thought.

"He'll be all right," Ulf assured her. Then he smiled at Anna. "You did a great job out there. You saved my brother's life."

"I didn't do it. You did."

"We did it together," Ulf said. Then he reached over and touched her hand. His touch was warm and exciting. He smiled. "Together," he repeated. Then, in a soft voice, he added, "Yes?"

She nodded, unable to speak.

CHAPTER FIFTY-NINE

When Anna looked up, her eyes met Mattie, who was standing over her glaring. There was a deep furrow between her brows, but she managed a smile and, in a high-pitched voice, said, "Well, bravo to you, little nanny. You did a good job today."

"Thank you," Anna said. There was no doubt that Mattie's undertones were condescending. "I'm just relieved that Klaus is all right."

"Of course you are, and I am sure you are quite taken with Ulf's bravery and charm. I know him well, and I know how he comes across, but believe me, he is not as charming as he seems. Especially when you are planning to marry him, and he seems to be taken with another girl. One far below his station—"

"Really? What a lousy thing to say," Ulf said to Mattie in mock anger.

"I didn't mean it that way," Mattie said. "I meant—"

"It doesn't matter what you meant," Ulf said, dismissing her. "All that matters is that Klaus is all right, and all is well."

"Yes, I suppose so. Now that you're done here, why don't we go back to our blanket? Our friends are waiting," Mattie said with a touch of warning in her voice.

"I must go," Ulf turned to Anna, then he added casually. "You did a very good job today."

Anna nodded and smiled.

Ulf stood up. Mattie wrapped her arm through Ulf's arm as they headed back to their blanket. Ulf was shirtless; he wore only a pair of navy-blue swimming trunks. During the incident, Anna hadn't noticed how well-built he was. Now that she could actually take a moment to look at him, she saw that he was built beautifully. The muscles in his arms and stomach made her feel weak and helpless. *I must remember that he likes me, but he really doesn't think of me that way, and I shouldn't think of him that way either. He's engaged, and I am nothing but a nanny. He flirts, but I don't believe he's seriously interested. Not with a fiancée who is so pretty.*

Klaus did not move as he lay on the blanket on his side with his eyes closed, spent by the incident. Gynther was wide awake. He sat between his brother and Anna.

"Do you think he will be all right? Ulf said he would be all right." Gynther asked, And Anna could see he was worried.

"He's fine. I promise you. He's just worn out," Anna said.

"I just want to lie here for a few minutes," Klaus said.

"Of course. Then, when you are feeling a little better, perhaps you will eat something," Anna said.

Klaus nodded. Then, in a strained voice, he said to Anna, "I know I have been difficult for you, but I realize now that I should have been nicer to you."

"You're just a boy, being a boy." She smiled.

He managed a smile and said, "Thank you. Thank you for saving my life. I was really scared."

"Of course you were. Anyone would be."

He nodded. "I want you to know that I'm glad you came to spend the summer with us."

"Well, thank you. So, am I."

"And I'm glad my brother Ulf likes you." He closed his eyes and lay quiet.

Gynther turned to look at Anna. "I am glad you were here today too. After all, you did save my brother." Then he patted her hand, and in a soft voice, he whispered, "I like you better than Mattie. Much better. You're kind and fun to be with, too. Mattie is stuck up."

Anna didn't answer. For a few minutes, the three of them sat there soaking up the sun, breathing in the warm air, and just trying to calm down. Anna was trying not to look at Ulf, but every so often, she would glance over to find him looking directly at her.

After a short time, Anna said, "Are you boys hungry?"

Gynther nodded, and Klaus sat up. "Yes, let's eat."

"Good idea. You look so much better," Anna said.

"I feel better," Klaus said.

CHAPTER SIXTY

That weekend, Anna tried to avoid him, but Ulf seemed to be everywhere. He found a reason to see Anna as often as he could. They talked for a few minutes each time they ran into each other, but it seemed that Mattie was always right around the corner. So, they never spent much time talking.

On Saturday, Anna's day off, she put on her prettiest dress and did her hair, then she went into the twin's room to say goodbye. "I'm going to meet my girlfriends for the afternoon, but I will see you boys tonight."

Klaus had changed since the incident at the lake. He was warmer towards Anna and no longer tried to find ways to upset her. "Ulf will be leaving tonight. Maybe you should get home a little early to say goodbye to him," Klaus suggested. "I like you so much better than Mattie."

"Yes, I think so too," Gynther agreed.

"Boys, don't be silly; your brother has a beautiful fiancée who is going to be your sister-in-law. He has no interest in me."

"I disagree with you," Klaus said. "I know Ulf. We both do, don't we, Gynther?"

"Yep. We know our brother very well. Take my word for it; he is interested in you. I'm sure you can tell both Klaus, and I are glad that he does. We like you. You're lots of fun and really nice. We don't like Mattie, and we don't want her to be our aunt."

"I don't know what to say," Anna said honestly.

"Well, don't say anything. Just come home early enough to say goodbye to Ulf. You look really pretty today. It would be good if he could see you in that nice dress," Gynther said.

Anna giggled. "You boys make me laugh. Anyway, my girlfriends are waiting, so I'm going to leave now. You boys be good, alright?"

Klaus and Gynther nodded.

"So, will you be home early?" Klaus asked.

"I'll be back before dinner. Is that early enough?"

"Yes, Ulf won't leave before dinner; mother won't let him," Gynther said.

"Very true," Klaus agreed.

Anna planted a kiss on each of their foreheads. Then she picked up her handbag and left.

As she walked into town to meet her girlfriends, Anna thought about Ulf. They hadn't had a real conversation since that day by the lake. She wondered if she was making too much of her feelings for him. Mattie was like a watchdog. If he got away from her for a moment, she was never far behind. *Mattie is one of those girls who show possession of her man by hanging on his arm constantly. She pretends to be confident, carefree, and cheerful, but I see right through it. Mattie is always laughing and acting like she hasn't got a care in the world, but I don't think she's secure in her relationship with Ulf. That is why she never lets him out of her sight. I wonder if he is always flirting with other girls or if I am special.*

CHAPTER SIXTY-ONE

Anna returned from her visit with her blood sisters earlier than usual that afternoon. Soon after, the twins knocked on the door to her room.

"Come in," she said.

"Bad news," Klaus shook his head. "Ulf is already gone. He and Mattie left for school a few hours ago."

"Oh, that's all right," Anna said, forcing a smile to hide her disappointment.

"You're disappointed. Aren't you?" Gynther asked.

She shrugged. "Yes, maybe a little, but there is no reason for me to be disappointed. Ulf is engaged to be married to another girl. So, what else could I have expected?"

"Eh, I know, my brother. He's not happy with Mattie. I can't imagine he'll marry her," Klaus said.

"So, why would he become engaged to her if he isn't happy with her?"

"Because it was expected of him," Gynther said. "He did it because my father expected him to. Mattie is from a good family. A wealthy family. My father knows her father, and they are friends, but

Klaus is right; I don't think he'll go through with the marriage because he isn't happy with her. And Ulf can be stubborn."

"Who said you boys can grow up so quickly? When did you learn to speak so maturely?" Anna let out a laugh. "Come on, boys, let's put this out of our minds and go to the lake. What do you say?"

"It's your day off. You don't have to spend it with us. You can relax and read or do whatever you want," Gynther said.

"I don't have to spend the day with you boys, but I want to," Anna smiled. "We have several hours until dinner. Do you want to go?"

"Of course," Klaus said.

"So, go put on your swimsuits. We'll go down to the lake for a quick swim."

The boys smiled at her, and Anna was happy that she had won them over.

Since that day at the lake when Klaus had almost drowned, a day that was both terrible and wonderful at the same time, the twins treated Anna like family. She was no longer an outsider. They listened to her most of the time and did what she asked, and Anna came to love them as if they were her own little brothers.

CHAPTER SIXTY-TWO

Elica returned to her room late that evening after spending her day off with her friends. She listened to her employers' arguing downstairs. Once again, the wife was accusing her husband of cheating on her with a younger woman. This same argument seemed to happen at least once a week. There was screaming, crying, and sometimes the sound of something breaking. Still, despite all of the arguing, the man never denied that he was unfaithful. Instead, he called his wife crazy; he said she was insane and that her constant nagging was pushing him away.

Elica sighed. She couldn't worry about them or the children in her care. She had troubles of her own.

Elica was miserable. Each day she woke up terrified of what her parents would say if they found that she was pregnant. To make matters worse, she was very nauseated all the time, and she found it hard to keep food down. Pimples had begun to pop up on her cheeks and chin, and her glorious hair was thinning, and instead of being shiny and bright, it was lackluster and greasy.

She stopped buying things when she went shopping with her

friends on her day off. Elica was saving every penny she earned for the illegal abortion she knew she must have. She had no idea where she might find someone who was capable of helping her get rid of this pregnancy. And how would she know if they were qualified? She shivered as she considered what could happen. An unqualified person performing major surgery on her was terrifying. Everyone knew that girls died from abortions all the time. Horror stories were whispered amongst young girls at school as warnings against sexual promiscuity.

Well, it's too late for me to be warned. Elica thought. *I never listened anyway, and now I am in trouble. If I were Jewish, I could have a legal abortion, but being that I am Aryan, it is forbidden, and so I must risk my life. I wish I could talk to Anna about this. Anna has always been the smartest of us blood sisters. She would know what to do. However, how can I tell Anna the truth that I have betrayed her? That Daniel has been my lover, and he is the father of my unborn child. Anna has always stood by me. She's been my best friend. But this could turn her away from me forever. How could I blame her?* Elica's thoughts turned to Bernie. *She is a good friend, but I know she would never understand. Besides, I've always known that Bernie is different than the rest of us girls. She has feelings for me that are unnatural. Feelings she knows I cannot return.*

I know she can't help it, and she is a good person, but she would be angry at me for betraying Anna. Bernie is always fair, and she would be appalled if she knew what I did, not because I am pregnant, not even because I love someone other than her, but because Daniel was Anna's boyfriend. Bernie would say that I should have thought about Anna's feelings before getting involved with him. She would probably be right, but it's too late now.

So, what about Dagna? She would listen. I think Dagna would try to help me financially to have an abortion. I believe she would give me any money she might have left over from working after the summer is over. But I know Dagna is too stupid to know what to do. She wouldn't be able to help me to find a qualified person to perform this abortion. And Dagna will drive me crazy with her judgments because I know she will never understand how I could allow myself to become pregnant by a Jew. She hates Jews. I know it's because she is jealous of them. She thinks they have all the money and all the privileges, and maybe she's right. But I love Daniel...

CHAPTER SIXTY-THREE

The following day, Anna was in the kitchen helping the cook to cut onions and potatoes for the evening meal when she overheard the twins' parents talking. They talked about the fact that the man of the house, the twins' father, had joined the party and was becoming directly involved with Adolf Hitler. Anna had never taken much interest in politics, so this was not a conversation that she found compelling. She wasn't surprised that Herr Fischer was a confirmed Nazi. He was a wealthy, influential man in Germany, and Anna assumed it was probably a good business move for him to join the party. Anna had heard him make remarks about Jews, and she knew that he didn't trust or care for the Jewish people, but he and his wife were not her main concerns that summer. She had been hired as a nanny for the twins.

As the hot, lazy days drifted by, she found she adored the twins. They were often challenging, but always kind and affectionate. Occasionally, she thought of Ulf, but as time went by, her feelings towards him grew weaker, and she accepted the fact that he was getting married, and their encounters with Ulf were little more than flirtatious moments that meant nothing.

Then, one afternoon, as she was playing a game of kickball with the boys in the yard, she saw Ulf coming towards them. She knew it was him immediately by his easy stride, and as he got closer, his confident smile. All of this made her feel clumsy and awkward.

Klaus saw Ulf before Gynther did. He yelled, "Ulf!" and ran towards his older brother.

Gynther turned around to see Ulf walking towards them. "Ulf! You've come home," Gynther said, his voice filled with delight.

Ulf let out a laugh, "Yes, I have." Ulf was tall and handsome, and today, he wore a uniform that fit him well and made him look even more attractive.

Anna gasped. It was as if a dam broke, and all of the feelings she'd been suppressing towards him were now flooding towards her like a raging river.

"Well, well, well," Ulf said when he was close enough for Anna to hear him. "How are you getting on with my two impossible brothers?" he reached over and mussed Klaus' hair.

Anna stammered, "F-Fine. Just fine."

"So, are the boys giving you any more trouble?"

"Actually, no."

"I'm glad to hear that. Because, to be quite honest, I've come home to visit the family, but I also came to see you."

"Me?" Anna said in surprise. "Me?"

"Yes, you."

"Oh? About what? I mean, why?"

A little smile came across his face. "I've given a lot of thought to things lately, and well, I've changed the path of my life," he said sincerely.

"I don't understand."

"You will," he said, smiling. He winked and turned away from her, leaving Anna bewildered. Then he turned to his brothers. "Klaus, Gynther, go inside for a while and read or find something to do. Just stay out of trouble, yes? I need a few minutes to speak with your nanny. All right?"

"Sure. All right." Klaus smiled.

"Sure," Gynther added.

Then the boys picked up the ball they'd been playing with and headed towards the house.

"Come, let's sit down," Ulf said to Anna. She followed him to a bench by a rosebush on the other side of the yard. The sweet fragrance of roses permeated the air.

"These are mother's favorite roses," he said, looking at the rose buds about to bloom. "They are a very lovely shade of pink."

Anna tried to smile, but her lips were quivering. She liked him. She liked him a lot, but she had to remember that he did not really know her. He knew a girl who he believed she was. But that girl was a *shiksa*. And Anna couldn't bear to think of what he might feel towards her if he ever found out she was Jewish.

He was looking at her face. His deep blue eyes filled with sincerity. Then, in a soft voice, he began to speak. "So, I'll begin by saying Mattie and I are through. We broke up."

"But why?"

"The truth?"

"Of course. I mean, it's none of my business. You don't have to tell me—" Anna stammered.

"You. You are the reason."

"Me? Why me? I am just a nanny."

"Because when I met you," he cleared his throat, "I saw the kind of girl I have been looking for all my life, and I realized Mattie is not for me. You are kind, gentle, and very good with children. Mattie is a nice person, but she's spoiled. She comes from wealthy parents, and she has grown up believing that she can do no wrong. In my humble opinion, that is not a good thing."

I, too, came from a wealthy family. Anna thought. *He thinks I am a girl from a poor family.*

"Now, don't get me wrong. Mattie has good qualities. She can run a household so long as she has servants and knows the latest fashion." He laughed a little. "But the truth is, Mattie is vain and, well," he hesitated, "rather demanding, I must admit. I gave it a lot of thought, and I don't see her and me making a good marriage, if you know what I mean."

Anna didn't know what to say. She just nodded her head.

"Besides that, I also felt that I needed a change. I was tired of school. I felt like I was attending because my parents expected it of me. But I didn't feel as if I was fulfilling my destiny. Do you know what I mean by that?"

"Not exactly," Anna said. Her heart was beating so fast that she felt a little nauseated.

"I mean, I am just not sure I want to get a degree in business and follow in my father's footsteps. As I am sure you know, there is a wonderful chancellor of Germany. I heard him speak one afternoon when some school chums and I were in Nuremberg. He is so charismatic, and he has good ideas for our country. I believe in my heart that he will be the strong leader that we need," Ulf said.

"I've been hearing bits and pieces about him," Anna said. "His name is Adolf Hitler, is that right?"

"It is," Ulf smiled. "When I heard him speak, it had such an effect on me that I dropped out of the university and joined the army."

"Oh, dear!" She exclaimed. "That was a very strong move on your part."

"Yes, it was," he said, "but I feel it's right for me."

I haven't heard much about this Hitler person. However, I know he hates the Jews. Anna thought.

"I am going away with the army in three weeks, but until then, I would love to get to know you better," He said, touching her hand.

She smiled shyly, but her heart was filled with joy. Anna had never in her wildest dreams believed that Ulf and his fiancée would break up. But she was ashamed of how happy it made her to know that he was free and available. In fact, Anna was so happy that she chose to ignore the words Ulf said about the new chancellor. All she could think of was that Ulf really liked her as much as she liked him. *I feel giddy, like a child. I know my parents would never approve. They would die if they knew how I was feeling about Ulf, but there is no harm in getting to know him. He isn't talking about marriage. We are only planning a couple of weeks of dating, which won't even be like real dating because his two younger brothers will always be with us. So, nothing can really happen. Nothing permanent, anyway.*

"You do realize that I am employed by your parents to take care of your brothers. So, they will be with us all the time."

"That's fine. I just want to get to know you," Ulf said innocently.

She studied him. His deep blue eyes, the dimples in his cheeks when he smiled, and his golden hair. *I thought Daniel was handsome, but Ulf is even more attractive.* She thought. *I wonder what he sees in me. I'll bet it has something to do with that old adage that opposites attract like magnets. Which reminds me that if he ever learned the truth about me, that I am a Jewish girl from a wealthy family, he would probably not want anything more to do with me. Right now, he likes me because he sees me as a poor girl from a good Christian family who is unlike his ex-fiancée, who is as rich and beautiful as he is. He thinks a girl like me would see a fellow like him as some kind of a god. I should probably walk away from this. I should tell him I am not interested. I know that would be the smart thing to do. But I just can't.*

"So, it will be fun to get to know you better, Ulf," she said, and because her voice sounded almost business-like, she giggled.

"What's so funny?" he asked.

"I don't know, actually," she said, shrugging her shoulders.

Then, to her surprise, he started laughing. And the sound of his laughter was so engaging that she began to laugh too.

CHAPTER SIXTY-FOUR

The following morning, as Anna sat in the kitchen eating a slice of dry toast and a cup of tea, Ulf walked in. "Good morning," he said cheerily.

"Good morning," she answered, then added, "the boys aren't awake yet." Immediately, she wondered why she'd said that. There was no reason, only that he made her feel awkward and clumsy.

"I know. That's what I was hoping for." He poured himself a cup of tea and sat down beside her.

"Do your parents know about your breakup with Mattie?"

"I haven't told them yet," he said. "They'll be upset. Our families are friends. They've been friends for years. My mother and Mattie's mother pretend to be the best of friends, but all the while, they are in constant competition with each other."

"What do you mean?"

"Oh, you know. They have the same friends and go to the same parties. So, they are always trying to figure out who has the most expensive dress and the biggest diamond. Crazy stuff like that," Ulf said. "Mattie's mother and my mother were children in the same neighborhood. You haven't met my mother yet. She and my father have been divorced for ten years. She is a good person, my mother, but there has been this strange one-upmanship between her and Mattie's mother. I don't like it, and I saw the same thing with Mattie and her girlfriends. Is that the way all girls are?"

"Not me. I only wish the very best for my friends, and I don't care if they have more material things than I do," Anna said sincerely, but she wondered if she felt that way because she had always been the rich one. The one who had the most material possessions. Maybe that was why she didn't care so much about material things.

"You are so different. I mean... you are a real person, not fake like the girls I've known in my past," he said boldly.

"You can't say that because you don't even really know me," she said, and she meant it in more ways than one.

"I can see how you are. I feel like I have known you for years. But I am ready to get to know you for real, in every sense of the word."

He is so bold and outspoken. I don't know what to do or say around him. Anna put her slice of bread down on the plate in front of her. Then she said, "You really move fast, don't you?"

"Why hesitate, huh? When something feels right, there is no need to wait."

"Oh, I don't know what you mean by that." *I think he means he wants to go to bed with me. I am not ready for that. That's for sure.*

"Not to worry. Don't be afraid, my little deep thinker. I am not going to push this thing between us any faster than you will allow." He smiled and touched her cheek. His fingers on her face felt like rays of heat that penetrated through her skin and down to her heart. "Now, how about today? I thought that perhaps we might take the boys to the zoo."

"I'd have to get permission from your mother."

"You can leave that to me. My stepmother adores me," he said with a smile. "I'll clear it with her. You just let the boys know what we are planning and tell them to be ready to go to the zoo right after breakfast."

CHAPTER SIXTY-FIVE

The boys were elated. They were excited about an outing to the zoo, and even more excited because Ulf would be with them. They ate their breakfast quickly and were ready to go when Ulf appeared in the dining room. Then they were off on their way to the zoo.

As they rode the bus, the twins were on their best behavior because they didn't want to do anything to disappoint Ulf. It felt strange to Anna. Almost like she and Ulf were married, and these were their children. Of course, she knew it was just a daydream. Yet it felt almost real, and in a very strange way, it felt right.

The boys loved the zoo. They ran from enclosure to enclosure in awe of the lions and tigers, laughing at the antics of the chimpanzees, and admiring the sheer beauty and grace of the gazelles. By noon, they were all starving. The cook had packed them a hearty lunch of ham sandwiches and hunks of cheese. There was warm beer for Anna and Ulf, even though she didn't drink much of it. And there was fruit juice for the boys. However, the boys begged Ulf to allow them to taste the beer. He agreed and let them each have a swig.

After lunch, the boys went to the reptile house to see the snakes and lizards, while Anna and Ulf relaxed on the lawn.

"My brothers love you. You don't know how many nannies my stepmother has gone through. Most of them say the boys are incorrigible," Ulf said.

"They are just children, and boys tend to be active, I suppose," Anna said, not knowing what else to say. Whenever she was around him, she found that she could not think of things to say. She had so many questions for him, yet she didn't have the courage to ask him.

"Tell me a little about you, Fraulein Anna," he said, smiling. His dimples made his face wildly attractive, yet this was the question she dreaded the most.

"What do you want to know?"

"Tell me all about your family, your dreams, your friends back home. I want to know everything, but first, I want to know if you have a boyfriend."

She blushed. "You are so bold." The words shot out of her mouth before she had the chance to stop them, and she was quite embarrassed.

"Am I? I suppose I am, but why make small talk? A person should say what they feel. They should ask questions they want to know the answers to rather than just talk for the sake of talking. Don't you agree?"

She contemplated what he said, then she nodded. "I suppose you're right. Well, I don't have a boyfriend. I was seeing someone for a while, but it didn't work out."

"Were you engaged?"

"No, we weren't that serious. Although I did like him."

"So, what happened?"

"He wanted too much too fast."

"Ahhh, so that's why you are concerned that I might be the same way."

"Well, my mother always said that boys were interested in one thing when it came to girls."

"I suppose we are talking about sex now."

She nodded, but she couldn't look at him. Her face was red hot.

"Sex is nice. It's beautiful when it's with the right person. But when a man matures, he knows that sex just for the sake of sex isn't gratifying."

She cleared her throat. "I wouldn't know," she said, looking away.

He smiled, then changed the subject. "What is your family like? Do you have brothers and sisters?"

"No, I'm an only child," she answered.

"And what do your parents do for a living?"

This was part of what she hoped to avoid. Ulf was asking about her parents. What if he asked about her church? Now, she was going to have to lie to him or find a way to change the subject.

"My parents?" she said softly. "My father works at a factory." *It is the truth. He works at a factory. I just left out the fact that he owns it.*

"And your mother is a house frau?"

"Yes," she said simply.

He nodded. "Let me guess, you are working this summer to pay for University?"

"That's right. How did you know?" Anna lied.

"I can tell. You are the type of girl who would want to get an education. I see that in you."

"I do. I love to learn. I love to read. And I want to do something great with my life, but I just don't know what that might be. I've heard that we all have a purpose for being here on earth. I wish I knew mine."

"I wish I knew mine too," he said frankly. "I think my purpose might be somehow wrapped up in this new chancellor. He has plans of making Germany great again. He wants to see our fatherland elevated back up to the status it was at before we lost the Great War."

"You are talking about Hitler?"

"Yes, have you read the papers? How much do you know about him?"

"Not much, I must admit," Anna said. *I know he hates Jews; that much is obvious. There are terrible posters all over the buildings here in Berlin about how bad Jews are.* Then she decided to feel him out, to see what Ulf thought about Jews. "I know he hates Jews."

"I wouldn't say he hates them. I would say he thinks they are bad for our country. They are *Untermenschen*, lower life forms. Not quite human. He is speaking of the Jews, Gypsies, you know that sort of thing."

"How do you feel about them?"

"I agree with him. However, I must admit to you, I don't know any personally."

"Then how can you say that they are *Untermenschen*?"

"Well, the Jews are responsible for our losing the war. And the gypsies that I have seen are filthy and have no respect for anything."

"But they are human beings."

"Well, that's the point I believe that Hitler is trying to make. He is saying that they are subhuman, not on the same level as you and I. And their behavior must be watched, so they don't bring our country down any more than they already have."

She felt like crying. At this moment in time, she wished she wasn't Jewish. She knew that if anything ever came of her relationship with Ulf, she would be forced to confess the truth to him. "I didn't think you were that close-minded."

"I'm not. All I know is that my country has been in trouble for a long time. We haven't had strong leadership. And, I just want what is best for Germany."

"And that means what exactly?" she said, and she could hear the anger in her voice. *I am feeling so defensive. I just want to scream at him.*

"It means that Jews and Gypsies, and other forms of *Untermenschen* must be kept under control. That's all. Really, Anna, this is nothing for you to be concerned about," he said gently.

There was a long silence. Then Ulf took her hand. "I'm sorry for spewing all politics at you. I didn't mean to be talking about such serious matters. After all, this is our first date, and rather than talk about Hitler, I would prefer to tell you how beautiful your eyes are."

She smiled and tried to hide how worried she was about his political beliefs. *What will he think of me if he ever learns the truth? Perhaps I should just enjoy our time together for the next few weeks, and once he is gone, I should forget him entirely.*

"Come, Ulf! Come, Anna! You have to see these black bears," Gynther said as he ran up to the blanket where Ulf and Anna were sitting.

"The bears, huh?" Ulf said.

"They are so big and strong," Gynther said. "One of them stood up on his back legs, and he was monstrous."

"Where is your brother?" Anna asked.

"He's standing in front of the bear's cage. I told him I was going to go and get the two of you."

"Very well. Go back and tell your brother that we are just cleaning up after lunch, and we'll be right there. Stay in front of the bears' cage, and don't move," Ulf said.

"All right," Gynther said.

Anna began to put everything back in the basket. Then she and Ulf folded the blanket. She was feeling so many different emotions. Anger that she was born Jewish. Fear that he would find out the truth. It also felt strangely wonderful to play house with him, to pretend in her own mind that she and he were married and that the twins were their children.

As they walked up to the bears' cage, one of the bears was standing on its hind legs.

"It is quite large," Anna said. "Gynther is right."

Ulf stood behind Gynther and mussed his hair gently. Then he turned to Anna and said, "Did you know that the Gypsies can teach bears to dance? Some of them keep them as pets."

"Bears? Really? Aren't they dangerous?" she asked.

"Of course they are. That's how you know that the Gypsies are subhuman. They are more like animals. That's why they can tame and befriend wild animals."

"Oh," she said, "I've never spoken to a gypsy, but a caravan of them did come through Vienna a few years ago. They were riding in wagons painted in bright colors and pulled by beautiful horses with long manes. My father and I watched them as they came riding through town. The women wore colorful dresses, and the men seemed so brave. I wanted to go down and see them at the camp they set up on the outskirts of town. They were telling fortunes, and I wanted to have mine told, but my parents refused to allow me to go to their camp."

"I must admit that they are an interesting lot. However, your parents were right in not allowing you to go. The Gypsies can be dangerous, and they are known to be thieves," he said, smiling. "Anyway, they are certainly subhuman and not equals to you and me, but like the wild animals here in the zoo, they are interesting."

Ulf and Anna stood behind the twins and watched the bears. One bear was extremely active that afternoon. It was a massive animal that stood over eight feet tall on its hind legs. It made a loud groan, then walked toward the front of the cage, where the guests watched him in fear and awe. Anna gasped.

"Don't be afraid. It can't get at you," Ulf assured her.

"It's frighteningly huge and also majestic."

"Yes, it's true. It is."

The bear let out another loud moan, and Anna jumped. Ulf put his hand on her shoulder. "Don't be afraid," he whispered in her ear.

Anna tingled all over. She turned to look up at him. He was smiling. Then he whispered, "You are so beautiful."

She felt herself blush. Ulf touched her cheek. *I wish this moment would last forever.* She thought.

But soon, the boys were bored, and they wanted to explore the rest of the zoo. Anna and Ulf followed their lead.

After a long, exhausting day of walking, they boarded the bus and rode home in silence. As the bus moved through the streets of

Berlin, Ulf reached for Anna's hand. She allowed him to hold her hand. He smiled at her, and she returned his smile. All the while, she was pushing thoughts of him finding out that she was Jewish out of her mind.

"Did you have a nice day?" he asked.

"I did. Did you?"

"I did. I had a lovely day, and now that we've spent an afternoon together, I am sure that I was right to break the engagement with Mattie. I never felt this way when I was with her."

Anna's heart swelled. She couldn't believe that he felt the same way about her as she felt about him. *How wonderful it would be if I were really Anna Baumgartner. If I were really just an ordinary gentile girl and he and I might have a future together.*

They were all silent the rest of the way home because they were all very tired. When they arrived at the house, Anna sent the boys to their room to get cleaned up for dinner. Then she turned to go upstairs. Ulf stopped her. "I would like to take you out for dinner on your night off. Would you like to go?"

It felt as if her heart was dancing. "I would love to," she said.

"Good, then let's plan on it."

"All right," she said.

The following day, Ulf did not come to breakfast. He slept late. But In the early afternoon, he found Anna outside in the backyard playing football with the twins.

"Look at you! A girl playing ball?"

"I try. I'm not as good as your brothers," she admitted.

"She's pretty good," Klaus said.

"I don't doubt that," Ulf said, winking at Klaus.

"Not really. I'm not much of an athlete."

"You are for a girl," Klaus said. "I haven't seen too many girls who are good at ball."

"Oh, yeah?" Anna said. "I know one. If you want to see a great female athlete, you should see my friend Bernie. Now she's an athlete. Me? I'm not so good." Then she turned to Ulf and added, "Your brothers let me win all the time."

Klaus winked at Ulf. Ulf laughed, then said to Klaus, "Go play with your brother. I want to talk to Anna."

"All right," Klaus said. He picked up the ball and ran out to where Gynther was waiting.

Ulf turned to Anna. "I like your hair in a braid. You look good when you are active and out in the sun. Your cheeks are rosy, and you are even more beautiful."

"Oh," she said, a little embarrassed, "I'm glad you like the braid. I braided it today so it wouldn't be in the way when I tried to play." She laughed a little.

"Tomorrow is your day off, yes? You are off on Saturdays?"

"Yes, tomorrow is my day off," she said.

"So, we shall go out for dinner?"

"I would like that. But in the morning I must meet my friends in town. They are expecting me."

"You've made friends here in Berlin?"

"No, they came with me from Austria for the summer to work in Berlin, just like I did. They work for families too."

"So, they are from your hometown?"

"Yes, we are all from Vienna. There are four of us girls."

"How nice." He smiled.

"Yes, it is. And we always meet in town in the morning on our day off. Then we spend the day shopping. Sometimes we stay later and have dinner together. However, this week I will return early so that I can get ready and have dinner with you."

Gynther and Klaus walked over. Klaus was carrying the ball.

"Are you going to come back and play, Anna?" Gynther asked. "Klaus and I are waiting for you."

"I am going to play very soon. I was just speaking with your brother."

"He can play too," Klaus said.

"Would you like to join us for a game?" Anna asked.

"Sure, why not," Ulf said. Then he turned to his brothers and said, "Look out, boys! The real competition is here now!"

By lunchtime, Anna was exhausted. Her face was flushed and lightly sunburned.

"The boys are right. You're not bad at this," Ulf said, laughing as they all went inside to eat.

CHAPTER SIXTY-SIX

The following morning, Anna met her friends at the cafe in town where they met every Saturday. When she walked in, all three of the girls had solemn expressions on their faces.

"What is it? Is something wrong?" Anna asked.

"It's Elica," Bernie said, "she's pregnant."

"Oh, my." Anna gasped. "Oh, my." She sat down in the open chair and reached over to take Elica's hand.

"Don't bother trying to ask her who the father is. She won't tell you. She won't tell any of us." Dagna scoffed.

"Does he know?" Anna asked Elica.

Elica shook her head, "No. I haven't told him."

"Is he here in Berlin? Or is he in Vienna?"

Again, Elica shook her head. "It doesn't matter where he is. I am not going to get him involved in this at all. I need to find a way to fix it," she said. "What I am saying is I need to get rid of it."

"Don't you think you should tell him first?" Anna said gently.

"No," Elica said, "I can't."

"I agree with Anna. I think you should," Bernie said. "I think you should give him an opportunity to help you."

"What if he abandons me when he finds out? And I know he will. Right now, he likes me a lot. If he finds out I am pregnant, he will run away from me."

"Why would you say that?" Anna asked.

"Because I know he will. I just know it. My mother says boys feel trapped by pregnancies. I am in love with him, and I don't want to lose him. I couldn't bear it if it was over between us."

"You can't be sure how he will react unless you tell him. I think you should write to him," Dagna said.

"I am so afraid I'll lose him," Elica said, "and I am so afraid of facing this on my own. I have to fix it. There is no other way."

"Don't be afraid," Anna said. "We're here. We'll help you. Won't we, girls? We're blood sisters, right?" Anna longed to tell them all about Ulf, but she didn't feel it was appropriate with all that Elica was going through. So, she decided to wait until the following week, hoping that there would be a time when it seemed right to talk about herself. Right now, everything was centered on Elica and her problem. And Anna decided that being a good friend meant keeping her focus on finding a way to help Elica rather than turning the conversation to herself.

"Forever," Bernie said. "Forever blood sisters."

The girls were in low spirits that day. No one felt much like shopping or going to a museum. So, they walked around for a short while and then returned to the homes of their respective employers.

CHAPTER SIXTY-SEVEN

When Elica arrived back at her room, she took off her dress and slipped on her robe. She was glad to have the afternoon to herself. She was tired, and the heat wasn't helping. Gazing out the window, her thoughts turned to her friends, her pregnancy, and Daniel.

Elica longed to tell them who the father of the baby was, but she couldn't. Bernie would be angry with her for sleeping with Anna's boyfriend, and Anna would feel betrayed. Even though Anna and Daniel were broken up, Elica was sure that Anna wasn't over him. Even Dagna would not be on her side. Dagna would think she was dirty for having taken a Jewish boy to her bed. *So, what am I to do? I will not tell them who the boy is, but I will let them help me. I know I must try to find someone to get rid of this pregnancy. But I have no idea how to begin to look for someone. It terrifies me to think of how dangerous it is to have this done. I could die; many women in my position have. But if I don't try to fix it, then what? My only other choice is to write and tell Daniel that I am pregnant. I know I can't trust that he will stand by me.*

Maybe everyone is right. Maybe I am not giving Daniel enough credit. Perhaps I should give him the opportunity to do the right thing. I could write him a letter and tell him the truth. But I wouldn't feel confident enough to send it until Anna reads it and says it doesn't sound stupid. I know I was wrong to betray her, but as long as she doesn't know it's Daniel I am writing to, she will help me to write a good letter. And I trust Anna's opinion above everyone else's. Of all of our friends, Anna is the one I wish I could be more like. She is levelheaded and so smart. She'll know if the letter is good enough to send. I feel like a real louse because I know I did wrong to her. But I am crazy about Daniel, and I couldn't help myself.

Still, I know that Anna will be so hurt by this if she ever finds out who the father of my baby is. Perhaps she will never find out. Or at least not now. Not until I see how he reacts to my being pregnant. Of course, she will find out if he marries me. But if that happens, I will deal with it then. Right now, I'll write a letter, but I'll address it to a fake boy's name so that Anna doesn't know it's Daniel. Then I will go to the house where she is working and ask her to read it before I mail it. I'll do that right now because I know she is still off from work until tomorrow morning.

Elica took a hardcovered book from the shelf and used it as a desk. Then she picked up a pen and paper and sat cross-legged on her bed. She began to write.

Dear Hans...

That's as good a name as any. I know so many boys named Hans that Anna will never know who I am writing to.

I know you have declared your love for me. But I am not sure you will feel the same way once you receive this letter. I really hope you do. I really hope that the information I am about to share with you doesn't change your feelings for me. I am very frightened as I write to you. But I am also all alone and desperately need your help. I hope you don't abandon me, but I am pregnant with your child. I am willing to get rid of it if that's what you want. I just don't know where to go to get it done or who to turn to. Please, don't turn away from me. Elica.

Elica read her letter over twice. Then she took a cool bath, got dressed, and walked over to the house where Anna was working.

Anna was standing beside a handsome young man. They were right outside the front door of the house as Elica headed up the walkway. Elica studied the man. *He is too young to be the father of the house, and Anna said the older brother was away at a university. So, I have no idea who that man might be. Anna is all dressed up. I hardly ever see her dress up. She's wearing one of the few dresses she purchased when we all went shopping together.* Anna's hair was caught up with a pearl comb in the back, and the front was perfectly waved around her face. The man wore a uniform, an army uniform that fit him well and made him look even more attractive. Anna and the handsome man were bending down to be at eye level with a young boy with whom they were speaking. *I should probably not bother Anna right now. And I wouldn't if I didn't need her so badly, but I can't go back to my employer's house without having Anna read this letter I wrote. I won't be able to rest until I send it to Daniel.* Elica thought.

Slowly Elica approached.

"Elica?" Anna said. She was clearly surprised to see Elica.

"Yes, I hope it's all right that I came by."

"Of course," Anna stammered, but Elica could see that Anna was only being polite. It was not all right that Elica dropped by, and Anna was uncomfortable. "This is Ulf," Anna said. "He is the oldest son of my employer. And this young man is Klaus. He's one of the twins that I told you about."

"Hello," Elica said shyly. Then she looked at Anna, "If you are busy, I will go."

"What is it? What's wrong?" Anna asked, concerned. "Do you feel all right?"

"Yes, I am fine. But is there some way that we speak alone for a moment?" Then Elica turned to look at Ulf. Her face was red with embarrassment, but she added, almost pleading, "I won't keep her long."

"Of course, of course," Ulf said.

Ulf put his arm around Klaus' shoulder and led him away. Once they were gone, Anna looked at Elica. "It's not like you to come here. What's wrong?"

Elica's voice was cracking as she said, "I wrote a letter to my boyfriend." She cleared her throat. "The boy who is the father of my baby. I wanted you to read it before I sent it. I know I am bothering you at your job, and I shouldn't be. But, Anna, you are the smartest one of all of us girls, and I just wanted to be sure that the letter doesn't sound foolish or... or... like I am begging."

"I understand."

"Please help me, Anna. I need your help." Tears started to form in her eyes.

Anna nodded. "I'll read it. Do you have it with you?"

"I do," Elica said. She opened her handbag and took out a sheet of paper, which she handed to Anna.

Anna was silent as she read the letter. When she finished, she looked up at Elica and then put her arms around her. Elica began to cry. "I am scared, Anna. I am really scared."

"I know," Anna said, "But you're not alone. I'm with you, and so is Bernie." Then she added, "Even Dagna will be here for you."

"Oh, Anna, I've been in agony trying to figure out what to do. I would prefer to have the baby, but my parents would be furious. They would throw me out of the house for sure. And I couldn't come and live with you. My mother would be livid. She would say I would be putting her job in jeopardy. And you know how she feels about that. I might go and live with Bernie or Dagna, but their parents would probably not allow it. After all, they come from poor families that can hardly afford to feed them. They wouldn't welcome me and an unborn baby.

"I thought about getting a real job and staying here in Berlin, but once you girls leave to go home, I would be all alone here. And when the time comes, I would have to give birth to my baby by myself."

She let out a long-ragged breath. Then she said, "It all depends on what my boyfriend says. If he thinks the best thing to do is get rid of it. I'll do what he says. If he wants to get married, I'll get married."

"But what do you want, Elica?"

"I don't know. That's why I am asking for your advice. Should I have the baby or try to find someone to help me get rid of it?"

Anna shook her head. "I wish I knew what to tell you to do. I can't make this decision. Only you can."

"Well, my boyfriend's response to the letter will help me to make a decision. So, now that you have read it, is the letter all right?"

Anna shrugged. "Yes, I guess so. I don't know what else you could say."

There was a long silence, then Elica said, "Are you and that young man going out together?"

"Yes," Anna said softly, "Ulf and I have a date."

"He's your employer's son? What does your employer say about this?"

"Nothing so far."

"He's very handsome," Elica said.

"Yes, he is."

"I wish something wonderful would happen to me," Elica said. "It never does, though. But it always happens to you."

"You said you're in love. That is something wonderful."

"It was, but now I am pregnant, and I don't know how he will respond when I tell him. If he wants to marry me, then everything will be beautiful. But if he can't cope with it, he will leave, and our relationship will turn from a great love affair into the most terrible thing that has ever happened to me."

"Oh, Elica, I hope he turns out to be everything you want him to be," Anna said sincerely. "I hope he declares his undying love for you and tells you how happy he is that you are going to have a baby. I wish you a long marriage filled with joy."

"Yes, Anna. I know you do, but what are the chances? It seems whenever I trust a man, it explodes in my face." Elica sighed. "Well, I've taken up enough of your time. I'm going to go back now, and I will leave you to your date. By the way, you look really pretty." Elica turned and walked slowly down the road. Her shoulders were slumped, and her head was down.

CHAPTER SIXTY-EIGHT

Elica felt worse about her predicament after seeing Anna so bright and carefree on her way out on a date with Ulf. Elica walked for a while until her legs hurt, then she walked over to the house where Dagna was working. She knocked on the back door, and the old man's daughter, who was visiting, let her in.

"I'm a friend of Dagna's. Is she here?"

"I don't know for sure. It is her day off," the middle-aged woman said.

"Yes, I know it's her day off. That's why I came," Elica said.

"All right then, wait here. I'll knock on the door to her room and see if she's here."

Elica sat down and waited. A few minutes later, Dagna came walking slowly into the kitchen. "What's wrong? Are you all right? You look pale."

"Yes, I'm all right. I'm just feeling sorry for myself," Elica said.

"Come on up to my room. We can talk there."

Elica followed Dagna up the stairs to a small, sparsely furnished but spotless room. She sat down on the bed. "I wrote a letter to the baby's father to tell him I am pregnant."

"That was a good idea," Dagna said.

"Then I went to see Anna to ask her to read the letter. You know how we all say she is so smart, right?"

"You and Bernie say she's smart. I don't think so. I think she's tricky, like the Jew that she is. But you girls don't want to believe me. I hope you don't ever find out that she has the true nature of a Jew, and by that, I mean she can't be trusted."

"Anyway, I was feeling frantic. I didn't want to send a letter that made me look foolish or desperate. So, I went to see Anna. I was just hoping she could give me some advice. But when I got to the house where she is working, she was walking out the door. Wait until you hear this... Anna was going out on a date with one of the most handsome boys I had ever seen. He is the oldest son of her employer. She didn't care much about my letter. She was too excited to go on her date."

"She never told us about him. She keeps secrets. I knew she was diabolical," Dagna said, "I've always known it."

"No, you're right; she didn't ever mention him. When I saw her with him, I felt so jealous. Why does it seem that Anna gets everything? She has wealthy parents, beautiful clothes, and a magnificent home. And now she has a wealthy and handsome boyfriend. He isn't even a Jew like her; He's one of us. He should be dating one of us, not her. She always gets everything that is good while you and I are always struggling," Elica said.

"That's because she is a Jew. Her parents stole all the money they have from the Christians. You know that the Jews killed Christ."

"Sometimes I am so jealous of her that I hate her," Elica said.

"I never liked her," Dagna said. "I never wanted her in our group."

"She's nice. She's kind, but I can't help but feel that she gets all the good things in life. While the rest of us struggle," Elica said. While in her mind, she was using this as a justification for having betrayed her best friend.

CHAPTER SIXTY-NINE

Anna was watching Elica walk down the winding road out to the street when Ulf came towards Anna.

"Everything all right?" he asked in a concerned voice.

She nodded. "Yes. Everything is fine." Anna looked up at him and managed a smile. She wished she could tell him how worried she was about Elica, so he would understand why she was so preoccupied. But this was their first official date, and Anna didn't want to scare him off by talking about her best friend being pregnant out of wedlock. So, she repeated in the cheeriest voice she could manage, "Everything is fine."

"Good. So, now let's go out and have some fun, yes?" Ulf said, smiling. He was so handsome when he smiled. She couldn't help but return the smile.

They walked into the town arm in arm without saying much. For Anna, it felt so good to be walking beside him. Everyone turned to look as they strolled by, and she knew that they made a handsome couple. Ulf in his uniform and Anna in her lovely new dress. He led her to a restaurant that had tables set up under a large awning. A musical band that consisted of three young men wearing traditional

German *lederhosen* was standing on a platform and playing German folk music. Several of the patrons were clearly drunk, and they were singing along. A couple were dancing in the corner. Ulf reached down and took Anna's hand, then he led her to a table as far away as he could get from the musicians. He pulled out her chair, and she sat down. He sat beside her and whispered in her ear, "I didn't want to be too close to the music because it's hard to talk over it, and I want to tell you so many things."

"Yes, it is difficult to talk over the music," she said, not knowing what else to say.

"This place is a lot of fun. I always come here when I am in town. In fact, I used to come here almost every week before I went to the university."

"It seems like fun," Anna said as she turned to look at him. He was smiling. She smiled. He patted her hand, and she did not pull away.

"I'll order a bunch of food and a pitcher of beer," he said. "Would that be all right with you? Do you like beer?"

"Yes," she said, even though she hardly ever drank, and when she did, it was always wine.

After Ulf placed the order, he began to softly massage Anna's hand. She felt so many emotions. Tentatively she said, "Ulf, I have to admit, all of this is rather strange to me. When I met you, you were engaged. Now, you are no longer getting married, and we are on a date. It seems so odd. I mean, I never considered dating you because I knew you were taken. But now, well... can I ask you why you broke up with Mattie?"

"It's a fair question," he said, nodding. "Mattie and I have known each other all of our lives. We were children together, grew up in the same neighborhood, attended the same schools, and had the same friends. Everyone always expected that someday we would get married. But... well... how do I say this?" He hesitated, looked into Anna's eyes, and said, "There was no magic between Mattie and me. I like Mattie very much. She is a good friend. More like a sister than a friend, really. But when I saw you, I knew I couldn't marry her. Do you know what I mean?"

"Not really."

"Well," He hesitated for a moment, then continued, "this is going to sound strange, but... have you ever met someone and felt like you have known them in another life? Somehow, you feel as if you have been searching for them your entire life. And then you find them, and you can't let them get away. You just can't. That's how I felt the first time I saw you."

"I don't know what to say," she muttered.

"I know by the way you looked at me the first time we saw each other that you felt something, too."

"I did. I was very attracted to you" Anna found it easier to talk to him about her feelings than it had ever been with Daniel.

"I knew it. There was a magic in the air between us."

"I must admit that I felt that magic very strongly that day at the lake when you rescued your brother," she said. "When you looked into my eyes."

He nodded. "Yes, I remember, but I knew before that." He smiled.

The waitress brought the beer and poured them each a glass.

"You like German beer?" he asked.

"You want the truth?" she asked.

"Of course I do."

"No, it's too bitter. But then again, I am not much of a beer drinker."

"Would you like a glass of wine?"

"I would," she admitted.

He called the waitress over, "A glass of white wine for the lady, please."

"Why did you leave school?" she asked.

"I felt like I was doing what everyone else expected of me, not what I wanted."

"And what do you want?"

"Well, I wanted to do something great with my life. I've always wanted a cause that I could champion, and the moment that I heard our chancellor speak, I knew he could restore Germany to her rightful place in the world. I really believe in him. And I want to be a part of it all. I want to see my country regain her pride and become great again."

"I think that the restoration of Germany is a wonderful goal, but I don't care for all the hatred he spews."

"It's not really hatred, sweetheart," he said, and the sincerity in his voice when he said 'sweetheart' made her tingle all over. "He just feels that the *Untermenschen* are bringing our country down, and he wants to make sure that they are kept under control. Hitler is a good man. He won't hurt anyone. I believe all he wants to do is just to keep a good watch on them. The Jews, the Gypsies, you know...."

She wanted to believe that nothing bad could ever happen. That night, with the stars twinkling overhead and the candles lit on the tables. That night with the music playing in the background and the electricity of his hand holding hers, her heart beating rapidly. His eyes locked on hers, warm and filled with sincerity. She found that she was far too enthralled with his dimples and the deep blue of his eyes to want to talk any more about the chancellor of Germany, the Jews, the Gypsies, or any of it. Instead, she longed to hear more of the lovely things he had to say about his feeling for her.

Anna was falling in love.

CHAPTER SEVENTY

They stayed in the *Biergarten* until it was well past midnight, and by the time they left, Anna had consumed far too much wine. It wasn't as if she hadn't had a glass of wine on the high holidays or at a wedding, but she wasn't used to drinking excessively. She felt good, giddy, and light. All the problems that had been plaguing her earlier about Ulf's political views and the problems with the hatred towards Jews in Germany seemed to melt away. Somehow, in her slightly drunken state, as he was telling her jokes and putting his arm around her, she thought he might be right about there being something very special between them. Something that had been there even before they met.

After they left the restaurant and were walking back home, Ulf leaned over and kissed her gently. She sighed and melted into his arms. It all felt so natural. It's as if I am at home in his arms, as if my entire life I have been searching for him, even though I didn't know it.

"Good night," he said when they arrived at the house, and she turned to go upstairs to her room.

"Good night," she whispered, then she tripped on a stair. Anna didn't fall, but a short giggle escaped her lips.

"Are you all right?" he asked. "I can help you upstairs if you'd like."

"No, that's not necessary. I'm fine. I just tripped." But then she tripped again. This time she slid down two stairs. Before she had a chance to protest, Ulf was at her side. He caught her before she fell to the bottom and lifted her, holding her tightly in his arms. *I feel so safe.* She thought as he helped her up the stairs.

When they were at the door to her room, he whispered, "I had a wonderful time tonight."

"So did I."

"It's a shame that it has to end," he said. "Shall I come in? We might talk for a bit longer."

"Yes, come in," she said.

He followed her into her room. Then, once she closed the door, he turned her around and kissed her. This kiss was deep and passionate. She was caught up in the magic of it. He kissed her again, his tongue tasting her mouth greedily. Anna began to breathe heavily as he lifted her and lay her on her bed. Then he lay down beside her and began planting warm wet kisses on her throat. She sighed. But as he unzipped her dress and moved down toward her breasts, she began to feel more sober.

"Oh, Ulf. I'm not ready for this."

"What do you mean?"

"We hardly know each other."

"I feel like I have known you forever."

"I'm sorry, but I need more time."

He sat up abruptly. At first, Anna thought he was angry, and she was frightened. *This is how I lost Daniel.* She thought. *But I am just not ready for this. This is serious.* He pushed away from her, then took a long deep breath and said, "All right. All right. I understand. I'll wait. I care about you deeply, so I'll wait. I'll give you as much time as you need."

She sat up and held her dress over her bra. "I'm sorry. I hope you aren't angry."

"I'm not angry. I was just caught up in the moment. But I understand, and I respect how you feel. However, it is late, and I think I had best be going to my own room now," Ulf said. "I will see you tomorrow."

"Yes," she said. "And Ulf…"

"Yes?" he turned to look at her as he headed for the door.

"Thank you for understanding."

The following morning, when the alarm rang, Anna awoke with a headache. Her mouth was dry, and she felt sick to her stomach. She had to drag herself out of bed. After she slipped on her robe, she headed to the bathroom to wash her face. It was then that she overheard Ulf's parents talking downstairs. When she heard Ulf's stepmother mention her name, she was intrigued. Instead of heading downstairs to the kitchen, Anna stopped and hid behind the door to her room to listen.

"Horst, your son is quite taken with Anna. I am afraid she is the reason he broke off his engagement to Matilda," Frau Fischer said.

"Don't worry too much about it. Matilda is a spoiled child, and she wouldn't have made a good wife anyway," Herr Fischer said.

"Yes, but she is from a good family. Anna is a nanny; she is not in his class. Certainly not marriage material for a boy like Wolfgang."

"You forget, my love, that you were once a hotel receptionist. I didn't care. I took one look at you, and I fell head over heels."

"But I am afraid that maybe she came to Berlin to find a rich husband, and Wolfgang is just falling into her trap."

"I don't think so. Don't worry so much, dear. Just let him have his fun. He is leaving for the army soon. Once he has gone, he will forget about her soon enough."

"And that's another thing. I know he is not my biological son, so it's probably none of my business. Still, I am very displeased that he left the university to join the army. That was a stupid thing to do."

"My dear, you are only protecting my interests. So, of course, it is your business. Everything I do is your business. But don't you worry your pretty little head about Wolfgang. He will be all right. He is young and full of romantic ideas, and he wants to be a hero to be admired. All young men feel that way, I think. At least I know I did. That's why I served in the Great War. But right now, the country is not at war, so he will serve a few years in the army, then return home and go back to school," Herr Fischer said calmly.

"And you are certain of all of this?"

"I am, dear. Our son is too wise not to return to school. I've been in the army, and I promise you that he will soon learn that heroics are not much fun. I know him. He's lazy, and the army doesn't tolerate laziness. So, please, don't worry too much. Let him keep seeing this girl so he can get her out of his system."

"You mean you think he must bed her, don't you?" Frau Fischer asked.

"Actually, yes, I do. Once he has bedded her, he will tire of her. You'll see. Every young man has one of those flings before he settles down with the right kind of woman."

"You tried with me; I was not that kind of girl. Even though I came from a poor family," she said proudly.

"I knew you were a lady right away."

"You wanted me so badly."

"I still do," He groaned.

"Oh, why don't you show me?" she laughed.

"Let's go upstairs," he said.

Anna retreated into her room and shut the door quietly. She felt hot tears sting her cheeks. *Dear God, please help me. I think I am falling in love with him. We almost made love last night. If we had, would he have gotten tired of me? I don't know, because I have never done that before, but that's what his father said. I don't understand. For me, love is not a game. It's serious. Very serious. And I am afraid that if something like that happened, I would be heartbroken forever. His parents don't really know me because I am living a lie right now. They think I am some girl from a poor family who their son is smitten with, a Christian girl. And from what they said, they wouldn't even accept a Christian girl if she was not from a wealthy family. But if they knew the truth about me, I am sure their feelings towards me would be even worse.*

CHAPTER SEVENTY-ONE

Dagna had always resented Anna for having been born into a family that was financially comfortable, and she'd made no secret of her feelings. She had never liked Anna. Not only was Anna a Jew, but she was spoiled. So, when Elica came to visit Dagna that evening after she saw Anna with Ulf, and she told Dagna that she saw Anna going out on a date with the son of her employers, a boy who was handsome and wealthy, Dagna was wild with jealousy. She and Elica had spent over two hours commiserating about how they had to struggle for everything they got and how good things always seemed to come easily to Anna.

Meanwhile, the old man who was Dagna's employer called for her at least four times. He needed some pain medicine. He needed a blanket. He wanted some water. *It is my day off, and he won't leave me alone for a minute.*

"I'll be right back," Dagna told Elica.

Elica nodded.

Dagna walked into the old man's room. He was sitting up in bed. "Yes?" she said impatiently.

"I am hungry," he said.

"I left you a sandwich."

"I ate it."

"It's my day off. My friend is here visiting with me," Dagna said, "and you keep calling for me. I am thinking about going out just to get away from you."

He ignored what she said and smiled. "So, who is your friend? A fellow?" he asked.

He's so nosey. "It's my girlfriend from Vienna," she said. "Now, if I bring you a sandwich, will you please leave me alone for a while?"

He laughed. "Of course. Bring me a beer too."

Dagna made a quick cheese sandwich and brought it to the old man's room. He smiled when he saw her. *I hate him.* She thought. *I would like to kill him.* She placed the sandwich and beer on a tray by his bed. "Now, please leave me alone for the rest of the night."

"You wouldn't want me to tell my son how mean you are to me, would you?"

"I am not mean to you. It's my day off."

"All right, all right," the old man conceded, "but don't forget, I like my breakfast early in the morning."

"Of course. How could I forget? You tell me every day," she said as she walked away from the old man's room. Tears threatened to fall, but she wiped her eyes with her thumbs. *Old coot.*

"I'm sorry, but it's getting late, and I have to get back. My employer will get worried," Elica said.

"I know," Dagna said. "Well, I'll see you next Saturday?"

"Of course."

"Are you going to send the letter to your boyfriend?"

"I haven't decided yet, but I must say that Anna was no help. I thought she would be, but she was so wrapped up in herself that she didn't really care about my letter."

"Well, why don't you just wait until next Saturday before you send it? We can take some time and think about it a little bit more."

"I don't know. I have no idea what I am going to do yet. I'll have to wait and see. But thank you for being here to listen to me. You're a good friend, Dagna."

"I am your best friend. I want you to know that. I am always on your side. Always."

"I know that," Elica said.

Dagna walked Elica to the door.

After Elica left, Dagna made herself a sandwich and went to her room. She ate quickly, washed her face, and brushed her teeth. Then, she lay down in bed but couldn't fall asleep. *I must try and get some sleep. That old man will be screaming for me before sunrise.* Her mind was on Anna. She was consumed with jealousy and churning hatred.

Life is so hard for me. I am not pretty. I am very overweight. I got the worst job of all my friends here in Berlin. Damn Anna. Why is it that Anna always seems to always get the best of everything? The most handsome boys, the wealthy parents? Why? Elica is prettier than Anna with her white blonde hair. You would think she would have better luck, but she doesn't have any luck either. I might not be beautiful, but I am still a pure Aryan woman. Don't girls like Elica and I deserve more than that dirty Jew? The four of us came here to Berlin to have an exciting, adventurous summer.

Elica is not having an adventure; she's too worried about dying from an abortion, and I can't blame her. As far as Bernie is concerned, I wouldn't expect her to have much of an adventure. She's got a problem that no one wants to discuss. She's a lesbian, and she's still in love with Elica. And me? I am having a terrible summer. I work for the most infuri-ating old man who is bothering me constantly. But Anna? Things always work out for Anna. Look at her now. She isn't even supposed to be here in Berlin. She's living under an assumed name, working for an Aryan family. If they knew she was a Jew, they would probably die. I can't believe it, but Anna has captured the attention of a wealthy Aryan boy. Her employer's son. It just isn't fair.

Dagna knew she should get some sleep. But she just couldn't rest. The jealousy felt like a cancer that was eating at her. It was so strong that it overshadowed the worry she felt about Elica's unwanted pregnancy. Dagna tossed and turned until her bed linens were twisted into knots. Then she got up to straighten them. It wasn't until the sun began to rise that she drifted off to sleep. She awoke to the old man calling her name even before her alarm clock rang. Dagna groaned and forced herself to get up. *Damn Anna, she kept me up all night.* She went into the bathroom to wash her face and brush her teeth, but the old man was still calling for her.

"Dagna. Where are you? I had to do everything for myself yesterday. And now, you are so late with my breakfast. What are you doing?"

She stopped what she was doing and called out to him, "I'm just getting dressed, Herr Halpmann. I'll have your breakfast ready in a few minutes."

"Well, hurry!" he yelled.

She quickly finished getting dressed. Then she ran downstairs to make his coffee and hot cereal. *I don't want him to tell his son that I am not doing a good job because if he does, his son will send me back home to Vienna. I want to stay here with Elica.* Quickly, she placed the cereal and coffee on a tray and brought it up to him.

He was sitting up in bed. When he saw Dagna, he scowled at her. "Young people don't take their jobs seriously these days," he said as he sat up in bed and began to eat.

Dagna wanted to slap him. *I should have put poison in his food.*

"It's cold," he said.

"It can't be cold. I brought it up here to you as soon as it was ready," Dagna said, almost in tears. *I wish I could knock him right out of that bed and beat him until he learned to shut his damn mouth.* She thought. But she said, "I'm sorry, Herr Halpmann."

"All right. All right. I'll eat it as it is. But next time, make sure it's hot before you bring it to me."

"Yes, Herr Halpmann."

He shook his head. "Go now," he said.

She turned and left the room. Dagna was in a foul mood that entire day. And it didn't help that her employer was always more demanding on the days following her day off. Her spirits were low, and the more Herr Halpmann demanded of her, the darker her mood became.

Herr Halpmann complained of being tired that day. He blamed his exhaustion on having to take care of himself the day before. So Dagna gave him an early dinner. It was still light outside when Dagna put the old man to sleep for the night. She was glad that he went to bed early, and for a while, he was not driving her crazy with his constant demands.

But her bitterness towards Anna had not subsided at all. She sat at the window watching the birds outside, and a plan came to mind.

The old man took his pain pills after he ate, and that should keep him asleep for the rest of the night. If I am quiet, I can sneak out of this house without him knowing I ever left. Then I can go and carry out my plan.

CHAPTER SEVENTY-TWO

Anna inspected the twins' mouths to make sure that they both brushed their teeth. She smiled at them when she saw they had. "All right, boys. Get into bed, and I'll read you a story before you go to sleep."

Klaus led the way, with Gynther following behind him. They jumped onto their respective beds as Anna settled into the rocking chair they had in their room since they were infants. She looked at the bookshelf in the boy's room. It was mostly empty. There were only a few books left. They all seemed to be derogatory books about Jews. Especially one called *The Poison Mushroom*.

"Don't you boys have any other books?"

"No, I'm sure you must have heard about the book burnings here in Germany," Gynther said. "We aren't allowed to have too many different books. We had to get rid of lots of books because they were forbidden."

"I haven't heard about the burnings, I am afraid. What happened?"

"We were too little to know about it when it happened, but the teachers at school still talk about it," Gynther said. "Several years ago, I guess it was in 1933, when our chancellor was appointed there. There was a big book burning here in Germany. Every book that was forbidden was burned. Our teachers say that there were big bonfires. So, now we are limited as to what we can read."

"I see," Anna said. *I have been so caught up with my own life, I never realized that this was happening here in a country so close to Austria.* She thought. "Perhaps I should just tell you a story. What do you think?"

But before the boys could answer, Anna heard a knock at the door downstairs. "I wonder who's here," Gynther said.

Then Anna heard Dagna's voice. She stood up.

"What's wrong?" Klaus asked.

"My friend Dagna is here, and I can't imagine why," Anna said.

"Ulf, there is someone here to see you," the maid called out.

Anna opened the door to the boy's room just in time to see Ulf bounding down the stairs. "Who is it?" he asked the maid.

"Dagna?" Anna said. She was standing at the top of the stairs, shocked to see her friend standing in the living room of her employer's home. "What are you doing here?"

Dagna ignored Anna and turned to Ulf. "I came to tell you something that you should know. You are dating a Jew."

"What do you mean?"

Anna grabbed the post at the top of the stairs. Her knees felt weak, and she was afraid she might fall.

"I mean, Anna is a liar. I never approved of her lying, but she made up a lie, so she could come to Berlin to work for the summer. Her papers are false, and her real name is not Baumgartner. It's Levinstein. I didn't think it would cause any harm. I thought she would just come here and work for the summer. That was until my friend Elica told me she saw you and Anna going on a date. Then I knew I must tell you the truth. It was the only right thing to do. So, I came here this evening to tell you that Anna is a liar and a Jew."

"That's impossible," Ulf said.

"It's not impossible. It's true. I swear it is," Dagna declared.

"Anna?" Ulf said, his face was as pale as parchment paper. "Tell me it's a lie. I'll believe whatever you say. I'll believe you."

Anna still stood at the top of the stairs. She felt her eyes sting with tears, her shoulders fell, and her head hung low. "It's true," she said in a soft voice. "You might as well know; it's true."

"But why? I understand that you wanted to come to work here in Berlin. But why would you not tell me? Why would you lie to me?"

Anna shrugged. Tears ran down her cheeks. "I was afraid," she said in a small voice.

Ulf's mother walked into the room. She assessed the situation and fixed a questioning gaze upon Ulf. He did not acknowledge her. The twins came rushing out of their room to stand beside Anna.

"Go back to your room," Ulf's mother said to the two boys.

"But what is going on here?" Klaus asked.

"I said go to your room," Ulf's mother repeated.

"You deceived me," Ulf said, his eyes burning into Anna.

"What difference does it make if I am Jewish or not? I am still the same person I was yesterday."

"It makes all the difference in the world," he said. "You tricked me."

Anna glanced over at Dagna, who had a satisfied smile. "I hate you," she said to Dagna, "I have forgiven you for everything you've done to me all of these years, but I will never forgive you for this."

"I thought you said you weren't ashamed to be a Jew?" Dagna said sarcastically. "I didn't think you would mind my telling your beau."

"You knew what you were doing," Anna growled. "You wanted to hurt me, and you did. Now, get out of my life and stay away from me. I never want to see your face again." Then Anna turned to look at Ulf. Her body was trembling with rage. "As for you," she said. "You hate Jews. You say you don't, but you do and have no real reason why. Only that some man in a political office tells you that you should hate me and people like me. Well, Ulf, I must say that I'm sorry for you. I thought you were a stronger person. A man who could make up his own mind, but you're a puppet just like her." She pointed to Dagna.

Anna continued, "You believe what someone tells you to believe, and that is pathetic. I was wrong to lie to you. I had begun to feel things I had never felt for anyone else and was afraid of losing you. I thought you cared for me. I wanted to believe it. I would have told you, eventually. I just thought it would be best if you got to know me a little first.

"I was wrong for deceiving you, and I am sorry. But now, I see you are not the man I thought you were. I know because something as small as this could change your mind about me, about us. So, I know we are not meant for each other. All those things you said to me about how you believed we were destined for each other were meant for another girl who wasn't Jewish. The girl who you thought I was."

He was speechless. He stood there looking at Anna, shaking his head.

"I think you should pack your things and take the next train home," Frau Fischer said to Anna in a soft but firm voice. "And you, young lady," she turned to Dagna, "leave my home right this minute."

Anna was stunned. She could not take her eyes off Dagna. She knew Dagna was cruel, but she had never wanted to believe that Dagna would actually go out of her way to hurt her.

Dagna looked directly at Anna and gave her one last smirk, then she turned and walked out the door. Anna was trembling as she went to her room to pack her things.

CHAPTER SEVENTY-THREE

The driver did not speak as he drove Anna to the train station. He did not open her door or help her with her suitcase. When they arrived at the train station, he stopped. "This is it."

"Thank you." She got out of the car, and without another word, he sped away. His whole demeanor towards her changed. It was hard to say whether it was because she was Jewish or because she lied. But it didn't matter anyway. It didn't even make any difference to her that he didn't say goodbye. Right now, nothing mattered to her more than getting as far away as she could from Berlin, and especially from Ulf. She would miss the boys, the twins, who had become her friends and allies. Now, even that was irrelevant.

The Fischers wanted nothing to do with her. Frau Fischer had fired her. Was it because she was a Jew or because she had lied? It didn't matter. She was no longer welcome in their home. Anna wondered if the boys would ever forgive her. She would never know. Ulf had turned on her like a viper, and it hurt so deeply. If she even thought about it for a moment, the ache in her chest was so painful that she had to think about something else.

Anna walked up to the ticket booth and bought her ticket back to Vienna. Then she took a seat on the wooden bench where she would wait three hours for the next train. It arrived on time. The sound of the whistle, which had sounded so exciting when she'd been leaving Vienna to come to Berlin, now sounded mournful. Picking up her small valise, she climbed the stairs and boarded the train. There was a deep, painful emptiness in her gut as she found a seat in the back of the train car.

I wish I had the opportunity to speak to Elica and Bernie to tell them I was going home. I don't know if Dagna will tell them or not. I suppose the only thing I can do is send them each a letter once I am home.

CHAPTER SEVENTY-FOUR

Dagna did not tell Bernie or Elica what she had done. When they received their letters from Anna, Bernie confronted Dagna. She was furious. "Why would you do that?" she asked when the girls met on their day off the following week.

"Because Anna always gets the best of everything. I was sick and tired of it," Dagna growled.

Elica looked away.

"What do you think, Elica?" Bernie asked.

"She agrees with me," Dagna said. "She said it to me the night before I went to Anna's employers to tell on Anna."

"Elica, you can't think that what Dagna did was right. This was no way to treat a blood sister."

Elica didn't answer, but she was crying softly.

"She's a Jew," Dagna said in a self-righteous tone. "She shouldn't be a blood sister with any of us. Her blood is tainted."

"Stop reading that stuff. It's horrible," Bernie said.

"It's my fault," Elica said. "I wish I had not said those things to Dagna. I was feeling sorry for myself. I was feeling jealous. But I never thought that Dagna would do this."

"But she did. Dagna ruined the summer for all of us," Bernie said. Then she stood up. She took a few marks out of her bag and put them on the table to pay her portion of the bill. Then, without another word, Bernie turned and left the restaurant, leaving Elica and Dagna staring after her.

CHAPTER SEVENTY-FIVE

There were three weeks left before the girls were scheduled to return to Vienna. That would give them a week to get ready before school was to start. During those three weeks, Bernie no longer met Dagna and Elica at the coffee shop in the mornings on their day off. Although Elica and Dagna continued to meet. That same week that Anna returned home, Elica sent Daniel the letter she had written to him. But by the following Saturday, when she met Dagna at the coffee shop, she still had not had any response. Dagna did not know that it was Daniel who was Elica's lover. Elica referred to him as Hans, and Dagna was led to believe that he was one of the gentile boys who worked at the factory. Elica knew she dared not tell Dagna that she was pregnant by a Jewish man.

As Dagna and Elica sat at the coffee shop one Saturday morning, the pregnancy was all Elica could talk about. She was terrified and obsessed, weighing her options over and over, but still not sure what to do. Even so, Dagna didn't seem to mind. She seemed to enjoy having Elica all to herself. And she loved the fact that Elica was dependent on her for advice.

"I don't know how to go about getting this pregnancy fixed. I don't know anyone who could help me," Elica said.

"What about your family, doctor?" Dagna asked. "You could ask him when we get home."

"Yes, but I don't think he will do it. Even worse, he'd probably tell my parents."

"You could have the baby. You and I could get an apartment somewhere. We could find jobs. I would help you with the baby," Dagna said.

Elica considered this. *It is the best idea I've heard. It's better than dying from an abortion. Dagna and I would be forced to leave school a year early, but Dagna doesn't seem to mind. And if we are both working, we could afford to have someone look after the baby in the afternoon while we work. It wouldn't be easy, and I am sure we wouldn't have much money left over after we paid all of our bills, but it could be done.*

"Are you sure you want to do this?" Elica asked.

Dagna smiled a bright, full smile. "Yes, I am quite sure."

Elica let out a long sigh. "Then this is what we will do. I have some money saved from working this summer. It's not enough to get a flat, though."

"Don't worry. I have money, too," Dagna said. "We'll do this together. After all, I've always been your best friend. Your only real true friend."

CHAPTER SEVENTY-SIX

Anna returned home feeling betrayed and miserable. Not only had Elica conspired with Dagna to destroy her, but Ulf, the man she thought she might be falling in love with, had turned on her so easily. He told her that he was following the chancellor and didn't like Jews. It was that she had refused to believe him. Deep in her heart, she had hoped against all odds that when he discovered that she was Jewish, he would change his mind about his feelings towards Jews. It didn't happen, and she knew she should never have expected it.

She had hoped that her mother would not question her too much about why she had returned home early. And because her brother Anselm had been sick again, her mother was too distracted to ask anything about Berlin. This was both good and bad. It was good that Anna didn't have to make up a story about what happened. However, once again, Anselm suffered and spent two weeks in a hospital. He had only just returned home two days before Anna's arrival. He was thin, weak, and very pale. It was a dark and bleak time for Anna. She spent most of her days at her brother's bedside, reading to him. But at night, she wondered what Klaus and Gynther thought of her now. *Do they talk about me? Do they hate me for being Jewish?* She tried not to think of Ulf or Elica. It was too painful. Instead, when she wasn't with Anselm, she put all of her efforts into practicing her piano.

Two weeks later, right after lunch, when Anselm lay down for his afternoon nap, Anna went outside to sit in the yard. She had always felt a sense of loss whenever the summer was ending. Until this year, there had been no real reason for it. Usually, it had just been the knowing that the cold winter was on the way. As she looked at the golden sun burned grass, she closed her eyes. *Even though this summer was painful, I am glad I went. I am glad I met Ulf. I never knew I could feel that way about another person, and now I know I can.*

"Anna..." It was a familiar voice.

Anna opened her eyes. "Bernie?"

"Yes, I got home from Berlin this morning. I am so sorry about what happened to you with Dagna."

"So, you read my letter?"

"Of course, and I felt terrible. I think that Elica and Dagna behaved terribly toward you. And that boy, what is his name? He is despicable." Bernie sat down in a chair beside Anna.

"Ulf," she said sadly.

"Yes, Ulf. What a silly name," Bernie said, smiling.

"It's short for Wolfgang. His brothers, the twins, nicknamed him Ulf," Anna said in a sad voice.

"You still like him, don't you?" Bernie asked.

"Of course, you can't turn feelings on and off like a water faucet. I still have feelings for him, and it's hard for me to believe that he could be so small-minded. But, the truth is, he is small-minded. He hates Jews, not to mention Gypsies and everyone else that the crazy chancellor of Germany tells him to hate."

"He's so political, sort of like Dagna. She is all caught up with that chancellor of Germany and his political party, too."

"Yes, I know. Dagna can't hurt me because I never thought of her as a real friend. But Elica is different. I thought she and I were like sisters. We've had our differences, but we have also had our good times. Her betrayal hurts even more than losing Ulf."

"I can understand. And..." Bernie hesitated. Then she took a long breath. "There is something else you should know."

"Oh?"

"Yes."

"Tell me, please."

"I've agonized as to whether to tell you or to mind my business. But I think you should know."

"Know what, Bernie? Tell me."

"As you know, Elica was pregnant when you left."

"Yes."

"After you were gone, she came to my employer's house and told me who the father of her baby is. I don't know if she ever told Dagna, but I doubt she would, considering he's Jewish."

"Who is it?"

"Daniel."

Anna felt faint. Everything turned black and began to spin. She closed her eyes hard, trying to stay calm. "My Daniel?" she asked in a soft voice.

"Yes."

"When, how? I never knew she was seeing him. Another betrayal." Anna shook her head. "Elica was never my friend. I suppose I need to face that fact."

"I wouldn't say that she wasn't your friend. She was always very jealous of you, and so was Dagna. They were too jealous to be good friends."

"And you, Bernie, were you jealous of me?"

"No, I was glad to have a friend like you who had the money to help Elica and Dagna out when they got into trouble, a friend who I could be honest with and count on. And, most of all, a friend who I could tell about my feelings toward Elica, knowing you would not judge me."

"I never judged you," Anna said. "I never judged Elica either." She sighed.

"Do you still care for Daniel?"

"I'll always care for him. But if I really think about it after what happened between Ulf and me, my feelings for Daniel are more like a sister than a girlfriend. And as far as his relationship with Elica is concerned, I am just shocked. I had no idea. So, this all comes as a rather painful surprise."

"Yes. It's understandable."

"Is Daniel with Elica now?"

"No, he never answered her letter."

"Did she fix the pregnancy?"

"Actually, no. She and Dagna are renting a rundown flat in the seedy part of Vienna. Elica is planning to have the baby."

"Oh, my." Anna put her hand on her throat. "Do her parents know?"

"Yes, they know. They would have thrown her out, but she moved in with Dagna when they returned from Berlin last week."

Anna shook her head. She tried to remember if she had noticed any difference in Frau Frey. "Frau Frey has not said a word to me."

"Of course not. Frau Frey is your maid. She needs her job. So, she dare not say anything to you."

"I guess the blood sisters are no more," Anna said with a sad smile.

"We, you and I, are still blood sisters," Bernie said.

"Yes, that's true, and maybe someday, Elica will apologize. Hopefully, you'll find it in your heart to forgive her."

"Time will tell. Right now, I don't want to see her."

"I can't say that I blame you."

"I will be gone for a short while. I am going to take a trip to Italy."

"What about school?" Anna asked

"I'll take a little time off. I want to do this. I've dreamed of it my entire life."

"I understand. Have a wonderful time, and be safe, my blood sister." Anna said, giving Bernie a hug.

CHAPTER SEVENTY-SEVEN

After Bernie left, Anna thought about Ulf. She decided she had not behaved properly. He had hurt her with the words he's said about Jews. Still, she felt she was wrong for lying to him. So she decided to write him a letter.

She went upstairs to her room and sat down at her desk. She thought about Daniel and Elica. Then she thought about Ulf. She was consumed with emotions. She began to write Ulf a letter. She wrote about how angry she was at him. But then she told him that somehow, even after the terrible things he said, her feelings for him were still there. She said that she hoped that he had time to think about what happened, and perhaps he realized that his love for her was stronger than his hatred for her people. She added that she wished he didn't feel this way about Jews. She told him that she knew it was wrong to lie to him and use a fake name.

She ended the letter with...

My real name is Anna Levinstein. Yes, I am a Jew. I might have lied to you, but my feelings were real. Please find it in your heart to forgive me. I know that day on the sand when we saved your brother and you looked into my eyes; we both felt the same. If you still feel the same, please write to me. Please find me.

Anna.

CHAPTER SEVENTY-EIGHT

A few weeks passed, and Anna began to feel that her letter to Ulf would be ignored. She decided that he no longer cared, and she would be forced to get over him. But then, on a Tuesday afternoon, she received a letter. She ran to her room and locked the door. Then she sat down on her bed and tore the envelope open.

> Anna,
>
> I can't believe that you would have the nerve to write to Wolfgang, Ulf, as you call him, after what you did. You are a liar and an imposter. To make matters worse, you are a Jew. Wolfgang wants nothing to do with you, believe me. We are trying to work things out between us. If you had not come into our lives and cast a Jew spell on him, everything would have been fine. I warn you to stay away from him. Now I have your real name and your address. My father is an important man in the government. If I find out that you have made any attempt to contact Wolfgang again, I will see to it you are punished. Remember, you are a Jew, and these are dangerous times for Jews. Be smart and stay out of our lives.

Mattie.

CHAPTER SEVENTY-NINE

Winter 1938

On the first of February, in a small apartment without sufficient heat, and with the help of a midwife who took pity on her because she did not have enough money to pay, Elica gave birth to a son. He was a strong, healthy boy who resembled his mother with tiny bits of wheat-colored peach fuzz that covered his little head, long legs, long arms, and a hearty cry.

When the midwife handed the baby to his mother. Elica, she looked into the child's face, then she held him to her breast and wept. She wept for joy that her child was alive and well, and she wept for sadness because he had been born into such poverty. His life would be harder even than hers had been. At least she had grown up with two working parents, but her son had only her to depend on. His father had never even acknowledged her pregnancy, and she had not had the courage to go to him in person.

It had not been easy for Elica to work all day at a factory while trying her best to hide her heavy belly and hold her urine. It seemed she always had a full bladder and needed to go to the bathroom, but she was afraid to go. She couldn't risk getting fired from this job for having to use the bathroom so often, so she held it as long as she could. Elica sighed. At least, all of that was behind her now. Her son was here in her arms. Her body would heal; she was young. She would be healthy and strong again.

However, now she knew she must face another demon. Now that she held this helpless little one in her arms, she realized how much she loved him. That love terrified her because she knew that in order for them both to survive, she would be forced to leave him with strangers so she could go to work and pay the bills. How she wished Daniel had taken responsibility for her pregnancy. *If only he were here beside me. If only he could see how beautiful his son is, he would surely want to be a father. I thought I didn't want this baby, but now that I have seen him with his tiny fingers and little ears and held his warm little body in my arms, I know that I have never loved anyone or anything as much as I love this child. I think Daniel would feel the same if only he were here.*

Dagna and Elica had moved in together when they returned from Berlin. Neither of them went back to school to finish their last year. Instead, they both got jobs at a factory. As the months went by and Elica grew larger, Dagna became demanding and mean. Dagna knew she had Elica where she wanted her, and Dagna loved the power. Elica could not survive without Dagna's income. Because she was pregnant, her parents would never allow her to return home.

One afternoon Dagna had threatened to leave if Elica did not tell her who the baby's father was. Elica had no choice but to tell her, so she told her it was Daniel. Dagna was appalled, not because Elica had betrayed Anna, but because Elica was carrying a half-Jewish child.

Before they moved in together, Elica was carefree and beautiful, desired by most men, and Dagna had admired her. Dagna felt that if she and Elica were good friends, then people would see them as being alike. Therefore, Dagna wanted Elica's friendship more than anything. But now, Elica was no longer carefree, and her beauty was fading. Besides, Dagna had the upper hand, so she treated Elica badly, constantly reminding Elica that she was doing her a favor by being there.

Whenever something went wrong in the apartment, like the closet door broke or there was no hot water, Dagna would turn to Elica and say, "You realize that this is all your fault. If you hadn't been such a tramp and gotten yourself in trouble with that Jew, we wouldn't be stuck in this lousy apartment." However, even though Dagna was ill-tempered and constantly threatened to leave, she did not. She enjoyed the power she held over Elica. After all, without Dagna to help her pay the rent, Elica would have been out on the street, pregnant and alone. And now that the baby was born, it was even more important that Elica had a place for her child to live.

CHAPTER EIGHTY

Since their return from Berlin, Anna and Bernie had forged a deeper friendship. They saw each other at least twice a week. Anna introduced Bernie to her parents. At first, they were not receptive, but as they got to know Bernie, they liked her. Anna's father said Bernie was a girl with a good head on her shoulders, and to Anna's surprise and delight, her mother agreed.

They had a new maid, a young girl. Frau Frey, Elica's mother, left her employment at Anna's home in early November 1937. She gave no reason, but even before she left, she had grown cold toward Anna. Frau Frey refused to discuss Elica whenever Anna tried to ask her how Elica was doing.

Anna knew that Bernie kept in touch with Elica and Dagna even though she told Anna how disappointed she was in both of them.

"They should never have done that to you," Bernie said. "They conspired to make your employer let you go. That was despicable. I don't care for Dagna at all, I never did, but Elica surprised me. I never thought she would do that to a blood sister. I still speak to them both, but I don't think my friendship with Elica will ever be as strong as it was before all of this."

On a Sunday afternoon in mid-February, Bernie came over to visit with Anna. They sat down at the table in the dining room. The new maid brought out a tray of refreshments.

"Elica had a boy," Bernie blurted out.

"Oh!" Anna said excitedly.

"On the first of the month. The baby is healthy. I saw him. He's precious."

"And Daniel? Has anyone told him?" Anna asked.

"No, no one. I don't think so, anyway. I doubt that Dagna would go to him, and I know for certain that Elica has not had any contact with him since she sent him that letter telling him she was pregnant. She told me as much."

Anna stirred her tea. She watched the milk swirl around as she spun her spoon over and over. Then she looked up at Bernie. "Would you think I was a fool if I told you that I am thinking of going to speak with Daniel? I think he needs to know he has a son."

"But why would you do that after Elica betrayed you?"

"To help Elica. We were best friends for years."

"Yes, but Elica and Dagna both treated you so badly. Elica slept with your boyfriend. And then they turned on you and told your employer that you lied to get that job. That was just wrong, in my opinion. There is no excuse," Bernie said.

Anna shrugged her shoulders, "We are blood sisters. I guess."

"You forgive her? Elica, I mean."

"Maybe I shouldn't. But I do."

"Are you going to go and see the baby?" Bernie asked.

"No, I wouldn't feel welcome there, but I think Daniel should know about it. If he doesn't want to marry her, that's his choice, but he should at least help her with the expenses. After all, she didn't make this baby by herself. He is responsible too. Don't you think so?"

"Of course."

The following day it snowed, a light snow that didn't stick. It was still snowing when school let out. White flakes were drifting through the icy wind as Anna walked to Daniel's house.

She knocked on the door. It was several minutes before a middle-aged woman in a maid's uniform opened the door. "Yes, can I help you?" the maid asked.

"I'm here to see Daniel."

"Come in, please."

Anna walked inside. It was warm and welcoming. A fire crackled in the fireplace, and the smell of freshly baked bread filled the air.

"Please sit down," the maid instructed.

Anna smiled and sat down in front of the fire.

"And who shall I tell him is here to see him?"

"Anna. He'll know me."

"Yes, Fräulein Anna. I will go and tell him. Wait here; I'll be right back."

Daniel came into the living room a few minutes later. "Anna," he said as he sat down in a plush chair across from her. "How are you?"

"I'm fine."

"It's good to see you. You look beautiful as always," Daniel said, smiling.

She managed a smile. "I'm here because I have something important to tell you."

"Oh," he frowned.

"Yes, can we talk freely here?" she asked.

"Sure. My parents aren't home. What is it?" he asked.

"It's about Elica."

Daniel's face turned red. "What about Elica?"

"She has had the baby. You have a son."

"A son!" he said, more to himself than to her. "I have a son?"

"Yes."

"Is he all right?"

"He's fine. He's healthy."

"I didn't know you knew about Elica and me," Daniel said.

"I found out."

"I'm sorry," he said in a soft voice. "I never meant to hurt you."

"It doesn't matter. What does matter is that Elica and your son are living in poverty. I don't expect you to marry her or anything like that unless you want to. But either way, you could help her financially. It would be the right thing to do, Daniel."

"Yes, you're right. I will go and see her."

"She's not at her home. After we got back from Berlin last summer, she moved into an apartment with Dagna. I'll give you the address."

Daniel stood up. He left the room for a second, then he returned with a pencil and paper.

Anna wrote the address for him. He was pale, and his hands were trembling as he took the paper from her.

"I got her letter last summer telling me she was pregnant. I didn't know what to do. I was scared, so I never answered. I know it was the cowardly thing to do, but I was shocked and—"

"It's all right. That's in the past. Go and see your son." Then she added, "Daniel, go and make this right."

CHAPTER EIGHTY-ONE

Elica had returned to work less than a week after her son was born. She had no choice. She needed the money, and she couldn't risk losing her job. So, she made arrangements to pay a woman to watch her child. Her name was Anita, and she was a plain-looking girl. But she was young, close to the same age as Elica. Since she, too, had recently had a baby, she seemed to understand how hard it was for Elica to leave her son with a stranger. This made Elica more comfortable with Anita. Anita lived upstairs of Elica and Dagna in an apartment that was just as wretched as the one where Elica and Dagna lived. But she was married, and her husband provided for her, so she was able to stay at home with her child. Anita and her husband were glad to have the extra money for watching Elica's baby.

Anita did a good job of caring for Theo, and Elica felt confident in her ability. But then Anita's husband, who was a strong supporter of Hitler, was awarded a promotion, and the couple was given a better apartment in a nicer part of town.

Before Anita left, she told Elica about the state daycare system.

"As long as Theo is a pure Aryan child, and he is, they will watch Theo for you so that you can work."

Elica had no choice; she went to the state day care and swore that her son was the child of a pure Aryan soldier who she'd met and shared one night with. When asked for his name, she said she didn't remember.

And so Theo spent his days in the state daycare with other children who had no one to watch them while their mothers went to work.

Elica missed her son terribly, and each day she found herself watching the clock, waiting for the moment when she could leave the factory and hurry back home to her child.

It seemed like forever until the factory bell rang, releasing Elica from her station. After she punched her card at the punch clock, she made her way outside. Usually, she would have walked home to save the bus fare, but it was snowing heavily. It was coming down so hard that she could hardly see in front of her. As she stood shivering at the bus stop, snow covering her thin wool coat and her long greasy hair, she counted the money she would have to pay for riding the bus, and she almost started to cry. Every cent was accounted for, and this was a luxury she knew she could not afford. Yet it seemed almost impossible to walk home. Again, she counted the coins in her purse, and then, wrapping her scarf tightly around her neck and face, she began to walk home.

It seemed to take forever. She slipped on a patch of ice and fell, scrapping her knee. It was bleeding, but she didn't have anything to wipe away the blood. She stopped at the state day care to pick up Theo.

"Your little man is waiting for you," the young woman at the door said. Then she noticed the blood on Elica's knee. "You're bleeding."

"I slipped on the ice."

"Come in and wipe that off," the girl said, handing her a rag.

"Thank you," Elica said, taking the rag and wiping away the

blood. Then she bundled Theo up in his hat and coat and hugged him close as she carried him out of the center. Her hands were almost numb by the time she arrived at her building. She ran into the vestibule and searched for her keys. Then someone walked inside behind her and said her name, "Elica?"

"Daniel?" She spun around, not believing that he was really there.

He nodded. He still looked so handsome in his heavy black coat and black and white scarf. "Can I come in?"

"Yes. Yes, of course," she said. She noticed he hadn't changed. Then, as she passed a mirror in the hallway, she was reminded of how much she had changed. There was little trace of the beautiful, carefree girl with hair the color of winter wheat. The woman she saw in the mirror looked worn and old. There were fine lines around her blue eyes which no longer had a magical twinkle. She pushed her greasy, unwashed hair back off of her face. She was ashamed of it, but she couldn't wash it because it was too cold in the apartment to have wet hair. *I am ugly.* She thought. *He must think so, and I am sure of it. He is probably sorry he came.*

They walked up three steep flights of stairs. "This is my apartment. I share it with Dagna, but she's not home. Come in. Please," Elica said as she fumbled with the key in the lock.

The apartment was dark and cold. Elica turned on the light, which was a single bulb in the middle of the room. Dirty yellowing paint was flaking off the walls. She placed the baby in his crib that she and Dagna had made out of an old broken dresser drawer. Then she slipped off her coat. The baby had started crying, so she picked him up. "Daniel, this is Theodore. I call him Theo. He's your son." Daniel looked at the baby and gasped. Neither he nor Elica said another word.

CHAPTER EIGHTY-TWO

Daniel felt his body tremble as he looked at the infant in Elica's arms.

"Would you like to hold him?" she asked timidly.

Daniel nodded and reached out. Carefully, Elica placed the baby in his arms.

For a few moments, there was silence. Daniel looked at the tiny ears and the wee fingers that gripped his hand, then he realized that he was crying.

"He's my son," he breathed.

"Yes," Elica said.

There was silence in the room, save for the buzzing of the ineffectual heater. Daniel looked up into Elica's eyes. "Marry me," he said. "I want to take care of you both."

"Yes," she said. "Oh, yes, I will." She began to cry. "It's been so hard, Daniel. I prayed for this moment. I prayed and prayed that you would come to me, but I never believed that it would really happen." She was choking and sobbing. Then, in a soft voice, she whispered, "how did you find me?"

"Anna," he said, choking, "Anna. She came to my house and told me where you were living. She said I had a son."

"Anna?"

"Yes."

"And what about your parents? Do they know?" Elica asked. "Have you told them?"

"Not yet, but I will. They will know today. Because we are going to see them, the three of us. You and me and Theo. At first, my father will be angry, but don't be put off. Once they realize that Theo is my son, they will accept him. After all, I am their only child, and he is their grandson."

"I must get ready, and I must change Theo. Then we can go."

"Of course. I'll sit here and wait."

And so it was. Daniel's parents were resistant at first. His father called him irresponsible. His mother asked him how he could have done such a thing with a *shiksa*, a non-Jewish woman, no less. But when they saw Theo, when they looked into his eyes. When they held him in their arms, everything changed. He was their grandson. Daniel's mother began to cry. And Daniel's father said a prayer thanking God for the healthy baby in his arms.

Elica and Daniel were married in a private ceremony at Daniel's home. Then Elica and Theo moved in with Daniel and his parents. Dagna, unable to afford the rent by herself, moved back home.

CHAPTER EIGHTY-THREE

Bernie told Anna what had happened between Daniel and Elica. She was glad that the baby would have a home and a father. Although she did not speak of Ulf, she missed him. *I am too forgiving.* She thought. *I am trying to make excuses for the way he behaved. I want to believe that he only hates Jewish people because he was raised that way. I don't want to believe that he is really so small-minded as to believe all the propaganda that was being spewed against the Jews in Germany.* But she knew in her heart that he believed it and was not the man she had hoped he was.

There was talk that Germany was planning to take over Austria, which had fallen into a deep financial depression. Jobs were scarce, and food and money were difficult to come by. Each day, beggars came to the door of Anna's home. They were people of all ages who had fallen on hard times. Her mother told the cook to give them soup, bread, or whatever was available. But each day, more and more arrived. And whenever Anna was out in public, either waiting for a bus or going to the market, she would overhear people saying that they hoped Germany would come and take over Austria so they might help Austria get back on her feet. People were excited for the Germans to arrive. But not Anna's parents.

They were worried. Her father had heard that Jews were not being treated well in Germany. Anna remembered the anti-Jewish newspapers she'd seen when she was in Berlin. And Now, every day, more and more of their Jewish friends and neighbors were leaving the country. Anna's mother begged her husband to go, but Anna's father owned a factory, which he had built single-handedly through painstaking work when he and Anna's mother had escaped from Russia and come to Vienna penniless. And He refused to leave it. One morning at the breakfast table, Anna's parents were having a heated discussion when Anna's father told her mother that his factory was his life, and he couldn't just leave it behind.

"I will not be driven from my home. We'll just have to stay here in Vienna and weather this storm. We are wealthy, and we will be all right."

Anna's mother looked like she was going to cry. Her eyes were dark with worry as she studied her husband. "There is fighting between the communists and the National Socialists in the streets every day. This isn't good for us, especially because we are Jews. If Hitler takes over, we will be in trouble. I've read the papers. He hates Jews, and he is making their lives miserable in Germany. What will he do here?"

"Don't be afraid," Anna's father said comfortingly. "This Hitler is too radical a leader; he won't last. You'll see. Everything will be all right. Right now, the Austrians think that Hitler has saved Germany. Maybe he has helped with the unemployment there. However, he is so fanatical that he will not last. He must be overthrown. You'll see."

CHAPTER EIGHTY-FOUR

In March 1938, Hitler sent Himmler to Austria to arrest any opposing forces, including many Austrian Jews. Daniel's father was among them as well as several important men who lived in the same neighborhood as Anna and her family. Her mother, seeing this and having lived through a pogrom in Russia, was on edge. When her husband returned home from work that day, she was in hysterics as she begged him to leave the country, but he remained calm.

"This is Austria. A civilized nation. It's not barbaric like Russia. There may be a few demonstrations, but all in all, everything will be fine."

"But what about the Jews that were arrested?"

"We don't know why they were arrested. Do we?" Anna's father asked as he hung up his coat.

"Because they are Jewish, and we are next," her mother said.

"No, dear. I am sure that those people spoke out against the Germans. We will just lay low, keep our mouths shut, and we'll be fine."

Then, on the twelfth day of March, Hitler rode into Austria in a blaze of glory. He was greeted by flowers and salutes as Austria fell into his waiting arms.

By the fifteenth, he'd made his way into Vienna, where he gave a speech at Heldenplatz, the Heroes' Square. There were celebrations and dancing in the streets as the Austrians rejoiced. Their savior Hitler had come to save them.

A month later, at the end of April, a new law was decreed. All Jews were forced to register any property or belongings valued at over five thousand reichsmarks. Anna's parents complied with the law because they believed that if they did, no harm would come to them.

Meanwhile, more Jews were arrested.

CHAPTER EIGHTY-FIVE

Then on November 8, there were riots in the streets. Rioters smashed all the windows of Anna's home. It was a night of terror like none other. The violence lasted for another day. And Anna and her family hid in the closet until it finally passed.

And then, in February 1939, a band of Nazis came to Anna's father's business. They walked into his office and told him that he must leave immediately. He wanted to ask why, but he'd heard of several Jewish business owners being sent to Mauthausen, a concentration camp in Austria, so he dared not say a word. His heart broke as he watched them take possession of his beloved factory. They forced him to open the safe in his office, and they took all of his money. One of the soldiers simply said that he must leave the factory immediately. He told him that the business was to be Aryanized. Which meant that the small factory was to be given to a young Aryan man and his brother.

Michael Levinstein forgot his fear for a moment. This factory had been his entire life. He'd built it on his own sweat and hard work. He was almost in tears as he grabbed the sleeve of one of the Nazi officers. "Please, I beg you. Don't do this. I have done nothing wrong."

The Nazi shook Herr Levinstein off. Then he took the butt of his gun and hit Herr Levinstein in the face. Blood spurted from Anna's father's nose. He fell to the ground. "Now get out of here if you know what's good for you," he said.

Michael Levinstein managed to get up. He took one last look around, then slowly walked out of the factory that he had painstakingly built and headed home. When Michael Levinstein returned home with blood all over him, his wife began shaking and screaming. "We must get out of here. We must leave Austria as soon as we can."

Michael agreed with his wife, but now there was no money. The Nazis had taken it all. Without funds, it would be impossible to make arrangements to leave the country. Anna's mother was beyond distraught. She was almost hysterical, staying in bed and weeping all day. Her father was at a loss. He no longer worked, so he sat at the dining room table all day and looked down, drumming his fingers without speaking to anyone.

CHAPTER EIGHTY-SIX

The Levinsteins had lost everything. They were living in a small apartment with two other Jewish families, and both had small children. There was no privacy and no room to breathe. The children ran around all day. They played, they screamed, and they unnerved the Levinsteins. Anselm grew sicker, and Anna worried that the noise and unrest were doing him harm. The children were always hungry, and they stole the small amount of food that the Levinsteins purchased. Anna's mother complained to the other mothers, but they said there was nothing they could do. "They are babies, and they're hungry. They see food; they take it. What can we do?"

There was no point in arguing. Anna's father tried to hide the food as much as possible. He wanted to get them out of there, but there was no place to go. They were almost out of money, and her father had been unemployed for a long time now. Anna had tried to get work, but no one was hiring Jews. If they had more money than they did, they might have tried to get out of the country. But as it was, they were all out of options.

Anna got dressed one Sunday morning and went to see Bernie to beg for help.

"Please, you must take us in until my father can make other arrangements."

"You mean to hide you?" Bernie said.

"Yes. Hide us until my father can come up with some sort of plan. I know it's a lot to ask. I know you would be putting your mother and yourself at risk. But I have no other choice, no one else to turn to. My father doesn't have any non-Jewish friends, and neither does my mother. Their friends have either left the country or are looking for a place to hide. We have lost everything. Soon, the Nazis will come and take our house like they have done to so many of our neighbors. They will imprison us."

Bernie's eyes were filled with compassion. "I'll talk to my mother. Don't worry. I am sure she will understand. I know she will agree to help you. So, the answer is yes. Come tonight with your family. The attic is not as clean as I would like it to be. I'll do my best to clean it up today. It isn't very large, and I know that there are four of you. I wish I could offer more, but at least it's safe."

"I am so grateful for this. You don't know how grateful I am."

That night, the proud Michael Levinstein, his wife Lilian, his son Anselm, and his daughter Anna all left the cramped apartment. They carried no baggage, only the clothing they could layer on their bodies. Lilian sewed all of her jewelry into the hems of her clothes. But The silver and the crystal were all left behind as the Levinstein family moved into the tiny attic in Bernie's house.

It was cold and cramped, but the Levinsteins were grateful.

CHAPTER EIGHTY-SEVEN

1940

Bernie was working hard. She finished school and then got a job at a factory. She never went into teaching as she had once hoped to do because she couldn't imagine teaching under German rule. Each night, she sneaked up into the attic to visit with Anna.

Anna had never been able to finish school, and she wanted to know about the changes that had taken place after the German invasion and what had caused Bernie to change her mind about becoming a teacher. Bernie told her that things had changed. There were no Jewish students in schools anymore, and all crucifixes were removed from the classrooms. The crucifixes were replaced with Hitler's pictures.

The weather grew warmer, and Anna lost track of time. Her father lost his pride, and her mother lost hope. Anselm grew weaker and sicker with each passing day.

Then, late one night, the door to the attic opened. Anna's mother gasped.

"I'm sorry to wake all of you." It was Bernie. "But, Elica is here. She wanted to see Anna, and she was afraid to come during the day. We didn't want anyone to see us coming up to the attic, so she came now."

The room was dark, but Anna's eyes were used to the dark. She looked up to see Elica standing by the opening to the attic. "Come in," she whispered.

Elica followed the sound of Anna's voice. She carried something in her arms, but Anna could not make out what it was. It had been a long time since she'd last seen Elica. The last time they'd seen each other was that day in Berlin, when Elica had brought the letter for Anna to read. Suddenly, a trickle of fear ran through Anna. *What if she turns us in?* She thought. "How did you find us?" Anna asked.

"I told Bernie I needed to see you, and she brought me here."

"Does Dagna know?" Anna asked.

"No, and no one would ever tell her. You are safe. I would not tell anyone where you are. I swear it," Elica said. "I know what you did for me and Daniel and for our son. That was very kind. Especially after how I behaved." She cleared her throat. "I am sorry."

"I know. I know you are."

"I fell in love with him. I was wrong to do what I did to you, but at the time, I was young and foolish. I know it's no excuse."

"It's all right. You and Daniel were meant to be together."

"He's been arrested, and I am protecting our son. I am going to the police to try to find him. I am leaving Theo, my son, with Bernie. I have to make sure they do not find out that he is Daniel's child. I have a good start on this. I already pledged that he is the son of a pure Aryan man. I had to do that before Daniel and I were back together. I had to lie because before Daniel's parents accepted us, Theo and I didn't have a dime. I was sharing an apartment with Dagna. I had to work, and I needed to use the state daycare to watch my baby all day while I worked. It felt like a betrayal to the Jewish people, but I couldn't do anything else.

"But then, once Daniel and I were officially together, and his parents saw Theo, they fell in love with him. They finally accepted me, and we moved in with them. They were helping us financially, but they are gone now too. The Germans took them. Oh, Anna, it's just horrible. I can't even begin to tell you how terrible this has been. I am glad I was forced to make up this story about Theo when he was a tiny baby so that I would be able to work. They would never have allowed him into the state daycare if they had known that his father was Jewish. And this story may very well have saved his life. Since Daniel and I were married by a rabbi, there are no records of our marriage, so the Nazis have no way of finding out who Theo's father is. I feel like a traitor to Daniel. I am not ashamed that my husband is a Jew, but I doubt it would help Daniel if I told the Germans the truth. It would only hurt Theo. For all I know, Daniel is dead." She let out a tortured sigh. "God forbid, but I haven't seen or heard from him since he was arrested."

"When was he arrested?"

"Two weeks ago. His mother too. We were trying to figure out what to do and where to go. We wanted to get away from here, but we were too late. The Nazis came for Daniel, and I hid with the baby."

"Oh, Elica. I am so sorry for you."

Elica began to ramble, almost as if she were talking to herself. "I am worried sick about him. I think about him constantly. He is my husband, yet I must lie to protect my son. I don't know what will become of us. I have no idea if I will ever see Daniel again."

"That's terrible. I am sorry," Anna said again.

"Well, I didn't come here to upset and scare you. I am sure this is hard enough for you without having to listen to my troubles. The truth is, I came here because I wanted to bring you this. Do you remember her?" Elica handed Anna a doll. "She was the doll in the window of the toy store when we were children. I wanted her so badly. But you got her for your birthday. I must admit I was jealous, but then you gave her to me because you said she reminded you of me. Do you remember?"

"Of course I do," Anna said.

"So, now I want to give her to you because although I cannot be here with you, I hope that when you look at her, you will be reminded of me, not of the bad times, but of the good times. And I also want you to know that after all we have been through, after all the mistakes I've made, I love you, Anna. You are always in my heart, and you are still and always will be my blood sister."

Anna took the doll. Then she put her arms around Elica, and the two of them wept.

"We will always be blood sisters, the three of us," Bernie said.

"Yes, the three of us," Elica repeated.

"And what about Dagna?" Anna asked.

"She's joined the Nazis. We always knew she would. I think she was responsible for having Daniel arrested. She was jealous of Daniel and me. She thought he took me away from her. And In many ways, he did. But he is my husband, the father of my child, and I am sick with worry about him. I can never forgive her. Never."

"Well, she was never really one of us blood sisters anyway," Bernie said. "I never liked her, and I never trusted her."

"I did. At one time, I trusted her completely. But now I despise her," Elica said.

"Just be careful of her," Anna warned. "Don't ever give her any information at all."

"I am going to leave my son with Bernie. I am going to tell Dagna that Theo died. I can't trust her not to turn him in as a half-Jewish child."

"Did Bernie agree to watch him for you?"

"Yes, she said I could leave him with her while I went to see Dagna. Dagna is my only chance of ever finding Daniel again. I must go to her."

"I know. I understand."

CHAPTER EIGHTY-EIGHT

I
t was hot in the attic. Summer brought extreme heat, and the heat made sleep nearly impossible. The days seemed endless, and the nights were lonely. Sometimes Anna shoved her face into her pillow to stifle the sounds of her weeping. She didn't want her family to hear her, although she thought they must know how depressed she had become. *It must show all over my face even though I try like mad to hide it. These are the best years of my life, and they are being stolen from me. I am confined to this small room with no idea when or if this will ever end. I never thought my life would be like this. I imagined myself going out with friends, getting married, and having a child. I never would have believed I would be forced to hide like a criminal.*

Bernie came up to the attic to visit as often as she could. She had taken on extra hours at work because she and her mother needed the money. Bernie brought food and water daily, making do with less so she could feed Anna and her family. Anna appreciated everything and told her over and over how grateful she was. Anna desperately longed to be outside, to feel the fresh air on her skin. She yearned for simple things, like a bath or swimming in the lake. But these simple pleasures were no longer available to her. Instead, for the last two years, she had to live by the rules created by her father to keep the family safe.

There was to be no peeking out the window. The family must stay away from the curtains just in case someone is walking outside. If that person walking by just happened to look up and catch a glimpse of someone in the attic, they could turn the family in. Not only would Anna and her family suffer, but Bernie and her mother would face severe punishment. Something as simple as a glance out the window could be the end of all of them. But that was not all; food and water were scarce, so they had to be rationed. No matter how hungry they were, the Levinsteins would make the supplies last until Bernie brought more. Anna's father made it clear no one was ever to ask Bernie or her mother when more food might arrive.

If they heard the door open downstairs or the doorbell ring, they must go to their beds and lie down. They dared not move because there was a good chance that someone other than Bernie or her mother was in the house. Absolute silence was crucial to their survival. If they must cough or sneeze, they must smother the sound with a pillow. *Rules, rules, rules.* Anna thought. *I am sick of all these rules. How I wish I could go to school or play the piano. I wonder if I will ever play again.*

"I brought you a couple of books," Bernie said when she came to the attic to see Anna one Sunday evening two weeks after the meeting with Elica.

"Thank you," Anna said. "You look so tan. Have you been out in the sun today?"

"Actually, yes. Anyone of school age is now required to attend National Youth day."

"What is that?"

"Well, it's kind of like a camp setting. First, we have to sit and listen for a couple of hours to all the political lies that the Nazis throw at us. Then, after they have bored us to tears, we get to play sports. You know how much I love sports. There is no charge for any of it, not even the equipment."

"Do they say bad things about Jews?" Anna asked.

"Yes, I'm sorry to say that they do. Most of the young people who attend are convinced that Jews are evil and dangerous. But you know I don't believe any of that."

"I know," Anna said, touching Bernie's hand.

"And..." Bernie whispered so that only Anna could hear. "I have to tell you something."

"Yes," Anna said.

"I still have not heard from Elica. It's been two weeks. I am worried. But I also know that I must get Theo out of our house. If, by some chance, Elica has made the mistake of trusting Dagna. If she has told her that Theo is alive and he is here, the Nazis will come, and we will all be in danger."

"Where are you taking him?"

"There is a woman who is very special to me. Do you remember when I went to Italy after we returned from Berlin?"

"I remember."

"Well, I met someone. Her name is Viola. We have been in contact through letters for the last two years. I believe she will help me."

"She is a friend?"

"She is more than a friend, Anna. You know how I am. You know how I feel about men and all of that."

"Yes, I know."

"Well, for years, I was in love with Elica. I will always care about Elica. But once I met Viola, I knew what real love was. Love that was reciprocated."

"That's wonderful," Anna said with tears of joy in her eyes.

"Yes, it is. And I know Viola will help me with Theo because, just like me, she thinks this terrible treatment of the Jewish people is despicable."

"But how long will you be gone?"

"I don't know. I'll return as quickly as I can. But until I get back, my mother will bring food and water up here to the attic for you and your family."

"Oh, Bernie. Please be careful."

CHAPTER EIGHTY-NINE

Bernie carefully climbed down the hidden stairs. Once she was back on the main floor of the house, she went to check on Theo. He was asleep. She chewed on her upper lip as she watched him.

"What a precious little boy you are," she whispered. "You didn't deserve the things that happened to you. You never did anything wrong to anyone. All you did was come into a world that is filled with hatred and danger. You should have grown up surrounded by people who love you. I happen to know that wherever she is, your mother loves you very much. And with God's help, she will find your father, and they will return. Then together, they will find you.

"But there are no guarantees in this sad world, my sweet boy. So, just in case I do not survive this journey, I must leave a message for your mother so she will know where to find you. I've told Anna, but I can't be sure that Anna will survive either. I pray that even if all of us are caught and executed, you will be spared. Somehow, some good will come to you. This is my prayer for you, Theo. Now, I must leave a note for Elica and hope that she remembers our special place where we left things of importance for each other when we were children."

Bernie sat down at her desk and wrote a letter to Elica telling her about Viola and the orphanage.

Dear Elica,

If you are reading this letter, it means that I did not survive. Please know that I waited for you to return for as long as I could. But I cannot wait any longer because not only is Theo in danger, but Anna and her family are as well. Every time I hear a siren, I am afraid that the Gestapo have come for Theo, and I can't bear to see them take him. He is such a sweet, happy baby. When I look into his eyes, so innocent and trusting, I know that I must do whatever I can to help him. I have always been brave. I've never feared death. But now, when I hold this precious young life in my arms, I am distraught with fear. I cannot allow them to take him. I simply cannot. So, I am doing something that terrifies me, but I must do it because it might save his life.

I am taking Theo to an orphanage in the mountains of Italy. I have a friend there who is in training to become a nun. I believe she will help me by caring for Theo and hiding his secret. I love you, Elica, and I always have. You were my blood sister and my closest friend, but besides that, I loved you. Perhaps People might call my feelings for you unnatural, but in my mind, love is love, no matter who is involved. A man and a woman, a man and a man, or even a woman and a woman. Love is always a gift from God. I pray for you every day. I pray that you will be all right, that you will find Daniel, and together you will bring Theo home and raise him with the love he deserves.

Goodbye, my dear and precious friend. My forever blood sister.

Yours always,

Bernie.

Bernie folded the letter and stuffed it into her pocket. Then she took Theo and left the house.

CHAPTER NINETY

The door sprung open. It had been kicked so hard that it flew off of its hinges. A man in a black leather coat who looked like a giant stood there, his eyes fixed on Anna. Anna stared at him. Although her bubbie had been dead for years, she heard her bubbie's voice.

"Annaleh," Bubbie said, "be brave."

"I can't, Bubbie. I am not brave like you," she answered aloud, as if her grandmother were standing right in front of her.

Who would have done this to us? Dagna? She's always hated me. But she doesn't know where we are. I can't believe Bernie or Elica would ever tell her. They know how she is. Could she have followed us? I don't know. And what about Bernie and her mother? They have been having a difficult time getting their hands on enough food to feed us. And they have been living with the constant fear of being caught. Yet, I can't imagine Bernie doing this. Elica has always been jealous of my family, but she is my best friend and blood sister. Yes, she betrayed me with Daniel, but she couldn't help it; she was in love. No, it wasn't Elica.

Love... Could it have been Ulf? He felt so betrayed, and I don't know if he ever received my letter apologizing. Mattie would not have given it to him. Mattie? And then there's Mattie. She had every reason in the world to turn us in. But why now? I haven't had any contact with her or Ulf. Who did this? Who? Anna couldn't breathe. She was overwhelmed with fear, and her mind was racing. Anna looked at the giant. He was the biggest, most terrifying man she'd ever seen. Then she fainted.

The sound of a gunshot, loud and intrusive, woke Anna. She found herself in the back of a black automobile. She lay on her mother, who was weeping softly. It was dark outside, but the lights from the automobile shined on a dead body covered in blood. It was a massive body, and Anna recognized it as the giant Nazi who had broken down the attic door. Anselm was so skinny and frail that at fifteen, he had the body of a nine-year-old and sat on their father's lap.

Do my eyes deceive me? Anna thought. *I must be seeing things.* She stared at the profile of the driver of the automobile. *It's not possible. It's not.* He wore the long black coat of the Gestapo and the hat with the death head symbol. But she would recognize him anywhere.

"Ulf?" she said. "Ulf?"

"Anna, do you know this man? This Nazi who has arrested us?" her father asked incredulously.

The German who was driving the car turned and glanced back for a single second.

Anna gasped. She could hardly catch her breath. "Yes, Papa. I do," Anna said. "I know this man."

AUTHORS NOTE

I always enjoy hearing from my readers, and your thoughts about my work are very important to me. If you enjoyed my novel, please consider telling your friends and posting a short review on Amazon. Word of mouth is an author's best friend.

Also, it would be my honor to have you join my mailing list. As my gift to you for joining, you will receive 3 **free** short stories and my USA Today award-winning novella complimentary in your email! To sign up, just go to my website at www.RobertaKagan.com

I send blessings to each and every one of you,

Roberta

Email: roberta@robertakagan.com

ABOUT THE AUTHOR

I wanted to take a moment to introduce myself. My name is Roberta, and I am an author of Historical Fiction, mainly based on World War 2 and the Holocaust. While I never discount the horrors of the Holocaust and the Nazis, my novels are constantly inspired by love, kindness, and the small special moments that make life worth living.

I always knew I wanted to reach people through art when I was younger. I just always thought I would be an actress. That dream died in my late 20's, after many attempts and failures. For the next several years, I tried so many different professions. I worked as a hairstylist and a wedding coordinator, amongst many other jobs. But I was never satisfied. Finally, in my 50's, I worked for a hospital on the PBX board. Every day I would drive to work, I would dread clocking in. I would count the hours until I clocked out. And, the next day, I would do it all over again. I couldn't see a way out, but I prayed, and I prayed, and then I prayed some more. Until one morning at 4 am, I woke up with a voice in my head, and you might know that voice as Detrick. He told me to write his story, and together we sat at the computer; we wrote the novel that is now known as All My Love, Detrick. I now have over 30 books published, and I have had the honor of being a USA Today Best-Selling Author. I have met such incredible people in this industry, and I am so blessed to be meeting you.

I tell this story a lot. And a lot of people think I am crazy, but it is true. I always found solace in books growing up but didn't start writing until I was in my late 50s. I try to tell this story to as many people as possible to inspire them. No matter where you are in your life, remember there is always a flicker of light no matter how dark it seems.

I send you many blessings, and I hope you enjoy my novels. They are all written with love.

Roberta

MORE BOOKS BY ROBERTA KAGAN
AVAILABLE ON AMAZON

The Blood Sisters Series

The Pact

My Sister's Betrayal

When Forever Ends

The Auschwitz Twins Series

The Children's Dream

Mengele's Apprentice

The Auschwitz Twins

Jews, The Third Reich, and a Web of Secrets

My Son's Secret

The Stolen Child

A Web of Secrets

A Jewish Family Saga

Not In America

They Never Saw It Coming

When The Dust Settled

The Syndrome That Saved Us

A Holocaust Story Series

The Smallest Crack

The Darkest Canyon

Millions Of Pebbles

Sarah and Solomon

All My Love, Detrick Series

All My Love, Detrick

You Are My Sunshine

The Promised Land

To Be An Israeli

Forever My Homeland

Michal's Destiny Series

Michal's Destiny

A Family Shattered

Watch Over My Child

Another Breath, Another Sunrise

Eidel's Story Series

And . . . Who Is The Real Mother?

Secrets Revealed

New Life, New Land

Another Generation

The Wrath of Eden Series

The Wrath Of Eden

The Angels Song

Stand Alone Novels

One Last Hope

A Flicker Of Light

The Heart Of A Gypsy